MONSTERVILLE

A LISSA BLACK PRODUCTION

MONSTERVILLE

A LISSA BLACK PRODUCTION

SARAH S. REIDA

Sky Pony Press
New York

First Edition

Sky Pony Press books may be purchased in bulk at special discounts for sales promotion, corporate gifts, fund-raising, or educational purposes. Special editions can also be created to specifications. For details, contact the Special Sales Department, Sky Pony Press, 307 West 36th Street, 11th Floor, New York, NY 10018 or info@skyhorsepublishing.com.

Sky Pony® is a registered trademark of Skyhorse Publishing, Inc.®, a Delaware corporation.

Visit our website at www.skyponypress.com.

Books authors, and more at www.skyponypressblog.com

www.lissablackproductions.com

10 9 8 7 6 5 4 3 2 1

Library of Congress Cataloging-in-Publication Data on file.

Cover illustration by Susana Diaz
Cover design by Georgia Morrissey

Hardcover ISBN: 978-1-5107-0733-7
Ebook ISBN: 978-1-5107-0736-8

Printed in the United States of America

To my love, the honey badger

CONTENTS

ACT ONE

ACT TWO

ACT THREE

ACT ONE

SCENE ONE:

A CREEPY WELCOME

If my life had a soundtrack, right now banjo music would be playing. When we pulled into the rocky driveway of our new house in Freeburg, Pennsylvania, all I saw for miles around were corn, cows, and woods. It was a miracle my cell phone still worked because I felt like I'd fallen off the face of the planet.

"We're here!" Dad crowed, pivoting in his seat to give Haylie and me a crazy grin. Which fit, considering he was bonkers for making us move from New York City to the sticks. I'd say he's having a midlife crisis, but he's not old enough yet.

Haylie kicked her legs in her car seat. "Lissy, help me!"

"Lissa, help your sister," Mom said, like I hadn't heard.

"One second, Hails." I unclicked my seat belt and opened my door. The glare of the sun hit me in the eyes and I ducked as I went to rescue Haylie.

"Are there cows?" she asked as I lifted her up. Her blonde hair tickled my nose while she squirmed, trying to get a better view.

"Not here," Mom said, "but next door there are. And piggies, and chickens, and—" She looked at me to finish the sentence.

"Dogs?" I asked, playing along. Even if this place was the bane of *my* existence, I wanted Haylie to be happy.

"Yes!" Mom clapped her hands and grinned at me, her smile widening when Dad looped his arms around her waist. I turned away from the sight of them kissing. Like there's anything grosser than your parents making out.

I put Haylie down and shaded my eyes to look "next door." It was the equivalent of a city block away—a backdrop of wooden buildings and animal pens against a line of trees. It looked like the scenery in a low-budget 1950s newsreel about farm life.

Dad moved to unlock the back of the U-Haul. "Hey everyone. We can go inside to check out our new house, and we don't have to worry about anyone stealing anything!"

"What about coyotes carrying our stuff away?" I grumbled.

"Coyotes?" Haylie's blue eyes lit up.

"There aren't any coyotes out here." Mom shot me a warning glare. "Nothing dangerous at all."

"You know, Mom, if this were a movie, you just doomed us."

Cardinal rule in movies: never say somewhere is safe. It's an invitation for disaster.

"Life isn't a movie, Lissa." It wasn't the first time she'd told me that.

"Well, mine definitely isn't. It's so boring, it would be the biggest box office bomb in history." I ignored Mom's warning look as I took a box from the U-Haul and walked up the cracked sidewalk to our sagging front porch. "Watch your step!" I called over my shoulder.

Haylie raced to catch up. "Lissy! Look!"

She pointed at the garden framing the porch. It was overgrown with grass and long stalks of thorny plants that choked the purple and pink bursts I assumed were legitimate flowers.

"A secret garden," I told her. "*Secret* meaning that to anyone looking, it's a dirt plot full of weeds."

Haylie waded through the weeds and picked a pink blossom. "I'm going to make a bouquet for our new house," she announced. She grabbed a handful of flowers and joined me on the porch, her cheeks as pink as the flowers. "Look!"

The flowers were wilted, drooping from the heat and lack of water. I took one and lifted it to my nose, inhaling the scent. "Nice," I lied.

Dad came clomping up the stairs with a stack of boxes. I rescued the top one. It was mine.

"Those are petunias. Aunt Lucy always loved petunias," he said. Aunt Lucy was the mysterious relative who had left us this house in her will.

This gift created the perfect horror movie setup: free house from mysterious relative equals death.

Aunt Lucy wasn't really mysterious—just a stranger. I'd only met her a few times, so when Dad told us about the house, my reaction was, "Lucy who?"

Haylie waved the flowers at me again, and I looked down at her. "Tell you what, Haylie. These stems are too short for a vase. Want me to put them in your hair instead?"

Her smile was blinding. Four-year-olds are so easy to please. "Yes! Yes! Yes! Yes!"

"Okay, keep your pants on." I kneeled on the porch and opened the box my best friends, Casey and Taylor, had filled with things to make sure I didn't forget them. Like that was possible. I pulled out the bedazzled bobby pins Taylor had stuck in a makeup bag of "essentials." "Here, hop up on the railing and I'll make you beautiful." I waved the bobby pins at Haylie.

She perched on the wooden railing, and I went to work pulling up strands of hair and fastening them with bobby pins. I stuck flowers wherever I could.

"Done!" I announced when I ran out of pins. "You look like a movie star."

Haylie giggled and felt her head. "I have flowers in my hair!"

"Flowers everywhere . . ." Dad sang in a baritone voice. He and Mom were already on their third load of boxes. He nudged open the front door with his foot and disappeared inside again.

"Come on, Hails," I said. "Let's go check out the new digs." I took a deep breath, picked up my box, and headed into the house.

I'd seen pictures of it before, but those didn't account for the mildewy smell. The place wasn't huge, but it was much bigger than our apartment. The house was a one-story, with a living room that opened into a dining room and then a kitchen. The bedrooms were in the back—three of them. Haylie and I would share a connecting bathroom.

"Look at all this space! And furniture!" Mom patted the coffee table. Aunt Lucy's furniture was clunky and dark.

"Yeah, lucky us."

The whole place felt alien. I already missed our condo's plush carpeting, and the cream-colored walls, and our kitchen counter with stools where Taylor, Casey, and I hung out and talked while scarfing down pizza.

I was one hundred percent sure that we couldn't get pizza delivered out here.

I carried my box down the narrow hallway and into my bedroom at the far end, setting it down on the bare floor. The box looked lonely all by itself.

"Lissa!" Mom called from the living room. "Look at the sky! It's going to storm! Help us get all this stuff in quick."

Sure enough, when I went back out to help, the temperature had dropped. The air had this calm, still feel to it, and I wondered if we were about to have a tornado. Maybe if one came, it would whisk me away to somewhere better, like Dorothy in *The Wizard of Oz*.

Mom, Dad, and I rushed back and forth across the front yard, moving boxes from the U-Haul and dumping them in the living room. We finished just as a huge crack of thunder sounded, followed by a low rumble. Big, fat drops started to fall, tapping against the windows. A loose shutter slapped against the side of the house.

I looked around the living room. Our stuff was everywhere—kitchen table in pieces on the floor, movies in boxes, Mom's tall Chinese vases wrapped in bubble paper.

"Well," I said. "I guess I'll go to my room."

"No!" Dad clapped his hands. "This is our first evening in our new house. Stella, get the sparkling cider I put in the fridge. I'll scrounge up Scrabble. We're celebrating!"

Mom and Dad genuinely thought we had a reason to. They'd grabbed at the chance to move to the country, going on and on about how good it would be for Haylie and me.

For the next few hours, we sat on the hardwood floor of our new dining room, playing Scrabble while Mom and Dad tactfully ignored my prison-themed word choices. Dad won because of his roughly four thousand IQ points.

When I finally went to my room for bed, I felt like a visitor there. I missed my favorite red blanket, which was still packed away somewhere. Boxes of clothes and books crowded the floor, and the walls were bare.

Crawling under the covers, I listened to the rain hitting the windows and pretended I was back in our apartment—the sound of the rain is universal. I imagined I was lying underneath my old ceiling with the glow-in-the-dark stars I'd stuck to it when I was ten. If I listened hard enough, I could almost hear the city traffic.

I'm fantastic at pretending, but it still took me half the night to fall asleep.

Little kids have security blankets. I had my box.

As soon as I woke up the next morning, I dug into Taylor and Casey's present. I'd been avoiding it, afraid I'd start bawling over the contents like a an over the top actress in a bad chick flick. (Like there's any such thing as a *good* chick flick.)

Along with a bunch of nostalgic stuff, like pictures and a signed playbill from *Wicked*, it had things I could use: a makeup bag so I could do my own makeup (since I wouldn't have Taylor to do it for me), a St. Mary's T-shirt, a pair of white sunglasses with purple lenses, a package of my favorite gummy bears, dangly earrings, and a blank journal for my screenwriting ideas.

I touched the purple cover of the journal, trying not to think about what I was missing at St. Mary's. Especially the fall play. The whole seventh grade would be preparing for it without me, even though I had written it. I'd won the sixth-grade playwriting contest at the end of last year.

If I'd stayed in NYC, I would have gotten to direct my very own play under the supervision of Roland Reed, the semi-famous TV writer St. Mary's was bringing in to help. He could have gotten me a job on a hip television show that needed a kid writer, which would have led to my first Golden Globe, which would have been the first step toward becoming an Oscar winner in multiple non-acting categories.

Instead, I'd be hanging out in cow country, doodling in my journal.

Thanks a lot, Mom and Dad.

They promised we'd go back to see my play. I couldn't decide if that was thoughtful or cruel. I mean, it was *literally* a display of what I was missing out on.

I put the notebook back in the box and closed the lid. After I got dressed, I headed down the hallway for breakfast. Mom was already in the kitchen, unloading appliances from a box and arranging them on the linoleum counter. She paused to hand me a package of Pop-Tarts.

"That's all I could find. And the store in Freeburg isn't open yet." She reached up to pull her hair into a ponytail.

"Here's an interesting factoid," I said as I ripped open the package. "The grocery store on our old street was always open."

"Right, so there was more time to rob it. Three times last year."

"*Nuh-uh.* The owner probably staged those robberies for the insurance money." Mom squinted at me. "Seriously! I've thought about it a lot."

I peered at our backyard through the dirty kitchen window. "Are we just unpacking all day or what?"

"Well, it needs to be done. But you can explore if you want. Or maybe go meet the neighbors."

"What neighbors?"

"The Griggs. They have a boy your age. And another in high school."

"Great." I figured I was obligated to be friends with them. Freeburg seemed like the kind of place where you had to be friends with anyone who lived within a five-mile radius.

"I'll start unpacking. And planning the redecorating," Mom said excitedly. "We can do anything we want! Imagine it!"

I scanned the kitchen, taking in the 1970s style of everything, including the yellow refrigerator. Back home, we had marble countertops and a stainless steel refrigerator that filtered water and made ice.

Maybe we could remodel this kitchen to look just like our old one, and I could pretend we'd never moved. I'd just never leave the house. If I did, it would be like in Tim Burton's *Beetlejuice*, where the main character opens her front door and falls into an alternate reality complete with a desert populated by killer sandworms.

Freeburg was my alternate reality.

"Great. Well, I guess I'll go exploring," I said. "Just, you know, roam around. Maybe check out the woods. Bag a deer, build a cabin."

Mom slit open a box with some scissors and pulled out our coffeemaker. "Hello, friend," she said to it, then waved me off. "Yes, go explore. But be back in an hour. We need your help."

I stuck my feet in a pair of flip-flops and headed outside. Even though the sun wasn't all the way up yet, it was already hot, sweat dampening my back under my T-shirt.

A noise at the end of our driveway caught my attention—this *RRRrrrrrr! RRRrrrrr! RRRrrrrr!* that kept getting louder.

I craned my head toward the noise, and five seconds later, a really pale kid on a red four-wheeler with square headlights came flying down the road. He wasn't wearing a helmet.

Maybe it was kind of mean, but I thought that was funny. It was like, *Oh, Freeburg's so safe and crime free so let me find ways to hurt myself all on my own.*

With nothing better to do, I walked to the end of our long driveway to check the mailbox. It was gray and the flag had been snapped off. I'd probably need a tetanus shot after touching it.

As I reached for the mailbox door, the *RRRrrrrrr! RRRrrrrr! RRRrrrrr!* started up again. A second later the pale kid came catapulting back over the hill, the four-wheeler's headlights glinting in the sun. He screeched to a stop in front of me.

"Hi," the kid panted. "You Lissa?"

"The one and only." I wasn't surprised he knew who I was. A new neighbor was probably as exciting as it got on Mine Haul Road.

"Sorry about your aunt. She was really nice."

"It's okay," I said awkwardly, because it's always uncomfortable when people say they're sorry for you. "I only met her twice. My dad says I look like her, though."

"That's cool." He pointed down the road at a white farmhouse. "I live right there. I'm Adam Griggs." He stretched to shake my hand hard. His palm was sweaty.

"So you're the one in high school?" I asked, discreetly wiping my hand off on my jean shorts. He looked really tall, even sitting down.

"Ha, nope. I'm in seventh grade. With you, right?" He smiled, and it occurred to me that even though he was way pale, he had very blue eyes and extremely white teeth. I always notice eyes and teeth.

"Yup. Livin' it up in the one-room schoolhouse."

Adam looked at me kind of hard, and I almost apologized. Instead, I pretended to be interested in checking the mail. The door screamed on rusty hinges and opened to a whole pile of junk—yellowed newspaper ads and big white envelopes. I closed the door without taking anything out.

"Didn't see anything you liked?" Adam asked.

"I'll grab it later. I was going to explore. Maybe in the woods."

"Yeah, you should do that. My brother and I go into your woods all the time. That's how we got half our badges."

"Badges?"

"Yeah. For Boy Scouts. I'm going to be an Eagle Scout in only two years." He sat up straighter when he said it, like he'd just announced that he'd cured Ebola.

"That's fantastic," I said, taking a closer look at him.

When I meet new people, I pretend I'm casting them for a movie. Adam was tough. On one hand, he had nice eyes and teeth. Plus he was tall, like every leading man ever (except for Tom Cruise). But then there was the Boy Scout thing, plus it looked like his mom cut his hair.

"What's your trespassing badge look like?" I asked, eyeing his jeans. They were way too short. Taylor could tell me if a makeover could save this guy. Unfortunately, she was three hundred miles away.

"Eh, it's all communal property around here."

"Remember that when I steal your goat."

"I don't have a goat. Just cows and pigs and chickens. What do you think I am, a hick?" He smirked.

I laughed, surprised. This guy was okay. "Well played, my friend."

Adam flashed his straight white teeth. "Thanks. Well, I gotta go help my dad with some stuff. Nice to meet you."

"Yeah, you too," I said as he hit the throttle, taking off down the road. He hit a huge puddle and sprayed muddy water everywhere. *Show-off.*

Still. I could have a worse neighbor. Even if by "help my dad," he meant "churn some butter" or "milk the cows."

I didn't want to go back to the house. Mom and Dad would be going on and on about their plans to remodel the kitchen. Plans that would make living in Freeburg a permanent condition.

I headed to the backyard. A frayed rope hung from the branch of a giant tree, probably left over from an old tire swing.

As I slipped into the woods, one of my flip-flops sank into goopy, cool mud hidden beneath a layer of dead leaves. I pulled my foot out with a big squishy sound, but the flip-flop stayed behind. *Gross.* I bent and rescued it from the reddish muck.

At that moment, I almost turned back—nothing about the wet and dark woods was inviting—but it still felt kind of peaceful there, and it was nice to be alone after last night's Mandatory Family Fun Time.

A bird cawed and then something skittered under the nearby brush. When I pushed my way through some branches, I saw that someone had bulldozed trails. Water pooled in the rutted tracks of the cleared ground.

Now, I know this is going to make me sound super wimpy, but this was my first time in real, honest-to-goodness wild woods. Central Park has woods, but it also has a carousel and carriage rides. And Dad had taken me "hiking" before, but those trails were made of concrete and had guardrails. Nothing like this.

Picking my way down the trail, I checked out the scenery. Maybe someone more nature-savvy could have identified the trees and bushes, but to me it was all: tall tree, short tree, scruffy bush, scruffier bush, repeat. The ground was littered with those gumball things—you know, those spiny little balls with stems sticking out of them—but I didn't know what kind of tree they'd fallen from. Stubby purple flowers poked up from the dirt, but I had no clue what they were. Ditto the waxy plants shaped like umbrellas. Umbrella plants?

Maybe I'd ask Adam to give me a tour. As a Boy Scout, wasn't it his job to know what plants you could eat and what could kill you? Also, we were neighbors now. He was supposed to be hospitable.

As I got deeper into the woods, I realized it had become quiet. It was a weird sound. Or non-sound, I guess.

In the city, there was always noise, no matter where I went. If I stopped on the sidewalk, closed my eyes,

17

and just listened, I'd hear taxi horns and voices and footsteps (plus someone would shove me and scream at me to get out of the way).

Standing in this silence made my skin crawl. It was weird to know I was the only person around. And even weirder to know these woods belonged to my family.

Continuing through the trees, I tilted my head back, taking in limbs so thick I could barely see through to the sky. Water burbled somewhere. A creek? *That* would be cool. Especially if there was a rock to lie out on, someplace quiet where I could work on my first real screenplay.

I fought past branches and brush toward the water, almost face-planting when I tripped on a root sticking up from the ground. Flip-flops had been a dumb idea.

Eventually, I saw the lip of a wide creek. I climbed down a steep, short hill to the water's edge, slipping a couple of times on the way.

"Wow!" I said aloud when I got to the bottom, my voice echoing.

It was really pretty down there. The creek's current was fast, racing over rocks and splashing against fallen limbs. About twenty feet farther down, there was a pile of tree branches and leaves in the middle of the creek. It looked like beavers had been building a dam. Water ran around it in deep currents, making a sucking sound.

I wished Casey and Taylor were here. We could hang out with lawn chairs and books, Casey sitting under a huge hat, slathered with SPF150 to protect her fair skin, and Taylor in baby oil to bring out her tan.

I picked up a rock and tried to skim it across the water's surface. It sank.

Suddenly, the hairs stood up on the back of my neck, and even though it made no sense at all, I had this crazy idea that someone was watching me. I could imagine exactly how I'd look as a camera captured my stalker's point of view—stepping hesitantly, slow. Vulnerable. Maybe seen in a flash frame, to show the stalker close . . . then closer . . . closer. . . .

I tried to shake off the feeling, but my heart drummed against my chest like my body was trying to warn my mind.

Even though I felt paranoid for doing it, I swiveled my head around, making sure everything was in order. You know, no one-eyed fisherman clutching an ax and giggling crazily behind a tree.

Nothing. The water kept burbling lazily in the creek and, far away, a bird called out. Through the gaps above in the trees, the clouds in the bright blue sky looked like cotton candy. In every way, it seemed like a beautiful day for a walk in the woods.

So how come the feeling was still there?

I decided to go back to the house. In movies, when

people go against their gut instinct, they end up biting it. I started to climb up the bank, using a root sticking out of the ground as leverage. It was hard going because my hands were shaking and my legs felt weak.

Water splashed in the creek. I froze, one hand grasping a root and the other gripping a handful of gritty mud. *What was that? A beaver? A deer? Or—*

Someone—or something—moaned. The sound came from near the beaver dam.

I reached for another root, but it snapped off in my hand. With a lurch, I grabbed for another one. Scrambling, not even caring about the mud that was getting all over my clothes, I crawled to the top of the hill.

Stealing a look over my shoulder, I saw bubbles rippling the water, and a huge dark form moving below the surface.

Maybe it's a turtle, I thought. But turtles don't thrash around like that, and they aren't six feet long.

All at once, the thing shot out of the water with a huge splash, like someone coming up after a dive. I screamed and fell backward, landing hard on my butt and rattling my teeth.

The creature had two arms and two legs like a person, but everything else was just . . . wrong. Fishlike. Water dripped from its scaly body, which shimmered in the sunlight. The creature lifted its green face, its flat nose quivering like it was smelling something.

It locked eyes with me. For what felt like forever, we were frozen, staring at each other. My heart hammered so loudly I was sure the creature could hear it.

What was this thing? It looked like the supernatural villain in a blockbuster film, but there was no mask, no zipper up the front of its body, no campy sound effects.

Meaning, it looked completely real. And this wasn't a movie. So, based on logic . . .

It opened its mouth, displaying sharp, triangular black teeth and a dark purple tongue."Don't come any closer!" I croaked.

Run! It was the first rule of monster movies. Run. Don't try to get a better look. But I was rooted to the spot. Monster bait.

The creature shook its head. It didn't have ears—just dark holes where each ear should have been.

I glared at it, trying to hide how scared I was. "What do you want?"

The creature licked its rubbery lips. When it spoke, its voice was a loud rasp. *"Brains."*

SCENE TWO:

THE EFFECTS OF MONSTER SPOTTING

I shot out of the woods faster than an Olympic sprinter. I even cleared a fallen tree. Toes pointed and everything.

It's true what they say: fear can make you *move your butt*. As I raced across the backyard, I barely felt my chest burning and my legs aching.

I clattered onto the back deck and locked the black latch on the wooden gate behind me, grimacing at myself. Stupid people in horror movies always do that—lock the door. Like that helps when the killer's got a chainsaw. Or teeth as sharp as razors. I slid open the glass doors and fell into the living room, gasping for air.

Sinking to the floor, I twisted to peer outside.

There was nothing in the backyard. Just shaggy grass dotted with dandelions. The tire-swing rope swayed lazily in the breeze.

Did I imagine the creature?

No. No way. I saw what I saw.

Music blared, and I jumped. Now, I know this is wrong on so many levels, but Mom loves classic Britney Spears. And right then, "Toxic" was turned up so loud I could barely register the blood churning through my ears.

I wrapped my arms around my knees and rocked back and forth, squeezing my fists to stop my hands from shaking. My nails bit into my palms.

I willed myself to calm down. I didn't want Mom or Dad to find me like this. I'd have to explain why I looked like I was on the verge of a nervous breakdown.

Footsteps stomped up the basement stairs and Dad emerged through the doorway. He carried a long piece of wood. "Look what I found in the basement!"

"What is it?" I asked through the marbles in my mouth.

"A headboard! Looks like maple. And check out that craftsmanship." He set the board down to rub his hand over the flowers carved into it. "You want it for your room?"

I shook my head. I couldn't think about decorating at a time like this.

"You're quiet." Dad set the headboard against the wall and moved toward me. "Honey? You okay? You're muddy. And what's on your forehead?" I put my hand there. When I pulled it back, my fingers were red.

"What happened?" Dad asked sharply. It was the same tone he used that one time Haylie ate a crayon and we took her to the ER.

"Nothing. I just . . . fell."

I hadn't meant to lie. I just did. Who would have believed the truth? Not my dad, the rational, level-headed, *sane* doctor.

Sane. That was the operative word here.

I shook my head again to clear it. Maybe I'd gotten heatstroke? Or had a seizure?

Mom came out of the kitchen, drying a plate with a dish towel. There was a dust smudge on her face. "Everything okay in here?" She frowned when she saw my forehead. "Aww, you poor kid. Who won? You or the tree?"

"I'm okay," I mumbled. "Just a little dizzy."

"You're a little pale, too. Ben? Is she dehydrated?"

"Maybe so." Dad hurrried to the kitchen sink and filled a glass. He raised it to my lips. "Drink," he commanded.

I wrapped my hands around the glass and tilted it up. I didn't realize how thirsty I was until the metallic-tasting water filled my mouth. My tongue was so dry it felt fuzzy, and my lips were cracked. The water was gone in ten seconds.

"Thanks," I wheezed, wiping my mouth.

Mom and Dad were still staring at me, their faces etched with worry.

"Better?" Mom asked, and I nodded.

Dad put his hand on my back and steered me to the bathroom. "Come on. Let's get you cleaned up and avoid an infection."

I perched on the counter, eyes fixed on the bathroom floor. It was made of hundreds of beige tiles, some cracked. *Most* were cracked, actually. When I looked to my right, I noticed a strip of faded red rose wallpaper sticking up and had to resist the urge to pick at it.

Dad hunted in a box under the sink. "Aha! Here it is!" Gently, he cleaned the cut on my forehead with a cotton ball and some peroxide, which stung. It reminded me of when he cleaned up the cuts and scrapes I got on the playground when I was little. I was always hurting myself.

Haylie appeared in the bathroom with her stuffed squirrel, Sammy. That thing looks like a piece of real roadkill since Haylie had used it for teething.

"What happened, Lissy?"

"Nothing," I said. "I'm fine, Hails."

"There." Dad stepped back so I could hop off the counter. "All fixed."

I touched the bandage. "Aww, that's too bad. I wanted a lightning-shaped scar like Harry Potter's."

"Maybe next time, kiddo."

I spent the rest of the day unpacking, dusting, and listening to Mom and Dad discuss color schemes and the pros and cons of knocking down the wall between the dining area and the living room. It was crazy boring, but at least it distracted me from that thing camped out in our creek.

Monster. That's what it was. I almost couldn't say the word, even in my head. Monsters only exist in movies and comic books.

And in crazy people's heads.

When there was a break in the manual labor, I escaped to my room and called Taylor.

"Lissa!" she screeched. Taylor doesn't say *hello* like normal people. "How's the country? Are you wearing overalls?"

"Is that an insult?"

"Why would that be an insult?"

"Because *you* would never wear overalls." Taylor doesn't wear much that isn't designer or "shabby chic," which means it's expensive but looks like garbage.

"That's only because they'd look weird on me. They'd look adorable on you."

"Especially if they have little sunflowers sewn onto them."

"Yes! On the butt. And then you could have those

little loop thingies to keep your hammers and other tools handy."

"Hammers and other tools?" I rolled over to glance in my dresser mirror. I was a mess. Well, at least there was no one here to see me. "I guess as long as I'm living here, I could learn a trade. Like carpentry, or something."

"That's the spirit!" Taylor's voice lowered. "A trade, *and* fresh air and nature!"

I sucked in my breath. I couldn't tell her, could I? If our situations were switched, I wouldn't believe her. No one believes in monsters. And I couldn't prove what I saw by showing her, since she wasn't *here*.

"We have wasps, too," I said instead. "Dad found them living in the rafters above our porch. So now he has to drive thirty minutes away to Home Depot to buy special wasp-killing spray."

"The country sounds exciting. *I've* never owned a real wasp's nest. Oh, hey." There was rustling on Taylor's end of the line. "I gotta go. Meeting Ian."

I picked at the fluff on my bedspread. "For the play?" Taylor had the lead.

"Yeah, we're running lines. I have *lines*, which *you* wrote. And they're fah-bulous!" Taylor said the last word in a British accent.

"Okay, then. I'll be here. Suffering."

After she hung up, I sighed. I hated that I couldn't tell her what had happened. Just another way I felt disconnected from her and Casey.

And I needed their help. Assuming what I saw was real—and it really seemed like it was—I didn't like the idea of a swamp creature trolling around our creek when Haylie was outside playing. Plus, I didn't like not knowing exactly what that *thing* was. It wanted "brains." According to every B-movie I'd ever seen, swamp creatures are never after brains. So what was I dealing with?

Then I thought of Adam. He'd trespassed in our woods. Maybe if I hinted at what I'd seen, he'd confess to seeing it, too. Seemed like a solid plan to me.

After a dinner of slightly burned pork chops and instant mashed potatoes, I went to find him. Country music twanged as I climbed the stairs to Adam's house. A fat brown dog lay on its side on the porch, sleeping. When I rang the doorbell, the dog grumbled without opening its eyes.

Adam's brother opened the door. Or at least I assumed he was Adam's brother and not his dad, since he was wearing a shirt that said THE VOICES TOLD ME TO.

"I know you," he said, smiling. He had blue eyes and pale skin, just like Adam. "You're the new neighbor kid."

I arched my eyebrows at him. If what Mom said was

true, he was only three years older than me. "Yeah, Lissa Black. Is Adam around?"

The guy leaned against the doorframe, his messy brown hair almost grazing the top of it. "Adam!" he screamed. "Lissa Black is here!"

"Thanks." I rolled my eyes.

"Here to serve." He opened the door wider. "Come in if you want. I'm Charlie, by the way. But you can call me Chuck. Like woodchuck. Or upchuck."

"Upchuck?"

"Yeah, you know, like vomit," he said as I walked into the front hall. Muddy work boots were jumbled together under a coatrack crammed with flannel jackets.

Adam appeared from a side room. "Hey! Lissa, what are you doing here?"

"Oh, I just thought maybe we could hang out." I ignored the smirk that spread across Upchuck's face. *Seriously, dude. Go groom a horse or something.*

"Sure. Want a fudge pop? We could sit on the porch."

"Sounds good." I waited while Adam ran to the kitchen. When he came back, he shoved the popsicle in my hand. "Here."

"Thanks." I followed him outside, tearing the white paper open. Chocolate smeared on my hand and I licked it off. Then I noticed Adam watching me.

"What? Feeding myself is hard." I took a bite. It tasted like an off-brand, but it was still good.

We sat on the porch steps, blinking in the glare of the setting sun. It was a mosaic of fiery pinks and oranges, and looked like something out of a painting.

I missed New York's art museums already, even if I hardly ever visited them. It was nice to have the option.

"So." I tried to sound casual. "Have you been in my woods lately?"

Adam scratched at a mosquito bite on his elbow. "Not since the real estate guys told us it was yours now. Promise."

I waved my fudge pop. "Oh, trespass all you want. I don't care. I was just wondering when you'd been there last. Especially the creek."

Adam smiled. "Your aunt was so cool. She gave us free run of the place. Charlie and I used to catch tadpoles there. And soft-shelled turtles, but those don't come out often. They're shy."

He hadn't taken the bait. He didn't seem to know about anything weird in the creek. And he seemed too—I don't know—*open*, to lie. I nodded, sticking my fudge pop back in my mouth so I wouldn't have to say anything right away.

Then it hit me. I didn't have to ask him to go *monster* hunting.

"So," I said, feeling sneaky and underhanded but at the same time really proud of myself for being so smart. "Want to help me find some turtles tomorrow morning?"

SCENE THREE:

RETURN TO THE WOODS

I have to break the fourth wall here, which is normally a lazy way to convey information in a movie—have the main character speak right to the audience.

But it's worth it to acknowledge, *honestly*, that I know what you're thinking: I was wrong for not fessing up to the real reason I was asking Adam to come with me into the woods. He was all excited, thinking he'd met a new friend, and here I was, leading him to certain death.

No wonder country people don't trust city folk.

But I'd already justified everything to myself: If the monster was a hallucination due to a tiny brain tumor missed during my last checkup, no harm, no foul. We'd go into the woods, splash around looking for turtles and tadpoles and whatever, and Adam would be none the wiser.

And if there really *was* a swamp creature, it wasn't like I'd stay and prance around, picking berries and smelling flowers. I'd be on alert for any sound or sight out of the ordinary, ready to vamoose and take Adam with me.

Finally, when it came down to it, Adam could kick a swamp creature's butt. The kid's built like an ox.

As any good Boy Scout, Adam showed up right on time the next morning, holding a bottle of water in each hand. I was still chewing my Cinnamon Toast Crunch when the doorbell rang. Even though I knew it was Adam, I looked through the peephole out of habit. It had the same view as looking through a fish-eye lens—Adam's head looked huge compared to the rest of his body. It was like a shot out of a Hitchcock movie.

I swung the door open. "Whoa, is that a fanny pack?" I pointed to the green pouch strapped around Adam's waist.

He held out a bottle of water. "Of course not. It's a waist pack."

"Huh." It looked exactly like the fanny pack Mom wore to Six Flags last year. "How is a waist pack different from a fanny pack?"

"A waist pack is a specially designed piece of survival equipment," Adam said. "It's fireproof, and waterproof, and it can hold up to fifteen pounds of supplies." He uncapped his water and took a huge swig.

"I see." I wondered why fifteen pounds of supplies

were necessary to splash around in a creek looking for turtles.

"Let's get a move on." Adam turned and walked around the side of our house. I followed, noticing that he wore galoshes—big yellow boots that squeaked with every step. I had to bite my lip not to comment on them.

The woods were totally Disneyfied. Yellow sunlight streamed through the trees, and birds chirped happily. I half-expected Thumper, the rabbit from *Bambi*, to come hopping through the leaves to hug my leg while bluebirds placed a garland of wildflowers around my neck.

Adam grabbed a big knobby stick from the ground. "You should pick out a walking stick, too," he said, waving his around. "They're good for swiping away spiderwebs and pushing back branches."

I scanned the ground but couldn't find anything long enough or strong enough to pass for a walking stick.

Adam held his out. "Here."

"Aww, you're being chivalrous. How adorable."

He grinned. "I handed you a big old stick. If you think that's chivalrous, you must have really low expectations."

I shrugged. "Then I'm never disappointed." Like I

knew anything about chivalry. Guys never paid attention to me, mainly because I was always with Taylor.

"How are you liking Freeburg?" Adam asked, snatching up another broken limb.

After my encounter with the swamp monster, I was done with being polite about this Podunk town. "Oh, you know." I pretended to strum a banjo, humming. "Good old country life."

"It's not *that* bad," Adam said. "You can't walk around the woods like this in the city."

"Tragic."

"Well, what do you normally do for fun?"

I shrugged. "Hang out with my friends. Watch movies. Write stuff."

"Can't you do all that here?"

"My parents wouldn't let me pack my friends in the U-Haul. Plus I wouldn't subject them to this."

"Nice attitude." He charged ahead with his stick, whacking at branches like we were fighting our way through a jungle with wild animals on the prowl.

"Hey," I said, jogging to catch up with him. "I'm not usually this grouchy. This is all just really—" *Depressing. Boring.* "—different."

"Gotcha." I couldn't read his tone.

After a short hike, we veered off the path toward the

creek. When I heard the burbling, I remembered why we were there. What we might see. My body tensed.

I fell back behind Adam. My heart was thumping so loudly I was afraid he'd hear it and ask me what was wrong.

He sidestepped down the creek's embankment, dropping onto the red clay below and landing heavily on the stones.

I surveyed the creek bed. The water sounded almost cheerful the way it bounced off the rocks. And little animals wouldn't be making noise in the bushes if something scary was around, right?

My body relaxed. I was safe here with Adam.

It occurred to me that Casey and Taylor would want to know about this. As long as Adam didn't hack me into little pieces and stuff me into his fanny pack, they'd be totally jealous that a guy took me for a walk in the woods.

I followed him into the creek, knees bent and arms out for balance. But the hill was slicker than I'd remembered, and my right foot slipped.

"Ahhh!"

My butt hit the mud so hard it knocked the wind out of me. I grabbed at the little roots jutting out of the mud but they snapped in my hands, and I slid all the way to the bottom of the creek bed.

"Wow," Adam said. "You're really not good at this nature stuff, are you?"

"I'm fine, thanks," I grumbled, letting Adam help me up. I stretched my arms and legs, checking for damage, but I seemed okay.

He glanced behind me and snorted.

"What?" I asked, brushing my butt. There was something wet there. When I pulled my hand away, it was covered in chocolate-brown mud.

"It looks like you pooped your pants." He bent down to pick up a rock, and then skipped it across the creek. It bounced four times before hitting the other side.

I decided that Casey and Taylor didn't need to know about this part of the walk. Or what Adam was like in general.

He shrugged. "Maybe if you'd worn galoshes, that wouldn't have happened." He picked up his foot, showing me the ridged sole of his boot. "See? They're good for climbing. They give you traction."

"Thanks for the tip." I kneeled to rinse my muddy hand in the creek. The water was cold and clear, but it got all cloudy when I rubbed my hands together.

I eyed the beaver dam—or whatever it was—farther down the bank. There was no sign of the swamp monster, but it had appeared suddenly last time. I clenched my fists, my legs tensing to run if need be. Water trickled over the stones, and a light wind rustled the leaves overhead. "Want to keep walking?" I asked.

"Didn't you want to look for turtles?"

Right, turtles. "Oh, yeah. Um, I don't know. I kind of feel like hiking more. Is that okay?"

"Yeah, sure. Follow the creek?"

I nodded and we started walking downstream, pebbles crunching under our feet.

With Adam there, the idea of a monster suddenly seemed dumb. This was just a creek. The water was shallow and clear. And the brush along the sides wasn't tall and dense enough to hide a monster.

Up ahead, a felled tree blocked the stream. It must have fallen pretty recently, because its leaves were still green and the trunk hadn't started rotting. Adam climbed on top. "Come on. There's something really cool I want to show you."

I scrambled up, clutching the rough bark. Some of it crumbled under my hands, and I teetered when I stood, holding out my arms for balance.

My heartbeat had slowed to normal by then. I couldn't explain what I'd seen the day before, but whatever it was, I must have imagined it.

You didn't imagine it, a little voice in my head nagged.

Shut up, little voice.

We jumped down from the fallen tree and continued on, walking for what felt like forever. Finally, Adam pointed up at a tree with a particularly thick trunk. "Dad and I made this a few years ago."

I shaded my eyes so I could look up. About ten short boards were nailed into the side of the tree—steps. They led to a wooden platform with a railing wrapped around it. "Cool, a tree house!"

Adam glanced at me scornfully. "It isn't a tree house. It's a deer stand. For deer hunting."

"Right. Of course I should have known that right away."

Adam ignored me, grabbing the lowest board and shinnying up to the platform. "Wanna come up? It'll hold both of us."

I climbed up to the platform and admired the view of wildflowers tangled together with weeds and roots. "Wow, pretty. This would look amazing in 3D. All the different colors popping out, you know?"

"I guess. I think it looks good the way it is." Adam unzipped his fanny pack, pulling out a package of beef jerky. "Want some?"

I shook my head. The idea of dried meat seemed so wrong. Like astronaut ice cream—what's the point?

Adam held the package out farther. "You sure? Good stuff."

"Nope, it's all yours."

He burped, tucking the package into his fanny pack. "What's up? You're staring off into space."

"Oh, sorry. Just thinking."

Adam squinted to the right, raising his hand slowly. "Shhhh!"

"What?" I whispered back, and he tilted his head.

"See?" he said softly.

It was like one of those optical illusion pictures—the kind where you look and, at first, there's nothing there except a bunch of colors and blobs. But when you stare long enough, the hidden picture pops out.

At first, all I saw was a bunch of green and brown all scrambled together. But when my eyes adjusted, I realized a deer was standing about a hundred feet from us. It had long, spindly legs and a few white spots on its back near its little nub of a tail. Its head was raised like it was listening for something.

"Cute," I breathed at the exact same time Adam whispered, "Dinner."

"Adam!" I said loudly. The deer startled and bounded away, disappearing into some bushes.

"Oh, well. Guess we'll have pizza instead of venison. That's deer meat, city girl."

"Ha, ha," I said, standing up and brushing myself off. "Should we keep walking?" I wanted to cover as much ground as possible. Staying in one spot was making me antsy.

We climbed down from the deer stand, and as I dropped onto the loose dirt, I heard a tree splinter and crash.

"What was that?" Adam asked sharply.

I pressed myself against the tree. "It's the—" Could a swamp monster knock down trees?

Another tree cracked and fell, closer now. Birds squawked and flew up and into the sky. Twigs snapped, branches broke, bushes shook, but I couldn't see a thing. Adam and I stayed planted at the base of the tree, craning our heads. I imagined what this would look like from an arc shot—the camera swiveling around us as we cowered, waiting for whatever came next.

There was a brown flash about thirty feet away. "Th-th-there," I stuttered, pointing.

"Quick!" Adam barked, grabbing my arm so hard it hurt. "Back up to the deer stand! Flat on the floor!"

We raced up the ladder, hitting the floor of the platform and pressing ourselves against the wood. I willed myself to stop shaking. *Happy thoughts, happy thoughts. Kittens. Chocolate. Best Original Screenplay Oscar.*

Loud footsteps boomed below us. They were far away at first, but getting closer, closer . . . I squeezed my eyes shut, breathing in the earthy smell of the deer stand.

The footsteps stopped right below us. I squeezed my eyes shut tighter, counting in my head. *One-Mississippi, two-Mississippi, three-Mississippi, four-Mississippi.*

I was up to fifty-seven Mississippis before I realized that not just the footsteps had gone quiet. *Everything* had. No more birds chirping, no woodpeckers pecking, no small animals rustling in the bushes.

I counted to one hundred and opened my eyes. A huge, furry brown *thing* was six inches away, staring at me. It had a wide, flat nose and sunken eyes. They reminded me a lot of the swamp creature's—brown and liquid.

"Adam," I tried to say, but nothing came out. I tried to lift my hand to poke him, but I couldn't move. Out of the corner of my eye, I saw that Adam was motionless beside me, his arms over his head like we were hiding under our desks for an earthquake drill.

"Adam," I mouthed again, this time managing a squeak. He lowered his arms and peeked at the monster. His face drained of color.

The monster leaned closer. Its breath smelled like hot, fifty-year-old garbage. The muscles in its massive neck tensed as it opened its mouth.

"Moooooooooooo!"

Adam and I scrambled down from the deer stand,

falling at the monster's furry brown feet. They were the size of tennis rackets. It grinned down at me, scratching at the matted fur on its back.

Adam shoved me. "Run!"

My limbs unlocked and I took off through the trees, sprinting until my chest tightened and the muscles in my legs felt like wound springs.

When I whacked my elbow on a tree, I cried out— yikes, that smarted! —but I never looked behind me. That's how you die in horror movies.

I could see light through trees up ahead. "Almost there," Adam called out. "Just a few more feet."

That's always when the monsters get you. When you think you're safe.

Stumbling on a root, I fell flat on my face. *"Oh!"* I scrambled to my feet and kept going.

Don't look behind you, don't look behind you, don't look behind you . . .

We burst from the edge of the woods, sprinted across my backyard, pounded up the steps to the deck, and yanked open the glass sliding door. I closed and latched it behind us, and we sank to the floor. It all felt like déjà vu.

Only today the house was empty. Everyone else must have gone into town.

The memory of the creature's brown eyes burned

in my head, and I hugged myself. It had been so close to me. *Close enough to—*

I wouldn't think about it.

"Holy cow." Adam rubbed the sweat from his forehead. "What *was* that? I've never seen an animal stand up on two legs like that before."

My arms were covered with red scratches, and a blue bruise was already forming on my elbow where I'd whacked it against a tree.

"I don't know," I said, panting, my mind flipping from the creature we'd seen today to the one I'd seen yesterday. "I think it was a Sasquatch."

Adam's brow furrowed. "You mean, like Bigfoot?"

I dropped my head into my hands. "I know! I know how crazy that sounds." I took a deep breath. "Adam, I have to tell you something." The words came out muffled.

"What?"

I spilled the beans—the whole story about the swamp monster rising up from the creek and staring at me and how I'd tricked Adam into scouting the area with me to investigate.

When I was finished, Adam didn't look angry, but he did look like someone had unhinged his jaw. Like he was a snake getting ready to eat a rat. It would have been hilarious if I wasn't so freaked out.

"I'm really sorry," I said feebly. "I should have told you why I wanted you to show me around the woods."

"It's okay."

"No, it's not. I should have warned you."

Adam picked a round, brown sticker-thing off his jeans. "Yeah, but I can understand why you didn't. Seeing is believing, right?"

I looked at him. Adam was exactly the kind of person I needed in a situation like this, and I had to ask him something I never imagined I'd ask anyone in a million years. I took a deep breath.

"Adam, will you help me catch some monsters?"

SCENE FOUR:

THE MONSTER TRAP

I wasn't that surprised when Adam agreed to help me. Boy Scouts are supposed to be helpful. Plus, capturing weird-looking creatures was probably right up his alley.

"What kind of trap do you think we should use?" I asked the next evening. We were hanging out next to the Griggs' cow pen, which was basically a fenced-in field adjacent to two big sheds. "Maybe we could try a bunch of different ones? Like, all over the woods?"

"Hmm," Adam said thoughtfully. He grunted as he hoisted up a bag of feed, spilling it through the wire fence and into a long trough. Cows lumbered over, and I stepped back. They seemed gentle, but they were big. Squish-you-flat big.

"Maybe we could dig a trench," I suggested, bending to pick a dandelion. It was soft under my fingers. "We could cover it with something really flimsy and put a bunch of grass on top of that. The . . . monster . . . would fall through to the bottom." It felt weird to say that word out loud. *Monster.*

"Sorry," Adam said. "This isn't a cartoon. That won't work. We need a snare."

"You mean something that pulls the monster up in the air when it steps in it?" I put the dandelion to my nose. It smelled sweet.

"Exactly," Adam said. "But you know, catching the monster's not the hard part."

"Oh, really? What's the hard part?"

"Figuring out what we're gonna do with it once we catch it."

"I have an idea," I said casually.

I'd been thinking a lot about this since last night, and it was more than an idea. I was sure it was the best idea in the history of ideas: we could make a movie!

It could be framed like a documentary that goes wrong. Adam and I could be bird-watchers who stumble upon a forest of monsters. We could shoot the whole thing with a handheld camera using shaky bad angles to make it look authentic.

The set would be free—it was right in my backyard. And we wouldn't even have to pay our actors, because they would be us.

But where would we distribute it? Maybe YouTube? Or maybe Taylor could ask Roland Reed to take a look. He might know someone we could pitch to. Or—

"I think we should keep the monster," Adam said, bringing me back to the present. "We can study it."

"What good would studying it do?"

Adam shrugged. "I don't know. It's probably a crossbreed. We can figure out what it's a mix of. Or it might be an entirely new species, and *we'd* be the ones to discover it." He jerked his head toward the woods. "Want to see where I think we should set the trap?"

"Sure," I said, trying to keep my voice even. Just the thought of going back into the woods freaked me out, but I couldn't send Adam in there alone.

After Adam grabbed his backpack from his house, I followed him through the woods, keeping so close I practically stepped on his heels. My entire body was tense. A twig snapped a few feet away and I flinched. "What was that?"

"A rabbit," Adam replied. "Trust me. We'll be in and out in twenty minutes." He didn't sound even a little afraid, and that made me relax. Kind of.

We weaved off from the trail and fought our way through bushes and weeds. Green stickers clung to my T-shirt. "Almost there," Adam said, whacking at a branch. "And . . . here we are!"

We were standing in a small clearing. In the middle was a half-crumbled red brick cabin backlit by sunlight. From a certain angle and with one eye closed and the other all squinted, it looked almost livable. But if I walked a step in any direction, I could see the roof was caved in and two of the four sides had fallen down. Weeds grew up in tufts from an old broken sidewalk and wildflowers covered the ground.

I pointed. "Hey, what kind of flowers are those?"

"The purplish blue ones are bluebells. And the white lacey ones are Queen Anne's lace."

"Pretty."

"Glad you think so, because this is our headquarters. We can use what's left of the cabin as a shelter, in case we come across our friend." Adam disappeared around the corner of the building.

"Wait!" I scrambled after him, careful not to slip on the broken sidewalk leading to what used to be the front door. "We should stick together!" I followed him through a gaping hole in the right side of the cabin Inside, it was just one room the bathroom walls had collapsed. I spotted the remnants of a metal toilet through the broken brick.

"Here's what I'm thinking," he said, swiping at a spiderweb. "We set up camp here, clear out all those old bricks and the junk outside. And then we set up the bait."

"What bait?" I asked, looking around. The place smelled musty, like someone's old attic, and something dark was clustered in a corner. I wrinkled my nose. Animal poop.

Adam shrugged. "What do you think it eats?"

"If it's really a Sasquatch, it's a vegetarian."

"According to who?"

"According to *what*, you mean. Monster movies. Sasquatches eat plants and berries."

"Huh. Then why did you run screaming for home?"

"Oh, I don't know. Because vegetarians can still be serial killers?"

That made me think, though. The Sasquatch could have ripped us to pieces when we were exposed on the deer stand, but it just stood there.

"Interesting logic," Adam said.

"You know, movies might help. They have rules. Especially horror movies."

"Like what?"

"Like, don't be a blonde and take a shower. Don't split off from a group." I ticked each rule off on my fingers. "When you shoot a monster, make sure it's dead. And, oh, no matter what, never, ever say 'I'll be right back.' Because you won't be."

Adam stroked his chin. "Huh. That's very interesting. But I gotta go check something. I'll be right back."

"You're not funny. I'm telling you, there are rules. And those rules will help us capture the monster."

"Looks like we might have a secret weapon: your big, juicy brain, full of useful rules. Unless zombies come. Then they'll eat it."

I paced in the small room, glancing up through

the gaping hole in the ceiling. "There's a problem, though."

"What's that?"

"The monsters I've seen here so far don't match their behaviors in the movies." I picked up a piece of rotten wood and hurled it outside. "What swamp creature wants brains? And I've never heard of a Sasquatch that moos. Maybe the rules are useless."

"Guess we'll find out, won't we?" Adam stepped through the gap in the wall to the outside. He slid his backpack off, unzipped it, and removed a bundle of rope.

"What's that for?"

"That's part of our snare." Adam reached into his backpack again and pulled out a big wire spring and a Swiss Army knife. "And this is the rest of it."

I watched Adam tie the rope into a loop. He hid the loop under a pile of leaves and threw the other end of the rope over a tree branch. "If the monster steps into the center of the loop, the spring snaps to launch it into the air."

I wrinkled my nose doubtfully. "Won't a Sasquatch be too big?"

"Maybe too big to dangle. But not too big to get caught."

"I just hope the knots don't come undone."

Adam looked at me like I'd insulted him. "Of

course they won't. I used a clove hitch." To demonstrate, he untied the knot, then retied it. Slowly, like it was important that I remember how to do it. Since I use complicated knots to catch monsters so often.

"Oh. Right. A *clove* hitch." I cleared my throat. "So how do we get the monster to step into the trap?"

Adam nudged more leaves and dirt over the loop with his foot. "With bait," he said, reaching into his waist pack and pulling out a shiny apple and a handful of trail mix. He placed them carefully on top of the leaves.

"There." He stepped back to admire his handiwork. "The hard part is over."

Adam wasn't the expert on monster movies, so I let it slide, but when someone says something like that, it means the trouble's just beginning.

SCENE FIVE:

MONSTER GAMES

My imagination kept running away with me over the next few days. Not about catching the monster or even my Oscar-worthy project, but about how my parents would react to seeing it. That was what *really* mattered, because there was no way my parents would make us stay in a town crawling with monsters.

I even wrote a scene of how it would play out:

FADE IN:
INTERIOR OUR HOUSE, LIVING ROOM

FAMILY WATCHING DVD. MOM'S AND DAD'S
EXPRESSIONS GROWING MORE AND MORE WORRIED.

MOM:
(Gasping, clutching chest, looking
  generally horrified and guilty)

Oh, my! You filmed that in *our* woods?
(Turns to where Dad sits on couch,

looking dumbstruck.)

Ben! Honey! Go online right now and buy us
tickets to fly home!

HOUSE INTERIOR, CONTINUOUS

DAD BUYING TICKETS, US PACKING, RUNNING
THROUGH HOUSE.

DAD:
Leave it! We'll buy new things! It's not safe here!

HOUSE EXTERIOR, CONTINUOUS

DAD BOARDING UP HOUSE, DAD STICKING
"FREE" SIGN IN FRONT YARD.

LONG SHOT

CAR PEELING AWAY FROM DRIVEWAY, BLACK
EXHAUST CLOUDS.

It was a nice scene. Maybe I could translate it to reality.

Problem was, it had been days and the monster still hadn't shown up. Adam and I checked the snare every morning and evening. Zilch. Seriously, where's a blood-thirsty, camera-ready creature when you need one?

On Sunday evening, I slouched on our couch, watching a rerun of *America's Next Top Model*. It was the forty-second season, or something, and Tyra Banks was reaching for ideas. (I'm sorry, but posing upside down in a wind tunnel is *not* a realistic modeling test.)

As I watched Tyra yell at one girl for "not wanting it enough," I tried to not think about how tomorrow I would begin a new school, and how tomorrow Taylor and Casey would start seventh grade without me.

Buddy movies never include a friend who's only available via Skype. What if they phased me out? Or, what if they walked into class tomorrow and found a fun, interesting girl who had just moved to Manhattan from Minneapolis, fidgeting at her desk, desperately in need of friends to help her adjust to the big, bad city?

I picked at a thread on the loveseat's cushion, shooting a glare at Mom, who was researching furniture on her laptop. "I don't think Crate & Barrel delivers this far," I offered, but she ignored me.

Dad was sitting next to Mom on the couch, and he kept snapping his newspaper and sighing, which was his way of passive-aggressively objecting to *America's Next Top Model*. Every time he did it, Haylie looked up from where she was playing with her Barbies on the floor.

Finally, he put his newspaper down. "Lissa, honey? Why don't you go down to the basement? See if you can find a game for us to play."

I shrugged, not tearing my eyes from the screen. "Nah, I'm good."

"It's not a request." Dad cleared his throat. "I bet Aunt Lucy has some good stuff down there."

"Fine." I hoisted myself off the recliner. "I'll be right back."

I smiled to myself. *I'll be right back.* Cue the spooky music.

I yanked on the metal chain attached to the basement light. The light flickered before turning on, casting long shadows down the wooden stairs. To my right, wobbly shelves were filled with rusty cans. They probably had killer spiders inside.

Carefully, I made my way down the stairs. Every step creaked, and I wondered exactly how many termites were gnawing on the wood.

I exhaled in relief when I got to the concrete floor, rubbing my bare arms. It was much colder down here. Plastic-covered furniture and piles of stuff were scattered all over the place. Something dripped in the far corner.

To my right was a box of old scrapbooks. I flipped one open to brittle, yellowed photos mounted on pages of construction paper. "Lucy, first day of high school," was scrawled beneath one. I peered at it closer and realized Dad was right. I *did* look a lot like Aunt Lucy. We had the same high forehead, dark eyes, and square jaw.

"Hey!" My voice echoed up the stairs. "Where should I look?"

"Check the table by the water heater." Dad sounded far away.

"Okay!" I replaced the photo album in the box and shuffled along the uneven floor until I saw a scratched-up coffee table. Faded, mouse-chewed games were stacked on top—Monopoly, Clue, Scrabble, Connect Four, Battleship. *Boring.*

But what was that at the bottom of the pile? It was a light-purple box, square and with black letters stenciled on the top. It was so dirty and dusty I couldn't make out the words.

With my right hand, I rubbed away the filth. *Monsterville.* Then, beneath it: *A Monster Around Every Corner.* The lower left-hand corner contained black initials: *L.B.* Probably for "Lucy Black."

I flipped the box, looking for a Parker Brothers or Milton Bradley logo, but there wasn't one.

I heard water dripping in the corner again. I looked up and glanced around. Long shadows stretched across the floor, and I couldn't see the far wall in the darkness.

Tucking Monsterville under my arm, I dashed across the concrete floor and pounded up the stairs.

"Find anything good?" Dad smiled innocently. He'd switched to a rerun of *The Office.*

"Just this." I shook the box before dropping it onto the coffee table, sending a cloud of dust into the air.

Haylie scooted over with her Barbies. "I want to play." She pried off the lid. "Neat!" She flattened the game board on the table and pulled out the little figurines.

Mom shut her laptop and put it on the coffee table. She rummaged for the game's instructions and handed them to Dad. "You do the honors."

"Put each monster in the proper habitat," he read from a yellowed piece of paper. "For example, the spiders in the hills, the troll near the bridge, the sandman in the desert, the mummy by the pyramids, the werewolf in the woods, the zombies in the town, the Loch Ness monster in the ocean, the blob guarding the cliffs."

Mom pursed her lips as Haylie placed each figurine in the right spot. "I don't know about this. . . . Are you sure this game's appropriate for Haylie?"

I leaned closer to inspect it. We had nothing to worry about. The monster figurines were too cartoonish to be scary. The blob looked like a ball of bright orange Jell-O with little nubs for arms. How was it supposed to grab you? "Looks fine to me," I said.

"Okay. But if Haylie has nightmares tonight, we're never playing this game again."

"I'm never scared," Haylie proclaimed, twirling one

long blonde strand around her finger and reaching for the gingerbread man-shaped player pieces. "Can I be the blue boy?"

"Um, sure." I was surprised that Haylie wanted to use the boy piece, since she loves anything glittery or pink or unicorny.

"Up to four players can play," Dad continued from the instructions. "Take your place at the beginning of the board, under the bed. Each player chooses a separate trail and battles his own monsters to rescue the kidnapped princess."

I examined the board. Whoever designed this thing hadn't made it fair. There were four trails, and they all had different numbers of spaces and levels of difficulty.

The left trail had forty-five spaces. You had to weave around glowing yellow dots in a foggy marsh and navigate a long bridge over the Loch Ness monster and the hydra—that's this seven-headed serpent-looking thing. Then, when you arrived on the other side, a blob and gigantic spiders waited among snow-covered cliffs.

The right trail had thirty-nine spaces. You had to escape a werewolf, the Abominable Snowman, and run from cave-dwelling zombies.

The middle left one looked easier. It had thirty-three spaces. You battled the sandman, the mummy, and stumbled across a zombie-infested town, but a bridge shortcut put you closer to the end.

The middle right one was the easiest, with twenty-five spaces. Other than two spots where you ran into nests of giant spiders, you only ran into the troll, which you'd encounter anyway on the other trails. All the paths merged into one before the troll appeared.

"Huh." Mom frowned at the board. "Haylie, sweetie, why don't you take this path?" She guided Haylie's hand to the easiest one.

"No, thank you," Haylie said politely. "I want the path with the doggy." She meant the werewolf.

"Okay, kiddo." Mom held out the game's wooden die. "You go first."

Haylie rolled the die and got a six. "One, two, three, four, five, six," she counted aloud, pushing her game piece across the board.

I went next, and I got a six, too. Only I landed on the space that made me face off with the sandman.

"Draw a card," Dad said, tapping the instructions.

Oh no, a zombie comes for you
With it in tow, a hungry crew
The way to escape the undead?
With all your might, swing for the head!

"But you're caught by the sandman," Dad said

unnecessarily, "so you have to wait until your next turn, and draw another card."

"Perfect," I grumbled, putting the card facedown. A wooden club was drawn on the back of it. I waited for everyone else to roll once, and then it was my turn again. I drew a card with a picture of an apple core on the back.

> *The troll won't sway, insists you pay*
> *Three silver coins to make your way*
> *But bargain yes, and you shall find*
> *He's happy with a mere fruit rind.*

"Well, at least you'll be prepared for later." Mom rolled the die. She landed on the space with the blob and let Haylie draw a card for her. Of course it was the card I needed.

> *The sandman's grabbed onto your shoe*
> *Down, down you sink, it feels like glue—*
> *But sprinkle moisture on the ground*
> *And life will grant another round.*

"Trade you," I offered, but Mom shook her head and placed the card facedown on the table.

"We have to play by the rules," she said, giving me a meaningful glance. We were supposed to be setting an example for Haylie.

The game was short. Dad won, since he had the easiest path. He even miscounted a few times so Haylie could catch up to him.

Haylie wasn't upset. She clapped when Dad landed on the purple tent at the end of the board. "Yay, you saved the princess!"

"Yup. And I got killed by the sandman," I said. I never got off that space. I made a big show of yawning. "Can I go to bed now?"

"Sure," Mom replied. "After you help us clean up."

I put the Monsterville pieces back in the box and brought the popcorn bowl to the kitchen. Mom took it from me and ran it under the faucet.

"Such an odd game," she said. "I wonder if they still make it."

"Hmm, that's an idea. It might be worth something. You know, if it's rare."

I headed to my room and changed into pajamas. After brushing my teeth, I fired up my laptop and did a search for *Monsterville* but nothing about a board game came up. Then I logged into my eBay account and searched for *Monsterville* under Toys and Hobbies. Nothing. It was like the game didn't exist.

Or maybe it was just unpopular. Who wants to play a game where there's no equal shot at winning?

Logging into my Gmail account, I stared at Taylor's

and Casey's grayed-out screen names. I wondered what they were doing. Were they asleep already?

I shut off my computer, jumped into bed, and burrowed under my red blanket, resting my cheek against the pillow. Even though I had real monsters to worry about, at that moment, starting a new school all alone scared me a lot more. I'd be lucky if I got any sleep at all.

SCENE SIX:

TRAUMATIZING EXPERIENCES

When I came into the kitchen for breakfast the next morning, Haylie was playing with Monsterville at the kitchen table. "A monster around every corner, a monster around every corner," she chanted while Mom tried to set plates and food around her. I swiped a piece of bacon.

"Good morning, sunshine," Dad said from behind *The New Yorker*. He subscribed to that back home but never had time to read it. The magazines would pile up in our hallway until Mom complained it was a fire hazard and threw them all out.

"Morning," I yawned, pulling out a chair. "Can I have some coffee?"

Mom paused, the spatula in her right hand. "You want coffee?"

"Yeah, sure." Drinking coffee seemed like a grown-up way to mark the first day of seventh grade. You know, to make it a little bit special. Kind of like how

Casey and Taylor were probably having lattes from Starbucks right now without me.

Mom shrugged and retrieved the #1 DAD mug from the top shelf. "Cream and sugar?"

"Load 'er up, please," I said, moving one of Monsterville's pieces to the starting line. "Haylie, can I play?"

She grinned. She had a bunch of plastic barrettes stuck in her hair and pulled one out, not wincing when a few blonde strands came with it. "This is for you."

"Wow, thanks." I clipped it into my bangs. "Does this look good?"

She giggled. It's so easy to make her laugh.

Mom set my coffee down in front of me and I took a sip. It had more sugar and cream in it than coffee. Delicious.

"Nervous?" she asked.

"A little," I admitted. "I haven't had to make new friends since kindergarten."

My stomach twisted when I thought of Casey and Taylor walking into St. Mary's without me. Last year, for the first day of school, we bought super ugly lime-green underwear to wear under our uniforms. Our private joke. This year, did they have one without me?

"It'll be fine," Dad said. "Just picture everyone

naked." He smiled and turned a page of his magazine, seeming pretty cheery about his own debut. It was his first day of work as a doctor at Chester County Hospital.

Haylie rolled the die. It bounced off the board and clinked against my coffee cup. "Three!" she said. When she moved her piece, she landed on the spider. "Card, please," she told me, and I obediently picked up a card and read it to her.

Werewolves suffer from bad press
They act with such gentleness!
But if one won't let you be
Give a piece of finery.

"Sorry, Haylie." I handed her the card. "Next time." I rolled the die. "Oh, look. I'm stuck, too." I'd landed on the Sandman monster.

Seven heads and poison flames,
The hydra never will be tamed
Do you face the hydra's wrath?
Don't be scared; stray from its path.

"We need to hurry, Lissa." Mom stood up with our plates. "I don't want you to be late."

Mom dropped Haylie off at nursery school, and then she pulled up in front of Freeburg Consolidated School. "You'll be great." She smiled like she meant it.

"Sure." I unbuckled my seat belt and took a deep breath, letting Mom lean over and kiss me on the forehead before I got out of the car.

Walking down the sidewalk, I pretended I was on my way to accepting an award. Or going on an audition. Sure, it felt like I was about to throw up, but I couldn't let that show. Confidence, baby!

A flag flapped on the flagpole. I walked past it and pushed open the glass doors.

Inside, kids mingled before the last bell. Some of them were really little.

That gave me a boost. It's hard to feel intimidated when you walk into a new school and the first thing you see is a seven-year-old by the trophy case, picking his nose.

I found my classroom and smiled automatically at the teacher sitting up front. The welcome letter had said her name was Ms. Green, and that she'd be teaching me *every subject*. She looked like the type to be cast as the teacher in a boring kids' show about peer pressure—all round and soft-looking.

"Oh, you're the new student!" she called, her face dimpling when she smiled. She adjusted her glasses and consulted a sheet of paper. "Lissa Black." She gestured around the room, and I saw Adam at a desk in the back. "Pick a seat."

"Thanks." I headed for Adam, checking out the other kids on the way.

One guy stood out. He had dark hair and blue eyes and a nose that looked like a creation by a very gifted plastic surgeon. I tried not to stare at him.

I plopped into the desk next to Adam's and dropped my backpack. "What's up?"

"I checked the snare this morning," he murmured. "Still nothing."

The bell rang. As Ms. Green hoisted herself from her chair, the chatter died down. "Time to take attendance," she chirped. I glanced at each person as she called names, scouting for potential friends. No one looked too promising, but at least no one had a forked tail or horns.

The cute guy was named Todd Walker. Of course. *Todd* was definitely a cute-guy name. Just like *Zac* and *Christian*. Parents, want to make sure your kid grows up hot? Name him one of those.

"Now, I see a lot of familiar faces around the room, and a few unfamiliar ones," Ms. Green said when she finished. "Well, just one unfamiliar one. Lissa, will you please come up here and introduce yourself?"

No teacher at St. Mary's would have embarrassed a new kid like this.

Reluctantly, I stood and walked to the front of the class. I don't mind public speaking, but I didn't appreciate being forced to be funny and awesome on command.

"Hi, everyone." I waved. "I'm Lissa Black. I just moved here."

Ms. Green touched my shoulder. Her hand was warm and soft. "Why don't you tell everyone a few things about yourself? Everyone! Lissa comes to us from New York City." She enunciated each word with as much enthusiasm as if announcing that I'd moved to Freeburg from Mars.

I shrugged. "There's not much to tell. I'm pretty normal." I paused, about to say something about life in New York.

Then I remembered my audience. These kids wouldn't appreciate the story of how Taylor and I got in trouble for putting on a street performance in Union Square. Or when Casey and I paid Ian to breakdance in front of the subway, and that homeless guy threw a hot dog at him.

When I didn't add anything, Ms. Green cleared her throat. "Ah. Well, we look forward to getting to know you. Now everyone, line up. It's time to visit the library. Ten minutes to find some books, and then everyone head to the computer room, okay?"

We all murmured our assent before pushing toward the door. Todd cut right in front of Adam.

A short blonde girl on Todd's right shoved him, not hard. "Raised in a barn much?"

"*Baaaaaahhh.*" Todd didn't look back.

The blonde girl swiveled to face me. "I'm so lucky. *I've* gotten to go to school with him for *seven whole years.*" She didn't seem at all bothered, though.

"I'm sure he's good for something. Like science experiments."

The girl laughed. "Yes! We can use him to test makeup. You hold him down, and I'll get the lipstick."

She had a great laugh—almost musical. It went with her big brown eyes and huge curls. In a movie, she'd be the main character's adorable sidekick. Thoughtful and supportive. Specializing in one-liners. *Hmmm.*

"I'm Candice," she said, which was helpful since I'd already forgotten her name from attendance.

"Lissa."

"Welcome to Freeburg."

We filed into the tiny library and scattered like cockroaches. I browsed through the books and grabbed *The Very Hungry Caterpillar* and *If You Give a Mouse a Cookie* for Haylie. We had them at home, but they were packed away somewhere. I headed for the checkout counter.

The librarian had long brown hair and looked about Mom's age. "You're new here?" She smiled at me. Her bottom front teeth were crooked.

"Yeah, we just moved."

"Oh, really? From where?"

"From New York. Upper East Side."

"Wow, Freeburg must be a change for you. Lots more open spaces."

You mean blank spaces, I thought silently.

"You like it so far?" she asked.

"I guess so." I struggled to think of a compliment for the Land of Nothing. Or Nothin', if you went by the locals. "It's . . . safer. My mother says we can keep our doors unlocked and not worry about it."

Her face darkened. "I wouldn't do that. Especially at night. Because—"

"Hey there, *Lisa*." I hadn't even heard Todd sneak up behind me.

"Lissa," I snapped, turning. For a cute guy, he sure was annoying. "Like Me*lissa*. Not that difficult."

"So can I call you Melissa then? I don't think *Lissa*'s a real name."

"Tell that to my parents."

"You want me to meet your parents? I'm not sure if I'm ready for that. We just met, Melinda."

"Whatever." Picking up my books, I smiled at the librarian. "I don't want to block the line. Thanks."

I nodded at Todd as I sailed past him. Hopefully he'd get tired of his wrong-name-game soon.

The rest of the day was uneventful.

No, that isn't an accurate way of putting it. It was *depressing*. According to my information packet, we weren't going *anywhere* fun for field trips. The cafeteria menu didn't include snack food, like hot pretzels with cheese. I'd already read the book they assigned us in Literature, and I hated that book.

Then, during PE, I discovered that the gym doubled as the auditorium. A dinky little stage was built into one of the walls in between the boys' and girls' locker rooms.

That was the first time I really felt like crying since arriving in Freeburg. Back at St. Mary's, our auditorium was a stand-alone building with real theater seats. I tried to imagine my play coming alive onstage at *this* gym. I couldn't.

When the day was over, Mom was parked outside the glass front doors of the school. "Well? How was it?"

I threw my backpack into the car and slid in.

"Everything I thought it would be." I looked out the window instead of at her.

"Oh, give me more. You must have *something* interesting to share."

"Nope." I was still staring out the window as we passed the community center. A white sign advertised a fish fry on September fourth. It was stupid, but that sign ticked me off. A fish fry? That was the most exciting thing going on in Freeburg?

"Nothing at all?" Mom prodded. I felt her eyes on me.

"Maybe if you find the *lack* of things interesting. Like a drama club. Not that I thought this hick school would have one."

Mom moved her sunglasses to the top of her head and looked at me. "Lissa . . ."

"What?"

"You know what. I didn't raise you to insult other people."

I slouched and stared out the window again.

We drove the rest of the way home in icy silence. I hated this. Mom and I have always gotten along. But not lately. Another side effect of this place.

"I'm going for a hike," I told her as soon as the car stopped in the driveway. "Bye." I slammed the car door, hard, leaving my backpack.

"Lissa—" Mom began, but I pretended not to hear

her. I skirted by Haylie's new plastic playhouse and disappeared through the trees.

The woods felt alive. Up ahead, a woodpecker was going nuts, drilling into a tree. And a bobwhite kept calling, over and over again—*wheet! wheet!* Adam had taught me some birdcalls, but that was the only one I remembered.

I bent to pick up a long stick. I needed a weapon in case I ran into the Sasquatch. It would be like the whack-a-mole game—bop it on the head and run like crazy. But, honestly, at this point I doubted the Sasquatch would show up. He'd probably looked around Freeburg and decided it was too boring to terrorize.

Marching quickly, pushing back branches and stepping over roots, I forgot about my argument with Mom. Instead, I focused on not tripping and on keeping hyper-focused in case another creature showed up.

I finally spotted the crumbling brick cabin Adam had shown me. Pushing aside a branch with the stick, I rounded the cabin, scanning the area.

I glanced at the tree where Adam had set up the snare and realized something was dangling there. Something alive! It thrashed and twisted, and I couldn't get a good look at it from so far away.

I dropped the walking stick, a scream catching in

my throat. What was I supposed I do? Run for Adam or take a closer look at this thing?

Even though my knees were shaking and my breath was coming in gasps, I couldn't resist. I picked up the stick again and tapped it against the brick cabin. "Hey!"

As I got closer, the creature twisted to look at me. "Help me!" it pleaded.

I lowered the stick. "Huh?"

This wasn't the Sasquatch. It was a skinny, hairless thing less than half my size, with long pointy ears and a snout.

How many monsters did my woods have?

"I'm so glad you came," it burbled in a squeaky voice. "I've been stuck up here for a long, long time. And my ankle hurts, and my leg's asleep—and—and—" It hiccupped, and then started sobbing. Snot ran from its nose.

"Um. Uh. . ." My eyes moved to its body. The creature wore a ratty pair of shorts.

Now what? In monster movies, this was Step One of three:

Step One: Monster begs Girl for help.
Step Two: Girl feels sorry for Monster and frees it.
Step Three: Monster eats Girl.

I knew the steps. But as I stood there looking into the creature's brown, sad eyes, I felt really bad for it. It was just so pathetic.

"I'll be right back," I found myself saying. "Promise."

"No!" it shrieked, crying harder. "Don't leave me!"

"I have to. I need to find something to cut you down."

The monster reached a gnarled hand toward me. "Hurry. *Please*."

I tore away as fast as I could, not slowing when thorns snagged my jeans. My heart was beating so fast I could actually hear it—*thud, thud, thud*—vibrating in my throat.

This is what they mean when they say "my heart was in my mouth," I thought stupidly as I flew out of the woods.

Adam was in his driveway, standing in the bed of his dad's pickup truck, hoisting big lumpy bags of grain down to Upchuck.

My feet kicked up gravel from the road. "Adam!" I screamed. "Adam, I need you!"

"What's up, Lissa?" Adam asked, grunting. He hoisted a bag into Upchuck's waiting arms. Upchuck took off in the direction of the barn, casting a look over his shoulder.

"I just came from the . . . place." I lowered my voice

when Adam's dad emerged from the barn. "And . . . we . . . got something!"

Adam's eyes widened. He kneeled to grab the last bag of feed, tossing it to his dad. "There. All done. Gotta go, Dad. Emergency." He hopped down from the truck and sprinted with me toward the woods.

"Wait!" I cried before we hit the trees. "Do you have your Swiss Army knife?"

Adam shook his head like I'd said something really dumb. "Lissa. I'm a *Boy Scout.*"

Tearing through the woods, we heard the creature before we could see it—sniffling and crying and carrying on.

"You've done it this time," he was mumbling to himself as we rounded the corner of the brick cabin. "You can't do anything right."

"Holy—" Adam stopped dead, his mouth falling open.

The thing twisted around to see us. "You came back! I can't believe it! Just like you promised!"

Adam looked at me. "You *talked* to it?"

"Yeah," I said sheepishly. "Do you blame me? Look at it!"

The creature's face was purple from dangling upside down. A puddle of tears and snot had pooled beneath it, drowning the bluebells growing there.

"Please let me down," the monster pleaded. "It hurts!"

I tugged on Adam's sleeve. "Maybe we can get it down and then tie it up?"

"Anything!" the creature cried. "I won't run away. I promise!"

"Oh, yeah?" Adam asked in a tough voice. "And how do we know you're not lying?"

The monster blinked at us. "My leg hurts," it said softly.

I stepped forward. A hundred monster movies had taught me to do the exact opposite of what I was about to do.

"Let it down, Adam. We can tie it to the tree."

Adam dug in his pocket for his Swiss Army knife. He shifted it from one hand to the other. "I don't know . . ."

"Oh, come on. You're like seven feet tall. You're telling me you can't handle this puny little thing?"

Adam bristled. "Of course I can. But what if this 'puny little thing' bites?"

The creature shook its head. "I won't! I promise! I promise!"

"And nothing else funny, either," I warned.

The monster sniffled. Adam stepped forward, bracing the monster with one hand while he sawed through the rope with the other. The rope gave and the monster dropped into Adam's arms. Quickly, Adam bound it against the tree.

"Wow," Adam said, rubbing his mouth. "This is really happening."

I wrapped my arms around my waist. "Guess so."

"So . . ." Adam said, not taking his eyes off the creature. "Any words of wisdom?"

"What do you mean?"

"You know, your monster rules. What should we do? Or not do?"

"Oh." I gazed into the creature's tear-filled eyes. "Well, we probably shouldn't trust anything it says. Or free it from its bindings."

"Check and check." Adam held the knife out. "Who are you?" he asked in the same tough-guy voice he'd used before.

The creature cringed against the tree. "Monster."

"We know you're a monster," Adam practically growled. He was good at this. "What kind of monster? Where'd you come from? And how do you exist in the first place?"

The monster blinked at us. "I-I'm not *any* kind of monster!" it wailed. "I can't decide!" It started sobbing all over again. Green snot bubbled from its nose.

"What do you mean, you can't decide?" I asked slowly, looking into its brown eyes. A thought was forming in my brain.

"I mean, I don't know what kind of monster I'd be good at being! I'm scared of everything. And I don't know what sounds to make."

The thought in my head clicked into place. "Wait a second. So you can change into different kinds of monsters?"

The monster fidgeted in the ropes, its skinny chest heaving. "Yes . . ." It dropped its eyes guiltily.

"So that swamp creature crawling out of the creek . . ." I trailed off, and it nodded. "And that Sasquatch that scared the bejeezus out of us a few weeks ago?"

"Yes . . . I can change shapes." The monster paused. "Did I scare you?"

"Are you kidding? I thought I was going to have a heart attack!"

It beamed proudly. "Maybe I'm not as bad at being a monster as I thought!"

"Sure," I said. "Only next time, remember that swamp creatures don't eat brains, and a Sasquatch doesn't moo."

"Great, Lissa," Adam said. "Give it tips."

"Sorry." I crouched to examine the monster. Its skin was pale—really pale—and mapped with spidery blue veins. It shrank away from me.

"I'm not going to hurt you." I stared at its long,

bony hands, its knobby knees. It was hard to believe that a monster could look so fragile.

"Okay," it said, its eyes wide. "I believe you. Since you came back."

"This might be kind of a rude question." I paused. "But . . . are you a boy or a girl?"

The monster wrinkled its wide forehead at me. "Boy, of course!" He sounded annoyed.

"Of course," I echoed, exhaling slowly. My heart still pounded, but now from excitement. The makings of an epic movie had just fallen into my lap. This was a *real monster*—one that talked and didn't seem human-hungry. And he could transform into different kinds of creatures.

"What should we do?" Adam asked me. "If anyone finds him, they'd lock him in a lab and experiment on him or something."

The monster's nostrils flared. "No! No zoo! No experiments! No one can know about us! That's what Atticus says!"

"Who's Atticus?" I asked. Was *he* camera-friendly?

The monster sucked in his breath. "No one."

Adam moved to tighten the ropes. "Really? No one?"

The monster dropped his head. "Atticus is in charge of all of us. In the beginning, we all look like me—

gobliny. But he was mad at me 'cause I couldn't figure out what kind of monster to be. I ran away to figure it out on my own."

"Ran away from where?" I asked.

"Down Below." The monster tapped his foot on the ground.

"You live . . . underground?" I asked. "How?"

The monster blinked at me. "I don't know. I just do. Well, we all do." He squirmed. "These ropes really hurt. Can you please untie me? I promise I won't run away."

Adam and I exchanged a look. "We need a minute to talk, Monster," I said. "Can we call you that? Or do you have a name?"

"Not yet," the monster said, starting to sniffle again. "Monsters don't get names until we figure out what kind of monsters we are."

I steered Adam into the abandoned cabin. "What do you think?" I whispered once we were out of ear-shot. "He seems harmless."

He seems harmless. Another rule. In a monster movie, the person who says that gets eaten first. Still, every instinct told me Monster wouldn't hurt us.

Adam puffed out his cheeks. "It's crazy, but I think you're right. He's too wimpy to be a real threat. I just don't know what we'd do with him."

"Are you kidding me? We'd make an amazing

movie! Or movies! Look around you." I bent down and picked a purple flower growing between two bricks. "We have a set that production companies would kill for. For free! Not using it would be the biggest waste ever."

"Just to be famous? I won the junior sharpshooter award at the county fair this summer. That's famous enough for me."

"I don't even know what to say to that."

"There's more to life than being famous."

"It's not about just being famous. It's about getting famous because you've done something amazing. A contribution that makes you worthy of fame." My stomach twisted as I thought of my play. *That* was supposed to be my first step toward fame.

"Contribution?" Adam raised his eyebrows.

"Yeah. Like writing a book or making a film or painting a picture. Giving something back to the world. That's what I want to do."

Adam stared at me until I looked away. "You're serious, aren't you? You really mean that."

"Of course I mean it," I said, trying to hide how embarrassed I felt. "Now, are you going to help me or not?"

He shrugged. "What's in it for me?"

"I'll make you the best boy!"

"Best boy? What's that?"

"It's the person who handles the power cables and runs the lights for the shots."

"Great, so I'll get electrocuted." Adam folded his arms. "If this is only a two-person production, shouldn't person number two have a better job?"

"Okay, fine. You can be the producer." He still didn't look impressed. "And you can have half the ancillary rights," I added reluctantly.

"Ancilla-what?"

"Ancillary rights. You know, the profits from T-shirts and posters and stuff. Ooh, maybe Mattel will want to make an action figure of Monster! One that can transform!"

"Oh, merchandising. You're so generous." Adam paused, looking at the ground. "I'll tell you what I want."

"What?" *All* the ancillary rights?

"I want you to make an effort. Let me show you around Freeburg. And in exchange, I'll help you with your little movie."

"Little? It's going to be huge!"

He raised his eyebrows. "We'll see. So. What's it going to be?"

"Whatever it takes. But . . . that's it? I just let you show me around Freeburg?" I resisted the urge to tell him I'd already been to the town's one gas station. And grocery store. Yahoo.

"Not just that. Give Freeburg a chance. And you can't whine or complain or act all snobby about how much better New York is."

"I'm not snobby!"

"Sometimes you are."

"Well, I'll stop." I smiled. "I will totally give Freeburg a chance. I'll go to bingo, and the fish fries, and pick some corn . . ."

"*Ahem.* Snobby!"

"Sorry." I stuck out my hand before Adam could change his mind. "I promise to give Freeburg a chance and not make fun of it or compare it to the city." *Though there's no comparison.*

"Deal." We shook on it and then returned to Monster, who was still squirming uncomfortably, almost like he needed to go to the bathroom. *Do monsters go to the bathroom?*

"Okay," I said. "We won't tell anyone about you. And we'll even help you decide what kind of monster you want to be so you can return to Down Below, wherever and whatever that is."

"Oh, thank you!" Monster said. He sounded so grateful that I felt a little guilty for having an ulterior motive. But hey, show business is cruel.

"You just have to promise that you won't scare anyone while you're here," Adam said in his tough-guy voice. "Otherwise you'll answer to *me*."

"Yes, yes, yes!" Monster nodded. "I promise."

Adam kneeled down to cut Monster's ropes. "I hope we don't regret this." He looked up at me. "Wait a second. Don't people in monster movies say things like that?"

"All the time."

"I'm not even going to ask how that turns out for them."

ACT TWO

A MONSTER INTERVIEW

The next day at school, I couldn't concentrate. Luckily, Ms. Green probably thought I looked confused because I was hopeless at Geometry and not because I was trying to figure out how an underground society of monsters operated or what their agenda was.

And, almost as important, how I could use my newfound knowledge of the world of monsters to create the first horror movie to win Best Picture since *The Silence of the Lambs*.

Adam was quiet on the bus ride home. When it dropped us off at the end of Mine Haul Road, he didn't head into the woods. Instead, he stepped into the ditch on the side of the road and motioned for me to follow him into the cornfield.

"Come on! I want to show you something!"

I stayed put on the road. "What?"

"Follow me and you'll see. And remember, a deal's a deal. No snobs allowed."

"I think we should check on Monster first."

"Just give me half an hour."

I sighed. "Fine." I followed Adam through green stalks and over clumps of dirt. It was like a maze. The corn was really tall and it was hard to break through one row to another with the stalks growing so close together.

"This is different," I muttered, reaching for an ear and tearing it from the stem. I peeled back the husk, brushing my hand against the soft tassel sticking out of the end.

Adam turned to grin at me. "Yeah. Isn't it great?"

"It's kind of peaceful," I admitted, right as a deer bug bit my arm. "Ow!" I swatted it away.

"Deerflies like corn. You'll get used to it." Adam turned and marched away, humming.

I followed him until the corn ended in a big, empty field. "Is this your parents' property?" I asked, scratching my new bug bite.

"Nope." Adam headed across the field toward a lake with an old wooden dock jutting out into it. When we got there, the dock creaked beneath our feet.

"Seems like you trespass a lot."

Adam shrugged. "People around here don't care. And I never hurt anything." He untied a canoe from a wooden post and stepped inside.

"What are you doing?" I asked as he plopped down.

"Taking advantage of one of the many free activities Freeburg has to offer." Adam leaned and extended an oar. "Here."

I stepped into the boat. It lurched, rocking back and forth. I sat down before it could pitch me overboard. The water smelled like fish and algae, and a green film covered the surface.

Adam pushed us away from the dock with his oar. Seconds later, we were paddling—Adam with four strokes for every one of mine.

"You're great at this," I said. "Maybe I should just leave the rowing to you." My arms already burned from the effort, and sweat was running down my back.

"Almost there," Adam grunted.

We turned a bend in the lake. "Holy cow!" I exclaimed.

Ducks were everywhere. Hundreds of them. Some brown and small, others black with orange beaks. There were even a few swans. And they weren't scared of us at all. A few darted toward us, their sleek feathery bodies cutting through the water.

Adam dropped his oar onto the floor of the boat. "Come to me, my feathered friends," he called out, raising his arms.

"They're not even afraid," I said in awe as I watched a little white duck bobbing alongside us. A brown goose, honking like crazy, plowed through the other birds as it took up a prime spot next to the boat. Ducks quacked in protest.

"Watch out, that one's Mother Goose," Adam said, pointing to the brown bird.

"Why is she called that?"

"Because she's the oldest and the crankiest."

"Ha. So she's like the geese in Central Park. Those things'll attack you."

We sat for a few minutes, watching the ducks. Above, cotton candy clouds moved across a blue sky. The boat rocked gently. It was the kind of quiet moment you never have in the city where things are always happening and there's always something different to see.

Finally, Adam picked up his oar again and sliced it through the water. "I guess we should get back. Your parents might worry."

I reached my hand toward the little white duck. "Oh, yeah. The librarian mentioned something about not keeping doors unlocked. What was up with that?"

Adam's mouth tightened. "We had something happen here last year."

"Really?"

"This little kid got kidnapped. Just four years old. His parents went to check on him in the morning and he was gone. Vanished. No signs of a break-in or anything."

"That's terrible," I murmured, thinking about Haylie. Once she crawled under a bush in the park to catch bugs, and Mom and I almost had a joint nervous breakdown when we couldn't find her.

"Yeah," Adam said, then cleared his throat like the subject made him uncomfortable. "And strange. Because, look around you. We're in paradise! Nothing bad happens here!"

The sky looked like a Pixar screenshot, and corn was lazily waving in the breeze. The lake's surface glinted in the afternoon sunlight.

"Well, the ducks don't look rabid. I'll give you that."

"Ducks can't get rabies."

In the water, a brown-speckled duck was quacking as it treaded water. "They seem hungry. I guess we'd better bring bread next time, huh?"

Adam grinned. "Or corn. Wonder where we could find that?"

I smiled and shook my head, sticking my oar into the water. Sure, I'd suggested coming back here, but so what? We had ducks in New York City, too. Who cared if they weren't as friendly?

Monster was waiting for us when we got to his home, sitting on the crumbled stoop. He reminded me of a kid waiting for the ice cream truck. A kid with pointy ears and light-blue skin.

"You came!" he cried, like he was surprised. His huge eyes zeroed in on our backpacks. "Did you bring me anything?"

I dropped mine on the ground. "Of course we did." I unzipped it and pulled out an unopened bag of potato chips. "Look, barbecue."

Monster grabbed the bag and stuffed it into his mouth, swallowing it whole like he was a boa constrictor.

Rats. I'd planned on using the potato chips as treats. One treat per question answered.

And boy, did I have a lot of questions: How old was Monster? Did he have any special abilities? How many other monsters were there? Could they leave Down Below any time? Could humans visit?

Monster burped. "I'm still hungry."

"Of course you are." I swiped my hair out of my eyes. Even in the middle of the woods it was hot. I reached into my backpack again. "How about an apple?" It was bruised, but Monster wouldn't care. After all, he'd just eaten potato chips still in the bag.

Monster reached for the apple. He tilted back his head and dropped it in, chewing once. *"Mmm."*

"Wow, it's like watching a living trash compactor." Adam removed a bottle of red Gatorade from his backpack and held it out to Monster. "Want to wash it down?"

"No!" I grabbed the bottle. "Don't give it to him yet."

"But I want it," Monster whined, reaching toward me. I held it high, out of his reach.

"You'll get it," I said in a soothing tone. "But first, we need you to answer a few questions."

"Like what?"

"Like, how'd you get in our woods? What is Down Below, and how'd you escape?"

Monster's eyes shifted nervously. "I don't know if I should tell you."

"It's okay." I kept my voice light. "Remember, you're a secret. Adam and I won't tell anyone."

"Can I have a drink first?"

"Fine." I handed him the Gatorade, and he clutched it in his knobby hands. With one long pull, the bottle was empty.

Monster burped loudly. It shook the trees. He cleared his throat and looked at the ground. "One night, I decided to escape. I knew where to go because I saw monsters using the portals before."

"Portals?" Adam asked.

"Yeah." Monster picked up his tail, holding it like a

95

security blanket. "Monsters use portals to go between Down Below and Up There."

"'Up There' is *here*, huh?" I asked.

He nodded. "And portals are the space below where someone sleeps. Like between the bottom of the bed and the floor, so long as there's room for monsters to crawl out from under it. It's like . . ." He tipped his head, frowning. "A door on the floor."

"Interesting," I said, shivering.

I imagined what that would look like from an aerial shot, the camera panning out to show some innocent kid lying in her bed beneath pink covers . . . and underneath her, a whole world of tunnels and darkness and snarling monsters.

"And, like a door," Monster said, picking up a stick and absentmindedly tapping it on the ground, "some portals are locked and some are unlocked."

"What's the difference?" Adam asked.

"If someone *doesn't believe* in monsters, monsters can't use their portal. From Down Below, it looks like a rusty trapdoor that's chained shut. But if someone *does believe* in monsters, the portal glows. All a monster has to do is pass through it. Well, so long as the person's in the bed. It can't be an empty bed."

"Which portal did you use to come up here?" I asked. "Do you remember?"

Monster sucked in his lips like he was trying to

decide whether to trust us. He exhaled, noisily. "I used a portal in the house by these woods. The one with the saggy wooden porch."

"You mean *my* house?"

I shouldn't have been so shocked. Monster had popped up in *my* woods, after all.

"I didn't see you there." Monster wrinkled his forehead. "The bed I used was a lady's. She had gray hair."

Adam grinned. "Well, it looks like Lucy believed in monsters. Told you your aunt was cool."

"That's crazy. Don't people grow out of believing in things like that?" I asked, my mind flitting to the Monsterville game. Aunt Lucy had probably played it a zillion times, never knowing that real monsters lived beneath her floorboards.

"Not if you know they're real. When I get older, I'm still going to believe we met this little guy." Adam reached into his backpack and handed a pack of gum to Monster. "Don't swallow it," he warned, but Monster had already gulped it down.

"So." I cleared my throat. "Do you use the portals all the time? And are humans allowed Down Below?" *Humans with film equipment?*

"Monsters don't come Up There that often," Monster said. "We don't want to get spotted. The portals are always guarded by elder monsters to make sure younger ones don't leave and expose them. I escaped when the guards were distracted." He poked at Adam's backpack, sniffing for more food.

"And . . . humans?" I prodded.

"Humans are only allowed Down Below one day a year."

"One day? What day?" I could film a movie in a day.

"I don't want to talk about this anymore," Monster announced. "Atticus would be mad. I'm done."

"But Monster—" I protested.

"I'm done!" He folded his arms across his chest.

"You don't have to throw a tantrum." But I was pretty happy with our conversation. Monster had given us a lot of information, and all we'd forked over in exchange was some junk food.

My brain was churning with ideas. My movie could be about monsters taking over the world. Or about a darker, alternate version of the real world. Like *Coraline*, only less creepy. More Tim Burton-esque. Exaggerated.

Or it could be a documentary disguised as fiction. But that would be cheating.

I checked my phone. "Oh, it's late! I have to get back for dinner." And a Skype date with Casey. I was dying for details on the play, which was all we had to talk about recently since I couldn't tell her about any of *this*. It felt weird not being able to share something with her.

"Dinner?" Monster was practically drooling.

"My dad's frying fish tonight," Adam said to him. "I'll bring you a plate."

"With tartar sauce."

Adam and I exchanged a look. "You know what tartar sauce is?"

"Yep."

"How?"

"When monsters come Up There, sometimes they take things. Things they know humans won't miss. Like old cans of food and extra bottles of ketchup. And sweaters that smell like they haven't been worn in a long time."

"Not a bad idea," I said. "We humans are pretty wasteful."

"I'll bring you some ketchup, too," Adam told Monster. "We have a bunch of extra packets."

Monster smiled so big I could see every single pointy tooth. "Thanks."

Wow. A monster with an appetite for fried fish and ketchup. There are some things you can't make up.

SCENE TWO:

HUMAN GAMES

Adam and I spent the next four days catering to Monster's every whim. Luckily, his needs were pretty simple—junk food and stories. I even brought him a plastic bag full of coloring books and paint-by-numbers, which made him happier than a rat with cheese.

We fixed up his house, too. Adam's parents had a bunch of old furniture in one of their sheds, and we stole things when no one was looking, including an air mattress, a musty-smelling rug with a burn mark, and a battered nightstand we nicked up even more when we carried it through the woods.

On Friday, Adam and I took the night off. After we left Monster with a huge plate of fried chicken and a stack of picture books, Upchuck drove us to the town fair in Smithton. This was in keeping with my promise to give country life a chance.

I kept my forehead pressed to the cool glass of the truck's window. Along with Upchuck's toxic cologne, the pickup smelled like Lucky, the Griggs' overweight Labrador.

If it were Friday night and I were back home in the city, I'd be sleeping over at Casey's. Before that, maybe we would have gone to a movie or window-shopped with Taylor's sister. There wasn't a decent movie theater or mall anywhere near Freeburg.

We drove along winding, bumpy roads through two little towns and miles of fields. I started to feel carsick, but I didn't say anything. Luckily, before I threw up in my lap, a Ferris wheel and a big yellow slide came into view. Upchuck eased behind a row of cars parked along the road and killed the engine.

"Check it out." Adam hopped down from the truck. "We went seven miles in ten minutes. How long would it take to go seven miles in the city?"

As I climbed out from the backseat, I took a deep breath of fresh air, relieved that I felt better already. "It's different. Everything's more spread out here."

"And we parked for free. How much would it cost to park in the city?"

I rolled my eyes. "I don't know." But I knew it cost three bucks an hour to park at most meters. And they're harder to find than a unicorn.

My phone vibrated, and I pulled it from my jacket pocket. Casey.

Skype? More crazy to share.

According to Casey during our Skype session the night before, Roland Reed was certifiably insane. When he wasn't folding origami in the back of the theater, he was yelling stage directions that didn't make any sense.

At least the scenery was shaping up. Casey had texted me pictures of the flats the theater crew had constructed—a kitchen and a park scene. Very nice.

"Look!" Adam strutted down the road. "I'm in the middle of the road. Think I'll get hit by a car?"

"Okay, okay, okay," I replied as I fumbled to text Casey.

At the fair with Adam. Later? Love to hear re: crazy!

That *did* make me feel better. Which was good, because the longer I was gone, the more I hated missing my play. Not just because I was missing the experience itself—but because the play reminded me of back home. Its plot was kind of an inside joke among me, Taylor, and Casey.

"Traffic's better here," I admitted to Adam. "You can have that. But there aren't symphonies, or city parks, or restaurants, or big libraries, or community centers, or malls, or—"

"Crime. Or pollution, or crowds." Adam lifted his arms. "Behold, the glory of living in the country."

He lowered them. "Oh, but wait. You can't. You're on your phone."

"I was *looking* at my phone." Casey had texted again: *When you & Adam have babies, can you name one Casey?*

I made a big show of sticking my phone back in my pocket and dusting off my hands. "There. Happy?"

"Sure."

My pocket vibrated, and I forced myself to ignore it, though another part of me was glad to let it go. The text would be another crack about Adam, and I was getting tired of explaining that he was just a friend.

Country music pulsed as we walked closer to the entrance. The fair was on a lot at the edge of town—basically a glorified square of asphalt. The Ferris wheel, painted white with orange lights strung on each car, was the tallest ride. Even from far away, it looked ready to collapse.

"Are the rides safe?" I asked.

Adam shook his head. "Would I take you here if they weren't?"

"Yes. Yes, you would." I shoved him in the shoulder. He didn't budge.

We walked through the crowd. The sun was setting, its orange glow making everything look softer.

Upchuck waved to someone. "Don't get lost. I'll meet you guys back here at ten, okay?"

"All right, Charlie," Adam said, and Upchuck disappeared into the crowd. Adam turned to me. "Come on, let's get ride tickets."

I followed him, my feet crunching on the gravel. Rows of bright lights decorated the metal stands, which opened to display fried food and carnival games. For a dollar, you could throw darts at balloons or grab a little yellow duck from a plastic blue pool.

Adam stopped at a white booth that said TICKETS in red letters across the front. "We'll try every ride, okay?"

I shrugged. "Sure."

"Nothing to be afraid of." Adam puffed out his chest when he said it.

I wasn't afraid of heights or speed. I was afraid of appearing in a newspaper article with the headline "Out-of-Towner Crushed in Tragic Tilt-a-Whirl Collapse."

But I'd promised Adam I'd give Freeburg a chance. Besides, getting on a rusty, poorly constructed, never-inspected carnival ride was *probably* not the most dangerous thing I'd ever do.

Adam handed me my string of red paper tickets, the kind you tear apart. We headed off to the closest ride—the swings.

"Get one on the outside," Adam told me as we ran for our seats.

"Whatever you say, Yoda." It was a compliment. *Star Wars* is my fourth-favorite movie franchise.

I hopped onto a swing and fastened the chain around my waist. It was just a metal clip. *Come on now—is the carnival company* trying *to get sued?*

The swings jerked into the air, circling around a metal cylinder. I twined my hands around the chain and pumped my legs.

"Let go and lean forward!" Adam yelled from the swing next to me.

"No, thank you!" The ride was picking up speed. Bright carnival lights passed by in a blur.

"Just try it!"

"Okay, fine!" Ignoring all common sense and desire for self-preservation, I leaned forward and let go of the chains.

It was like flying. I stared at the ground, memorizing it. There was a big crack in one part of the asphalt. Each time I whipped by it, I knew I had come full circle.

The carnival lights blurred together and I wondered what this scene would look like from a crane shot capturing the rotating middle cylinder and the flying swings. I bet the effect would be really cool, especially with the lights and the sound mix of the crowd and country music.

The swings slowed. "Aww, man!" I kicked my feet. "More!"

I came to a stop right on top of the big crack and fiddled to unhook the metal safety clip. When my feet touched the ground, the world tilted. "Whoa." I laughed, trying to stay upright as I stumbled out of the metal gate exit.

"Which one now?" Adam asked.

"The slide? Or maybe the Tilt-a-Whirl. But food first."

The picnic area was at the side of the lot. A country band played under a metal pavilion. I recognized "Hotel California" by the Eagles. As far as songs go, that one's pretty much a masterpiece.

I spotted Upchuck sitting on one of the picnic tables talking to a pretty, dark-haired girl wearing a Freeburg Bulldogs sweatshirt and jean shorts. They sat so close together their shoulders touched. Way to go, Upchuck.

Adam saw them, too. "Ha! Check it. That's why Charlie drowned himself in cologne. Lately he's been all about girls." Adam barreled toward the funnel cake line.

"Hey! Lissa and Adam!"

I recognized Candice's voice and turned to see her with Todd.

"Todd spotted you guys from the top of the slide," she said, pointing to the yellow contraption at the edge of the lot.

Todd bit off a piece of funnel cake, powdered sugar raining onto his sweatshirt. "It wasn't hard. Lurch is easy to see from a distance."

Lurch is a tall, gangly monster from *The Addams Family*, one of the only movies to do justice to the TV show it was based on. I was impressed Todd knew the franchise.

"How long you guys been here, *Melissa*?" he added, and I forgot about being impressed.

"Not long. And my name is Lissa. Get it right."

"Todd's dad is in charge of the raffle," Candice said. "We've been giving out cakes all night. It's fun."

"How does the raffle work?" I asked, but Todd shook his head. "There are better games. Wanna play?"

"Depends. What do you have in mind?" I asked suspiciously. I bet there was a dunking booth around here somewhere.

"I'll show you." Todd polished off his funnel cake and tossed the plastic plate into the trash. Then he led us through the crowd, stopping at one of the metal trailers.

Todd had picked a game where you aim a toy gun and shoot water at a target, which moves a jockey on a horse across the booth's back wall. Adam looked at me and raised an eyebrow, and I knew what he was thinking. He'd *kill* Todd at this.

After we sat on stools and paid the game attendant, Adam turned to Todd. "Let's make this interesting. How about a bet?"

"I'm game. What're we betting?"

"Here's what I want. If I win, you have to wear your Halloween costume from two years ago to school on Monday. Remember? The ninja?"

I clapped my hands together. "Yes! And if *I* win, you have to wear your ninja Halloween costume from two years ago to school on Monday."

Candice laughed and raised her hands. "I'm staying out of this one."

Todd looked from me to Adam, his mouth curving into a smile. "Okay, I see how it is. Well, tell you what. I win, and you both wear Halloween costumes on Monday. You as Peter Pan"—he pointed to me —"and you as Tinker Bell." He pointed at Adam.

"You're on," I said.

"And . . . go!" yelled the game attendant.

I bit my lower lip and aimed the water at the target. It was hopeless. *I* was hopeless. My poor horse stayed frozen at the starting line. Candice's horse didn't do much better. I guess growing up in the country doesn't always guarantee you'll be a crack shot.

Adam and Todd were neck and neck. "Go, Adam!" I murmured. My horse jerked an inch to the right.

At the last second, Adam pulled ahead. His horse hit the end of the board and a bell rang.

I cheered. "In ya *face!*" I jumped off my swivel chair and raised my arms in victory.

"Freak accident," Todd sulked.

"Number five, number five, pick a prize," called the attendant. He pushed a button to return the horses to their starting positions.

Adam nudged me. "Go ahead, pick one."

"Um." I scanned the booth's rows of cheap stuffed animals and pointed to a pink pony. "I guess that one." Todd snorted, and I rolled my eyes. "It's for my little sister." I snatched it. "She loves pink. And horses."

Adam swiveled in his stool and grinned at Todd. "Well, well, well. I look forward to Monday."

"Me, too," I said. "And I never look forward to Mondays."

"Whatever." Todd snorted, hopping off his stool. "Candice, wanna ride the Hammerhead?"

"Of course not. You know how I feel about being upside down. I'm going back to the raffle."

He sighed. "Okay. I'll come with you."

I waved as they walked away, then turned to Adam. "Thanks, ringer. Way to carry the team."

We celebrated by buying a ton of junk food. I dug into a funnel cake. "Holy cow, this is amazing!"

"I know." Adam took a long sip from his lemon shake-up. "Do you think Todd will actually dress like a ninja on Monday?"

I shrugged. "Maybe. But you know what? Even if he doesn't, we still know you beat him. And so does he."

"True." Adam looked up at the sky, and I followed his gaze. It was a clear night and the stars were out. "You know," Adam said after a while, "girls are always into Todd."

"Yeah, I'm not surprised."

"Really? Why not?" He was still looking at the star-lit sky.

"I don't know. Because he looks like he belongs in a boy band? Something called, like, Men 'N Progrezz?"

Adam snorted. "How about Boyz 'N Harmony?"

"Anything with an 'N instead of an *in*."

Adam took another sip, slurping when he got to the ice at the bottom. "What does that mean, though?"

"What does what mean?"

"That it looks like Todd belongs in a boy band."

"Oh." I felt my face turning red. "Well, Todd *is* objectively attractive."

"Huh."

"I'm just saying he's nice to look at. So long as he's not talking. That ruins the effect." I gathered my trash and stood up. "Come on. Let's go on another ride."

"Sure." Adam smiled and crumpled his napkin. "See? I knew you'd love the fair. What's up next?"

"I'm thinking the Tilt-a-Whirl," I said, following him through the crowd. "Hope I don't hack up a funnel cake."

"You better not. Here in these parts, we don't waste our food," he said in a country twang.

"One of the many ways the country's superior, right?"

"You got it."

When I got home, Mom and Dad were watching a movie in the living room. Something with Bill Murray, who everyone knows is amazing. And I hear he gets all his offers for roles through a voice mailbox. No agent, no manager, just "Hey guys, hope you know my phone number!"

"Hey, hon!" Mom turned to peer over the back of the couch. "Have a good time?"

"Yeah, it was fun." I hung up my jacket in the hall closet. "I've never seen so much fried food in one place."

"Well, I hope you took advantage," Mom said. "You won't always be able to eat everything you want and never gain a pound."

"Uh-huh." I slid my shoes off and got a glass of water from the kitchen. As I padded down the hallway to my room, I spotted a strip of light shining underneath Haylie's door. I wondered if Mom and Dad knew she was up so late.

I knocked softly. "Haylie?"

"Yeah?"

I pushed open the door and glanced around her room. It was purple and pink everywhere, with a Barbie dollhouse and armies of stuffed animals. Haylie sat cross-legged in bed, leaning over a piece of white poster board. Crayons and markers were strewn all over her purple bedspread, along with the Monsterville game. Who knew that a kid could cuddle with a board game like a stuffed animal?

"Whatcha doing up so late?" I asked, sitting next to her and pulling my legs up underneath me. "Drawing a masterpiece?"

Haylie looked up and pushed a lock of hair out of her face. "Trying to get them right," she said.

"Who?"

"The monsters."

"From the game?" I glanced at the box. Where did it fit in with Monster and Down Below?

Maybe it was just a game owned by some batty old lady. Maybe, since Aunt Lucy believed in supernatural stuff—which had allowed Monster to crawl out from under her bed—someone had bought her the game. And that was all there was to it. The game was just a red herring in this twisted mystery.

Haylie picked up a fat purple crayon. "My new friend says monsters are real."

I smiled. "Oh, yeah? You made a new friend in pre-school today?"

Haylie shook her head. "When I was drawer-ing. He wanted to borrow my crayons. And I said, 'I need all of them.'"

I looked at the packs of markers and crayons spread out all over the bed. "Haylie, you should always share. Otherwise, why would other kids share with you later?"

"That's what *he* said! He said if I gave him my crayons, he'd bring me flowers."

Ha, ha. My little sister was only four, and already dudes were bringing her flowers. She'd be unstoppable by the time she reached high school.

"So then what happened?" I asked, playing with her hair. Its softness reminded me of corn silk. Absentmindedly, I braided it, then dropped it and combed through it with my fingers.

"I gave him ten crayons." Haylie scribbled on the poster board. "Blue, pink, green, blue, um—pink, red . . . for ten flowers . . ." She trailed off, yawning.

"For ten flowers? That's a pretty good deal."

"I know." Haylie smiled happily. Then she yawned again, so wide I could see her tonsils.

"All right, Hails. Time for bed."

Haylie helped me put her poster board and crayons away in her little plastic desk. I tucked her under the covers and shut off the light.

"Good night, Haylie," I whispered from the door. But she was already asleep.

SCENE THREE:

DRESS REHEARSAL

The next day, Adam and I met up early to hang out with Monster. It was like preparing for camp—I emptied my backpack and filled it with food and books and other stuff to entertain us. And, of course, Dad's handheld camera. Adam carried three fold-up lawn chairs.

For now, I'd just focus on getting footage of Monster—experiment with different camera angles, try some dialogue I'd been working on. I liked the idea of ad-libbing part of the script. That can turn out awesome. Like in *Raiders of the Lost Ark*, where Indiana Jones flat out shoots the guy he's sword fighting. It wasn't supposed to go down like that. It was supposed to be a long drawn-out sword fight where Indiana Jones wins in the end, but Harrison Ford got food poisoning and was like, "enough of this—I've got a gun—*bang*!"

"Monster, we're here!" I hollered when we got to the brick cabin. "You asleep?" I unfolded one of the lawn chairs and placed it near the Queen Anne's lace and bluebells. They were everywhere.

Monster bounded out of the cabin. "Nope! I'm awake! And hungry!" He eyed our backpacks.

Adam sighed. "Monster, you need to learn to control your appetite." But he unzipped his backpack and dumped the contents on the ground. "Just don't eat it all at once."

Monster sat down and pawed through the pile. He tore open a package of Pop-Tarts and ate them in two seconds. Then he opened a can of soda and drank it in one gulp.

I unzipped my own backpack and pulled out the camera. "You guys ready?"

"What's that for?" Monster asked, one long finger brushing against the lens.

"To film you."

"Why?"

"Because later we can watch the video of you turning into different kinds of monsters. And you can pick which one you want to be. Based on what's scariest."

Monster's eyes widened. "Like a movie? Like *Finding Nemo*?"

Adam and I exchanged a glance. A chill traveled up my spine, despite the warm September day. "How do you know what *Finding Nemo* is?" I asked Monster.

"I don't . . . know." Monster wouldn't meet my eyes.

"Are you sure? What's it about?" I prodded.

"There's the orange fish that gets lost. And the funny blue fish who talks a lot." Then Monster sucked in his lips like he'd said too much.

"How do you know that?"

Monster plucked a dandelion from the ground and rubbed it between his fingers, turning the tips yellow. "Maybe Down Below, in the beginning. The other monsters did lots of things to make us feel better. They were very nice," he said mechanically. Something was off.

Adam didn't seem to notice. He leaned closer to Monster. "In the beginning? Beginning of what?"

Monster reached for a twig and snapped it in half. "Beginning of being a monster."

"So you *became* one?" Adam asked. "You weren't born one? Do you remember how?"

That was a question I'd been dying to ask Monster, but it seemed rude, like the time Ann Vater asked Taylor if she believed in God even though her family's from Ethiopia.

Monster looked at his bare feet. They were dirty from the ground. "I kind of remember," he said tentatively.

"You weren't hatched?" Adam asked.

"Nooo . . ."

"Well, what's the first thing you remember?" I

asked in the same nice, soft voice I use on Haylie when she's about to put something gross in her mouth.

"I remember . . . a flash of light. And a lot of other goblins. Some of them looked really upset. Then Atticus came and took four of us away."

I leaned forward in my chair. "Then what happened?"

Monster covered his ears. "No! I'm not talking about this anymore."

"But, Monster—"

"No!" he screeched so loud that birds flew out of the trees.

I put up my hands. "Okay, okay. We don't have to talk about it. Why don't we just start practicing?" With a pang, I thought of all the practicing Taylor and Casey were doing for the seventh grade play without me. Not just that—painting the set, hanging out with the crew . . . I was missing every single second.

"Turning," Monster corrected me.

"Turning?"

"That's what we call changing into different kinds of monsters. It has to be really quiet and really still."

"Okay," I said, folding my hands in my lap. I figured if Monster got upset enough, he might not let me film him.

He headed back inside his little red cabin, and Adam and I settled into our lawn chairs. I felt like we were gearing up to watch one of those goofy off-Broadway plays where the actors wander into the audience.

A minute crawled by and Monster still hadn't come outside.

"Come out, Monster!" Adam called. "We're ready to be scared!"

"Yeah, come out, Monster!" I yelled, hoisting the camcorder. "Action!"

I could hear shuffling footsteps from inside the cabin. Hairy brown paws curled around the door-frame. A long, furry brown face with red eyes and pointy teeth stuck its head out.

"Grrrrrrrrrr!" Monster's red eyes flashed.

"Oh no! A werewolf!" I screamed, trembling so the camcorder would shake. The footage was kind of cheesy, but I'd get better.

Monster dropped to all fours and loped over to us, bumping my knee with his head. Drool spattered onto my foot.

"Cut!" I shut off the camera. "Gross, Monster. Did you have to do that?"

Monster sat on his haunches and grinned, his tongue lolling out of his mouth. Gradually, he trans-formed—the fur disappearing back into his skin, his body shortening and getting skinnier, his ears pop-ping up. Soon he was back to his normal self.

Well, depending on what you defined as *normal*.

"Was that good?" he asked hopefully.

"Pretty good. I think that one could be really terrifying if you practiced more. Now"—I reached for my backpack and dug through it—"I think you should try a zombie." I pulled out a comic book and held it out, pointing to a page. "See how they drool on themselves and walk with their arms all sticking out? That's what you need to do."

Monster stared at the page, his forehead knitted.

Adam stood up and stretched. "Here, I'll show you." He dangled his arms in front of him and stumbled forward. "Braaiiiinns."

I rolled my eyes. "A little cliché, don't you think?"

Adam turned to me, his tongue hanging out of his mouth. "Brains?"

"Just because you don't have one, that doesn't mean you can take mine." I laughed at the blank look in Adam's eyes. "Seriously, that's a good zombie. Monster, take notes!"

I stood up and held out my arms, too. "See, you have to drool a little more," I told Adam. "And make sure you keep that glazed-over expression. That shouldn't be hard for you."

"Brains!" Adam launched himself at me, pushing me face-first into a pile of dead leaves. He sat on me. "Zombie. Win!"

"Ugh." I struggled to get up, but Adam was way too

heavy even though I could tell he wasn't putting all his weight on me. Finally he let me go, pulling me up easily with one hand.

"You fell down." He grinned at me while I brushed leaves and dirt off my jeans.

"Yeah, how'd that happen?" I grumbled, my face burning. I wasn't sure why. Falling down doesn't usually embarrass me.

Monster shifted from one foot to the other. "I think I'm ready to try." We took our seats. Quietly, I raised the camera and turned it on. "Action!"

Monster's body lengthened and widened. Tufts of brown hair sprang from his smooth scalp, and his ears shrank. His eyes sank farther into his head, and his skin tone changed from bluish-white to light green. His long, gnarled fingers became stubbier, the nails moldy and black.

As he reached for us, chunks of skin fell from his rotten arms. "Braiiinns!" he roared, so loud my hair blew back.

Adam and I applauded. "Great job!" I told him. "Now, drool on yourself."

Monster opened his mouth, but when he did, his jawbone dropped out and hit the ground. It bounced.

"Oops." He knelt down and stuck it back where it belonged. Instantly, he changed back into a goblin. I blinked and missed it.

"Still fantastic," I said. "That actually looked real. I can't wait to see your blob."

"Blob?"

"Yeah." I cleared my throat and recited the rhyme on the card:

"A blob's truly a disgusting slob
Like gelatin, a quivering glob.
You could pass by, but don't even try
Only a straight path keeps you alive."

Monster looked tired as he picked up a dead leaf with his knobby fingers. "I'll try that one later. But I did okay for now, right?"

"Yeah." I nodded encouragingly. "I totally believed you were a real zombie."

"Thank you," he said. I might as well have told him his hair looked nice.

Adam and I stayed with Monster until it was time for lunch, taking turns with the camcorder. Monster got some sharp footage of a woodpecker drilling a rotting sycamore tree. But eventually, Adam and I had to leave.

"We'll be back tonight," I said. "And look! We brought you more books! Ones with good pictures."

I pulled a stack of Haylie's favorites out of my backpack. There were Berenstain Bears books, with a few Dr. Seuss ones mixed in.

Monster reached for one with a bright orange cover. "Thanks." His lower lip jutted out.

I hated leaving him. I worried about wild animals, and if his cabin would hold up, and whether he was lonely or scared or hungry.

Adam and I headed through the woods and popped out in my backyard. Haylie was hanging out near her playhouse, lying on her stomach and scribbling on more poster board.

"Hey, Haylie," I called, but she didn't look up. I shrugged and headed for the kitchen with Adam. We ate a quick lunch and went back outside to tell Haylie to come in.

I poked my head into her pink house—which was about the size of my bathtub—and found her fast asleep, her chest rising and falling and her cheek tucked into Sammy Squirrel. A blanket was draped over her.

I smiled. She looked so sweet lying there, like a little angel.

"Haylie!" I whispered softly, tapping her shoulder. "Time to get up. Mom wants you to come inside. Is that okay?"

Haylie reached out her arms, and I scooped her

up. I staggered under her weight. "Oof! You're getting heavy."

"Am not." Haylie wrapped her arms around my neck. She smelled like animal crackers and baby powder.

"Sure, you aren't. Adam, can you grab her drawing? I don't want it getting rained on or anything."

"Got it." Adam stuck his head in the playhouse. He inhaled sharply, drawing his head back so fast he banged it on the doorway. "Ouch!"

"What?"

"Look in here," he said tightly.

I bent to peer through a window. In the corner of the house, in a neat little pile, was a cluster of flowers—bluebells and Queen Anne's lace and an umbrella plant. My throat constricted and I put Haylie down, gently, on the picnic table.

"Haylie," I said sweetly, trying to hide the tremor in my voice. "Those are pretty flowers."

She blinked up at me, kicking her legs. "Yes."

"Where did you get those pretty flowers?"

"I *told* you." Haylie raised her little shoulders. "From my friend."

"Does your friend have a name?"

Haylie pursed her lips and shook her head. "Not yet. So right now I call him Monster."

I closed my eyes. Monster had shown himself to

Haylie. Didn't he know how dangerous that could be? What if Mom looked out the back window and spotted him?

Adam looked as upset as I felt. His face was pinched, and he kept running his hands through his hair. "Haylie, you can't tell anyone about Monster. Do you understand?"

"Why not? He's my friend."

I thought quickly. "Yes, but he's a *secret* friend. Kind of like Clive, remember?"

Clive was Haylie's imaginary friend back when she was three. Don't ask me where she got that name. It was all, "Clive doesn't like that show," and "Clive needs chocolate," and "Clive says it's scary at night without two lights on." Then, one day, Haylie announced that Clive had moved to Pittsburgh, and that was the end of him.

"But with Monster," I told Haylie, "people *can* see him if you're not careful. So you need to make sure that people don't. Otherwise they might take him away."

Haylie's eyes got so big I felt terrible for scaring her, even if it was necessary. "Okay," she said in a small voice.

I smiled at her. "Now, come on." I picked her up again and carried her toward the house.

As we climbed the stairs to the back deck, I stole

125

a glance over my shoulder. It might have been my imagination, but I swore I saw something move at the edge of the woods. Something that was light blue, and short, with pointy ears.

Something that was in *big trouble*.

MONSTER DISCIPLINE

Adam had to help his dad with the yard, leaving me to discipline our new pet. I charged through the woods, getting madder every time a branch smacked me or a bush scratched me. Seriously, how dumb could he be?

"Monster!" I screamed when I got to his building. I stormed in.

"Eeek!" Monster leapt onto his mattress in the corner and tossed a blanket over his head. I grabbed a corner and tugged it off. Monster put his hands over his eyes.

"I didn't do anything! I didn't do anything!"

"Oh, yeah? Then how come you're acting scared of me?"

"Because you're acting mad." Monster kept his hands over his eyes. He trembled, fat tears splashing the mattress.

I sighed. "Monster, uncover your eyes. I'm not going to hurt you."

"But you're mad!"

"Yeah. Because you did something really stupid. You showed yourself to my sister. What if she was the kind of kid who cries and tattles?"

Monster lowered his hands. He looked annoyed. "Haylie would never tell on me. She's my friend."

"Well, yeah. But you didn't *know* that, did you?"

"No."

"See?"

"But she didn't." Monster hopped across his bed and pulled something out from underneath it gingerly. "And look what she made me."

It was the poster board Haylie had been coloring on, covered in blobs and scribbles.

"Wow. That's . . . colorful."

"I know! Isn't it pretty? It took her hours and hours. *Plus* she gave me her crayons." He looked triumphant.

"That's right," I remembered. "Ten crayons for ten flowers."

"Yup." Monster traced a long finger around a shape on the picture. "She gave me all the good colors."

I cracked a smile. "That sounds like Haylie." Then I shook my head. "No! You're distracting me. I'm trying to lecture you." I squatted down to be eye level with him. "Monster, you're lucky that Haylie didn't rat you out. But I'm telling you, letting people know about you is dangerous. You need to stay here, okay?"

Monster flopped onto his bed. "But it's boring here! And Haylie gave me crayons."

"Well, you can use them here. Right?"

Monster's lower lip jutted out. "It's not as fun, though. And Haylie said she'd bring coloring books next time. And Oreos."

I pinched the bridge of my nose and squeezed my eyes shut. "Monster, you're giving me a headache."

"I'm sorry," Monster said, putting his chin in his hands. "But I'm lonely."

I sat down next to him, putting an arm around his bony shoulders. "You won't be lonely forever. Adam and I will help you figure out what kind of monster you should be, and then you can go back Down Below to be with your friends."

"I guess." Monster looked away.

"What?"

"Nothing." He used the exact same tone Haylie uses when she wants me to ask her what's wrong.

I took the bait. "Monster, what's wrong?"

"It's just that I didn't have any friends Down Below. I was too new."

"Well, every new place stops being new at some point, right? And you find things you like about it. And people—or monsters—that you get along with. Soon it's not a new place anymore. It's home."

Ugh. I sounded like a school-mandated program on values.

"I guess so." Monster propped the poster board against the wall. "But I still want to see Haylie again. How about if I'm careful?"

I glanced around his little room. It was a total dump—lots of dust from broken bricks and giant gaping holes in the walls and ceilings. Adam and I had dressed it up with blankets and rugs and an air mattress, but it was still a rat hole.

"This plan is totally a recipe for disaster," I said, "but okay. You and Haylie can play together again. But on one big condition, okay?" When Monster nodded, I went on. "You only hang out when Adam and I arrange it. When the coast is clear. Because I'm telling you, if my dad thinks Haylie's in danger, *you're* in danger. Got it?"

Monster gave me a gap-toothed smile. "Got it!"

I smiled back tiredly at him. As much as I liked Monster and as badly as I wanted to make my movie, I knew that he needed to go back Down Below pretty soon. I didn't trust him not to search for Haylie when he was bored.

And I didn't trust that he wouldn't be spotted.

SCENE FIVE:

NIGHT ESCAPE

On Monday, Todd showed up in his ninja costume. He looked ridiculous.

"A bet's a bet," he told Adam and me.

I was surprised. The kid had honor.

That afternoon, Adam and I had serious work to do with Monster after school. "Monster," I directed. "Like we talked about. Come out of the building and pretend you're going to attack me! And then you hear a sound and run off, okay?"

I showed Adam how to hold the camera and took my spot in the foreground, sitting cross-legged on the ground and opening a book. *La la la, look at me, waiting to be killed. . . .*

"Action!" Adam called, and Monster-the-zombie shambled out of the house. I flipped a page in my book, willing my eyes not to stray. Director, writer, *and* actor—I was a triple threat!

Monster was so close I smelled his sour breath. "Now?" he asked.

I tossed the book. "Monster!"

"What?"

"You don't ask me when! And right before you're about to bite me, you pretend to hear something and run off. We'll add the sound later."

"Oh." By then, Monster had transformed back into his goblin-like self. "Can we do it later? I'm hungry. And I want you to read me *Green Eggs and Ham*."

I sighed and got to my feet. "Okay, fine."

Shooting went on like that for three days. Monster either ruined scenes or wasn't interested in doing them at all. Like a typical star, he delayed production.

I wished Casey and Taylor were here to help. Any excuse to be creative, we ran with it—like the improvised skits we filmed in Washington Square Park and the play we put on for Taylor's mom's birthday. They'd find a way to make Monster perform.

On Thursday afternoon, I was headed into the woods for another filming attempt when Haylie ran out from her playhouse.

"I want to come with you!"

"Oh." I glanced at the woods. "No, Haylie. It's too far. And you could fall and get hurt."

"But I want to see Monster."

"Well, Monster's . . . busy."

"Doing what?"

"I don't know. Monster stuff." But I knew that

whatever Monster was doing, he'd love to see Haylie. He asked about her every day.

"Like what?"

"I don't know. Hanging out in his monster house. Cleaning his monster room."

"I want to see it!"

"No, that's a terrible idea. Monster's house is really far into the woods. And there are dangerous things out there. Like . . . bears."

"Bears?" Haylie's mouth dropped open.

"Yes, bears. And bears love how little kids smell."

"They do?"

"Yes, but they can only smell kids from ten feet away or closer. So as long as you stay in the yard, you're totally safe."

Haylie scrunched up her face. "But what if I want to pet the bears?"

"You don't, Hails. Just trust me."

"Oh, okay. So can Monster come out and play?"

I sighed. Sometimes I wish Haylie wasn't so smart for her age. Other four-year-olds will forget a question if you distract them, but not Haylie.

"Tell you what. I'll bring Monster to play if you promise to keep him in the playhouse where Mom and Dad can't see him. Okay?"

Haylie nodded. "Okay, I promise." She paused. "Lissa?"

"What?"

"Why do we call Monster that?"

"Call him what?"

"Monster."

"Oh. Well, because that's what he is. He doesn't have a name yet."

"Why don't we give him one?"

She was right. Monster deserved a real name. I mean, how would I like it if people went around calling me *Girl* all the time?

"That's a great idea, Haylie. Do you have anything in mind?"

"No. I just thought he should have a name."

"Fair enough."

She went to grab her tea set, and I weaved through the trees to find Monster. He came with me happily. At the edge of the woods, I scouted the yard for my parents. When I saw that the coast was clear, Monster and I made a break for Haylie's playhouse. She was sitting outside at its picnic table, waiting, shielded from the sun by a pink, floppy hat.

I practically shoved Monster through the playhouse's tiny door.

"Ow!" he protested, but then he wrapped his gnarled hands around the bottom of the window frame and poked his head out. "Hi, Haylie."

"Hi, Monster!" Haylie tapped at her hat. The brim hid half her face. "Do you like my hat?"

"Sure. It's really . . . pink."

"Thanks! And you're really blue."

"I'm always blue."

Haylie tilted her chin up to look at me. "He's always blue," she repeated. "Blue."

She smiled.

In movies, directors show the passage of time with a montage—you know, like watching an actor training for the Olympics and the first shot is him struggling to lift a barbell, and then it shows leaves changing from green to yellow and in the ending shots he's lifting a way heavier barbell. So you're like, "Oh yeah! He's totally ready."

That kind of sequence couldn't be used with the progress on my movie. Because there was none. Everything I filmed was just—meh.

By mid-October, I had about twenty hours of footage of Blue. The problem was, none of it was anything special. It was a bunch of clips that didn't amount to something whole.

I couldn't blame everything on my star. It was my

fault, too. My ideas were all over the place, and none of them were great. No high-concept idea that would be a blockbuster.

One Friday evening before bed, I stared at my computer screen trying to will a good idea to come to me. I knew that praying for an amazing epiphany wasn't exactly how Francis Ford Coppola had come up with *The Godfather*, but I was desperate.

Why couldn't this be as easy as writing the seventh grade play? I wrote that whole thing in under two hours, inspired by the lameness of Casey's brother, Scott, and his obsession with *Call of Duty*. And cheered on by Casey and Taylor, as I perfected my snappy dialogue.

I'd barely even been trying then. But I was trying really hard now and getting absolutely nothing in return.

Sometimes being a Creative Person is really annoying.

My phone buzzed, and I grinned to see TAYLOR lit up on the screen. I grabbed it and punched TALK.

"Cheer me up," I instructed her.

"Only fourteen days until you get to see your play!"

"Trust me, I'm counting. Anything else?"

"Okay, here's the latest," she said, and I could picture her on the phone, curled up in her desk chair with her feet on her desk, frowning in concentration as she painted her toenails. "Mr. Reed wanted to rewrite your script."

It felt like I'd been punched in the gut. *"What?"*

Roland Reed thought I was a terrible writer. Talentless. That my script was single-ply toilet paper. Post-use.

Taylor laughed. "Don't worry about it. Mr. Kincaid wouldn't let him touch it."

Mr. Kincaid is an English teacher at St. Mary's. According to Casey and Taylor, he was asked to supervise the rehearsals, since Roland Reed treated his own appearance as optional.

"But Mr. Kincaid's not a screenwriter," I said through numb lips.

"He's also not a crazy person. Trust me. It's fine. "

That didn't make me feel better. It was like in bad romantic comedies, where the heroine's friends say she "can do *so* much better" after she gets dumped. Well, she's still alone, isn't she? And I had no backup screenwriter to confirm my talent, compared to how the heroine always has a way-better-but-previously-overlooked-for-silly-reasons guy friend.

"Okay," I said, but it didn't make me feel any better. Even if Roland Reed had a few screws loose, he still had street cred. "Did he say why?"

"He said it needed more angst and less heart. Then Mr. Kincaid was like, 'Mr. Reed, we value your opinion and your work. But this is a play for young people. We need heart.'"

"Then what happened?"

"Then Mr. Kincaid gave Mr. Reed money to get sodas for everyone. And he never came back!"

"Wow."

"Yeah. He's *special*. Don't worry about anything he says."

"I won't," I lied.

After we got off the phone, I went to Haylie's room, hoping she could cheer me up.

"Want to play Monsterville?" I asked.

Her eyes lit up. "Yes!" She was in bed with her dolls, and she jumped up. "A monster around every corner! A monster around every corner!" Soon every doll was knocked to the floor.

"Goodness. Calm down, Haylie." I retrieved the game from its spot on a shelf, and she flopped down on the bed.

Haylie beat me three times because I kept getting stuck. I even had to go down the big waterslide once.

When I landed on that space, Haylie said, *"I've* never gotten to go on the waterslide."

"Well, don't be too jealous. I'll lose for sure now. Because look—you've only got two spaces until you get to the princess."

Haylie rolled the die and got a three. "See? You win," I told her. "Ready for bed now?"

"Yes," she said smugly. "I won enough tonight."

That night, I couldn't sleep. I kept imagining Roland Reed ripping my script in half and throwing it into the garbage. And thinking about how much fun rehearsals must be. Casey and Taylor had posted a bunch of pictures on Facebook, tagging random objects as "Lissa Black." It was supposed to be funny, but it only reminded me that I was gone.

Plus, my room was stuffy, and an owl kept hooting. It sounded so close that it felt like a personal attack: *"Try to sleep! Hoot! Hoot! HAHAHAHAHA!"*

"Don't make me come out there," I grumbled, sticking my head under my pillow and wishing for earplugs. Or a slingshot.

Something *thwacked* against my window. I froze, listening. Another *thwack*.

Groaning, I rolled off my bed and went to the window. Adam was there, holding a handful of pine chips, the kind we had spread around our hedges. I unlatched the window and pushed it open.

"You're throwing pine chips at my window?" I called softly. "Couldn't you get pebbles?"

"Pebbles?" Adam looked down at his pine chips. He dropped them and rubbed his hands against his jeans.

"In movies, the prince always throws pebbles at the princess's window."

I could see Adam's grin even in the dark. "Yeah, but I'm not a prince. And I'm pretty sure you'd hit anyone who called you a princess."

"This is true." I leaned over the window ledge. "What's up?"

"I can't sleep."

"Neither can I."

"Good. Let's do something."

"What?"

Adam twisted, showing me the backpack he was wearing. "It's a surprise," he said mysteriously. "Want to climb out the window?"

"Can't I just walk out the front door?"

"You can, but then it would be less of an adventure."

"Okay, fine." I pulled on a pair of sneakers and put my desk chair beneath my window, using it to boost me through. I balanced, my butt on the ledge.

"Just ease down. Keep your knees bent."

I dropped, my knees buckling. "Ack!" I yelped as pine chips dug into my palms.

Adam held out a hand. "That was pathetic."

"Shhh! Someone might hear you!"

We weren't being that loud, and Mom and Dad probably couldn't hear a thing in their room—Dad sleeps like the dead, and Mom wears earplugs—but it was exciting to think that Dad could fling his window open and discover me sneaking out.

Adam might be a Boy Scout, but he had a dangerous side. I never would have guessed. And I kind of liked it.

We tiptoed around the corner of the house. It was damp outside, and wet grass squished under my sneakers. A slice of moon overhead cast just enough light to see the ground ahead.

"Where are we going?" I asked, wrapping my arms around me. It was chilly.

"To see Blue."

"At night?"

"Yeah. Don't you think he'd like a little company? I can't sleep, you can't sleep . . . what do you bet that he can't, either?"

"Okay, sure. And it's a weekend, anyway."

When we got to the edge of the trees, Adam fumbled in his backpack and handed me a flashlight. "Here, just don't aim it at your house."

"Of course not." That's a cardinal rule of horror movies: know when to use a light. Because if you're escaping from a killer and using a flashlight to cut through the woods, you might as well be screaming, "Here I am! Come get me!"

The woods were pitch black. I pulled my hood over my head and drew the strings so only my nose poked through. I kept picturing a twig popping one of my eyeballs out like a grape. I wasn't taking any chances.

I played the flashlight over the ground. Something slithered across the path, and I tried not to feel grossed out. A breeze whistled through the trees, and bullfrogs were croaking in the creek. They were talkative tonight.

Adam marched ahead as smoothly as if we were walking on a sidewalk in daylight. "Isn't this great? The woods are so peaceful at night."

"Yeah, sure. Until we're eaten by a werewolf. One we know personally."

I wondered how much Blue practiced at night. He swore he did—turning into different creatures and prowling the woods—but I knew a secret that made me suspect he was lying.

Adam had rigged a little lamp for Blue. It needed its batteries recharged almost every day. And they wouldn't need to be recharged if Blue weren't keeping the lamp on all night.

That's right. Blue—a *monster*—was afraid of the dark.

The walk to see Blue felt longer at night. When we finally reached the cabin, a dim light was glowing from inside.

"Blue?" I called quietly, aiming my flashlight at the doorway. "You there? It's us."

Blue crept out of the cabin. "Lissa? Adam? What are you doing here?" His grin was as wide as the Cheshire Cat's in the Disney iteration of *Alice in Wonderland*.

Adam dumped his backpack on the ground. "I thought it would be a good time to go camping. You know, before it gets too cold."

Winter would be coming in only a few months. We couldn't keep Blue in a broken-down shack when it was snowing and freezing outside. For his own good, Blue really needed to figure out what he wanted to be.

Blue poked the backpack with his long fingers. "What did you bring me?"

Adam nudged him away and reached into the pack. "Graham crackers, marshmallows, and choco-late. S'mores stuff. Lissa, can you get some dry leaves and sticks? You might have to hunt a bit."

I brought Adam an armful of dry sticks and pine needles. He selected a few sticks and leaned them together to form a crude teepee. Then he reached into his backpack and pulled out a roll of toilet paper.

"You need that for out here?" I asked him. "I didn't know Boy Scouts were so dainty."

Adam shook his head. He wadded the toilet paper and stuck it in between the sticks. Then he sifted through the pine needles and leaves, examining them like he was mining for gold. "We can't burn the green stuff. It'll smoke instead of catching fire."

I rolled my eyes. "Whatever you say, Scoutmaster."

I was curious about what he was doing, though. Taylor's parents have an electric fireplace—one you light by pressing a button on a remote control. It's way convenient, but it's pretty much just for decoration. The glass doors don't even get that hot.

Adam lit a match. I could smell the sulfur. Keeping his left hand cupped around the match, he lit the tissue in three places. The blue-red flames licked at the paper, snaking around the makeshift teepee.

Blue found three long sticks, and we each impaled a few marshmallows. I stuck mine right into the fire.

"Not an accident," I told them. "Marshmallows taste better all charred and black."

"Yeah, just don't wave it around to blow it out. Charlie lit himself on fire doing that."

"Charlie doesn't strike me as the type of guy who'd light himself on fire," I commented.

"He was eight. I remember it because I was four and thought he was invincible."

"Aww, that's cute. But bummer about Charlie getting hurt." I watched my marshmallows bubbling under the heat, turning amber before blackening. "Hey, want to tell ghost stories?"

"Okay," Adam said. "I mean, this is the perfect place for it. Who wants to go first?"

"I will," Blue said. He'd already eaten three entire Hershey's bars. The chocolate was smeared all around his mouth. It was a good thing Adam had brought two six-packs.

"Really, Blue?" I asked. "You know a ghost story?"

"Well, it's not a *real* ghost story," he said, his tail twitching. "But you'll think it's scary. Does that count?"

"Sure."

Blue stared into the fire, which was really crackling by then. One of the wooden sticks shifted, and red embers flew into the air.

"This is the story—" He hesitated, then swallowed and tried again. "This is the story of how monsters become monsters."

I forgot about the marshmallows melting at the end of my stick. My mouth went dry.

"I don't know the whole story," Blue said softly, "but I know enough."

"I thought you didn't remember how you became a goblin, though," I said, recalling Blue's outburst.

"I lied. I knew that if I told, and Atticus found out . . . bad things would happen," he finished in a whisper. "But you've been so nice, and I know you'd never tell. Right?" He looked up at me with huge, scared eyes.

"Of course not. You're safe. I promise."

Blue drew in a deep, shaky breath. "Okay. See, monsters live Down Below. And Down Below isn't safe. There are wars. And accidents, like up here. Monsters don't die unless something bad happens. But sometimes . . . something bad happens.

"Because of that, they need to get new monsters. Ones that are good for Down Below—ones that are smart or special in some way." Blue stared into the fire. Close to such bright light, his pale skin looked almost transparent.

"Every year, on Monster New Year, monsters add to their numbers. They scout for kids who would do well Down Below. Kids who aren't afraid. Who don't mind change. Kids who are smart and can make Down Below better."

Haylie, I thought instantly, and my throat tightened. My shoulder brushed against Adam's, and I realized I'd scooted closer to him.

"Before monsters take their targets, they show themselves to see how the kids react. If a kid screams for his parents, the monster leaves him alone. Monsters don't want to share Down Below with crybabies. But if the kid doesn't seem scared, that kid might make a good monster. He'll go on the *maybe* list, for the monsters' meeting before Monster New Year."

"Meeting?" Adam interjected. "What happens at the meeting?"

"They figure out how to add to their numbers. They talk about the kids on the list, and they vote on how many and who to take. But it's not a meeting for all the monsters—only the really important ones, like Atticus. The monsters have a map, and they mark where the kids live. The ones they want to take."

"What kind of a map?" I asked. "Of the United States? Or the whole world?"

Blue's eyes were sad when they met mine. "The Down Below I know, it's just the United States. But there are other places Down Below that are underneath other countries."

Adam and I looked at each other, horrified. Kidsnatching by monsters was a *global problem*.

"Then they decide which monsters will lead the kids Down Below," Blue continued. "On Monster New Year, those monsters crawl out from under the kids' beds. Always by midnight—kids can't be taken after midnight. I don't know why.

"The monsters usually send a monster that isn't scary. A monster that's big and fluffy and funny-looking, so the kid will want to follow. And then, once he gets Down Below and the kid sees how dark and scary it is, the monster is there to comfort him. It's like having a really big teddy bear for a bodyguard. One with pointy teeth.

"The teddy bear monster leads the kids to the Transformation Room. That's this special place Down Below where new monsters are formed. Or, I guess, *transformed*. There are games, and magic tricks, and lots of junk food . . . everything's used to distract the kids until daylight. Because as soon as daylight hits Up There, the kids Down Below turn into monsters."

"But when does daylight hit?" Adam asked in a hushed whisper. "Wouldn't it be at different times in different places?"

Blue wrinkled his nose. "It's based on the time zone the Transformation Room is under. One monster said the Transformation Room is under the capitol. Does that mean anything?"

"Yes! That's Washington, DC. So Eastern Time, then," I said. "Same time as it is here."

"Anyway," Blue continued, "the kids don't become just *any* kind of monster. Every new monster is a goblin, and later they pick the kind of monster they want to be. You can stay a goblin if you want to, though."

Blue fell silent, staring at the marshmallow at the end of his stick. I couldn't even imagine what he was thinking.

I looked into Blue's brown eyes. The first time I'd

looked into them, I'd been struck by how human they were. And I realized that during his entire story, he referred to the monsters as *they*. Not *we*.

"You were a kid once," I whispered.

BLUE REMEMBERS

Adam and I stayed with Blue until after dawn, letting him share what he remembered from his life Up There. Here.

A lot of his memories were gone, wiped away with each day spent Down Below. This included his name and where he'd come from. This was typical for monsters, and a reason Atticus was so special—he was one of the few whose memories had stayed intact. That helped when the monsters infiltrated Up There each year—Atticus "knew the enemy."

Once Blue had escaped to Up There, he stopped losing memories. And some of the ones he'd lost had come back.

He told us he remembered one thing really clearly—sitting on someone's lap—a lady with long blonde hair and a huge smile. She loved reading him Dr. Seuss books. No wonder those were his favorites.

"I think that lady's my mom." Blue's eyes welled with tears. "And I remember my dad, too. He worked in a car shop. When he came home, he always smelled like oil, and his hands were dirty. We kept special soap to wash out grease in our bathroom. It smelled like oranges."

I wanted to pull Blue onto my lap and hold him the same way I held Haylie when she was upset or didn't feel well. Just rock him back and forth and tell him that everything would be okay.

But I didn't know if everything *would* be okay. Blue was a kid, or at least he was before he was taken. He didn't belong out in the woods with us. He belonged at home in bed, sleeping under rocket ship blankets, with his parents in the next room.

"Is there anything we can do?" I asked hesitantly. "Is there any way to reverse your transformation?"

Blue dropped his head. "I don't know."

"I'm sorry," I said, feeling horrible. The only thing worse than a terrible situation is knowing you can't do anything about it.

"You know, Blue—" I stopped. "You had a real name once. Are you *sure* you don't remember it? Maybe if I brought a book of baby names and read them to you?"

"No." Blue wrapped his arms around his spindly legs, wiping away tears.

"Oh, Blue." I scooted closer to put my arm around him. "It'll be okay."

Adam's face was pinched. "On Monster New Year,"

he said, "the monsters will do this all over again. Steal kids, I mean. What day is Monster New Year?"

Blue shook his head. "I don't know."

"I do!" I exclaimed so loudly that Blue recoiled against me. "Halloween. It has to be Halloween."

Adam lit another match and held it to the fire. "Why?"

I shook my head. "Because Halloween had to have started for a reason. People noticed something weird about that particular day. Something spooky."

"Huh." Adam didn't sound convinced.

"Plus, that's a cardinal rule in monster movies. If something looks or feels wrong, it probably is wrong."

"I've never liked Halloween," Adam muttered, poking at the fire with a stick. "There's always a creepy vibe in the air."

"I love Halloween," I said. "At least, I used to."

"Halloween's coming in two weeks," Adam pointed out.

I chewed on my lower lip, thinking of all the kids who would be taken . . . and there was absolutely nothing I could do about it.

Well, that wasn't entirely true. I could protect Haylie.

"What can we do to help, Blue?" Adam asked. "All this time, we've been trying to help you figure out what kind of monster you should be when you shouldn't be one at all."

Blue shrugged his narrow shoulders. "You've already done a lot. If you hadn't caught me, I'd be living off berries and stealing apples. Or in a cage. Or back Down Below."

"The others have to know you're gone," I said. "Why haven't they come after you?"

Blue scratched at his knee. "I worry about that a lot. Maybe because they don't know where I am, and monsters stick to scouting out houses."

"Are you sure?" I didn't want to scare him, but I was certain the other monsters didn't want him up here. What if he got caught and exposed them? They had to know he was a risk.

"Yeah, what if the monsters go on a mission to find you?" Adam asked.

"Monster prison." Blue trembled at the idea.

My eyes felt hot, and I didn't want to get teary in front of Blue. If he was anything like Haylie, seeing me upset would make him upset."

"Don't worry, Blue," I said. "We'll find a way to make things right."

But I worried that was a lie.

SCENE SEVEN:

A BRILLIANT IDEA

My feet sank in wet grass as I crossed our yard, squinting at the orange sun rising above the cloud line. The sky was gray—still early, but it was more daytime than nighttime for sure.

I was totally late—in movies, kids who successfully sneak out at night get back *before* dawn.

I crept up the wooden porch stairs, avoiding the second step because it creaked. Slowly, I eased open the screen door, holding on to the doorknob so it wouldn't slam shut behind me.

"Someone's up early."

I jumped, my heart thumping. "Mom!" I put my hand over my chest. "You scared me."

She sat at the kitchen table, drinking coffee and flipping through *Vogue*. "Sneaking in is always stressful." A smile twitched at the corners of her mouth.

I wandered into the kitchen, wrapping my hands around one of our new high-backed chairs. "I just didn't want to wake anyone up. Adam and I got up early to go . . . fishing." I was too tired to come up with a better excuse.

"Fishing?" Mom raised her eyebrows. "Is that what the kids are calling it nowadays?"

"Gross, Mom."

Mom put her coffee cup down. "I'm just kidding, honey. But you've been spending a lot of time with Adam. And he *is* a boy."

"Yeah, but not a normal boy."

"What does that mean?"

I rubbed my hand across my face. It was too early for this conversation. Or too late. "I just don't like him that way, okay, Mom?"

"Sure." She smiled at me. It was the same way she used to smile at Dad when he said he'd be home for dinner instead of working late again. "Tell you what, honey. It's been a long time since we've had a day together. How about it?"

"A day?" I repeated. "What do you have in mind?"

"Maybe we could drive to Algonquin and check out the historic district."

All I knew about Algonquin was that it was an hour away. An hour there, an hour back . . . plus Mom would want to spend at least a few hours there to make the drive worth it. Ugh.

"That's okay," I said. "We don't have to."

"But I want to. And your father has the day off. He can watch Haylie."

I sighed. "I'll go take a shower."

Mom was waiting in the car when I emerged from the house. "Yay! A girls' day," she said. Gravel flew up from the tires as she put the car into reverse.

"Yay." I rubbed at my eyes, which felt gritty. A dull throb pulsed at my temples. I hadn't pulled an all-nighter since last New Year's Eve, when Casey and Taylor and I had a classic Jim Carrey marathon. Once the sun had come up, we'd immediately passed out.

"It's a great day for a drive," Mom chirped. "All the leaves are changing."

She was right. As we wove along country back roads, I stared out the window at the trees. They were all bright October colors—yellow and orange and brown—that blurred together.

"Isn't this peaceful?" Mom sighed contentedly. "You know, in New York City, I couldn't even get behind the wheel without tensing up. Here, a ride's a great way to relax."

"I can see that." I stifled a yawn, fiddling with the

radio dial. Gospel and country music. "Do you have any CDs?"

"Nothing you'd like. We might have to have an actual conversation." She smiled at me, the dimple in the right side of her cheek deepening. The blue shawl around her neck matched her eyes and made them look bluer than usual. She looked gorgeous, in a totally effortless way.

"Wow, Mom. You look really nice."

"It's the fresh air." She slowed to make a right-hand turn. "It makes me younger."

She was kidding, but I believed her. I hadn't heard her argue with Dad once since the move. The normal reasons they'd argue were gone—Dad didn't work nearly as many hours at Chester County Hospital. And Freeburg Consolidated School was free.

The ride didn't feel like it took an hour, and soon we came to a little green sign welcoming us to Algonquin. We drove through a covered bridge and into a colonial-looking town. Four paths led to a gazebo in the center of a square, and a courthouse with stone steps and a huge Big Ben-esque clock took up one side. It reminded me of the backlot Universal Studios used in the *Back to the Future* movies.

"Wow. This is adorable," I said as Mom parked along the curb of the cobblestone street. "Like stepping back in time." I opened my door and studied the signs.

"Most of the buildings around here have been declared historical landmarks," Mom explained. "Even if someone wanted to, they couldn't tear them down and build a McDonald's."

"Good."

Mom pointed to a restaurant with a green awning and purple flowers lining its walkway. "Brunch?"

My stomach rumbled, and I realized I hadn't eaten anything but marshmallows in almost twelve hours. "Sure."

A waitress came outside to refill someone's water glass. "Sit anywhere," she said, motioning to the tables covered in red-and-white-checkered tablecloths.

"Isn't this nice?" Mom asked as the waitress reappeared, handing us each a laminated menu.

"What's nice?" I asked.

"Going to brunch and getting a seat right away. Back in the Village, we'd wait an hour."

"You sound like Adam." I scanned the menu for French toast.

"How so?"

"Oh, nothing. He's just always going on about how much better Freeburg is than the city."

Mom put her menu down and folded her arms in front of her. Her wedding ring glittered. "Sounds like Adam wants you to like it here. Because he likes *you*."

"Yeah, he needs an extra pair of hands to help with the cow tipping."

"So you don't like anything about Freeburg? Like having a big yard instead of a three-foot balcony overlooking an alley?"

"Well, I have to admit, French toast is way cheaper than in New York."

After we ordered, Mom reached for her glass. "Lissa, I want you to know we didn't move to Freeburg to torture you. Your father and I honestly believed it would be good for everyone."

"I know." I took a sip of my water so I wouldn't have to say anything else.

"Being here isn't so bad, is it?"

"It's growing on me, a little," I admitted. "Like a fungus."

Mom smiled when the waitress deposited our food in front of us. It smelled amazing, and the cook had been generous with the powdered sugar on my French toast. It reminded me of the funnel cake at the fair.

"Let's not compare Freeburg to New York," Mom said. "It's a beautiful day. We're in Algonquin. Let's just enjoy it. And then *next* weekend, we can enjoy New York and your play."

My stomach flipped just thinking about it.

"Okay, fine." I pointed at a store across the street with my butter knife. "I want to go in there." According to the sign, it was Tom's Old Time Game Shop." It looked like the type of place that would sell jacks and marbles and discontinued board games.

"We can go in all the shops. That's why we're here."

After Mom paid, we hit up a candle store where Mom bought a peppermint candle, an indie clothing place where I bought a pair of dangly earrings, and an antiques shop where everything was too expensive.

Taylor would've *loved* the indie shop. I clicked a picture and sent it to her.

When we opened the door to the game shop, a bell tinkled overhead.

I breathed in a lungful of musty air. "Wow. So *this* is where old games come to die."

The store didn't look that big from the outside, but inside it was huge, filled with crooked rows of wooden shelves and mismatched tables piled high with thousands of board games.

It was the kind of place to find a treasure, like the cluttered bookstore in *The Neverending Story*.

A gray-haired guy with wire-rimmed glasses stood behind the counter. He looked like he belonged in an old-fashioned candy shop. Or *shoppe*.

"Welcome to Tom's Old Time Game Shop." He smiled, flashing a gold tooth. "I'm Tom."

"We're just browsing," Mom said. "Seems like we have a lot to look at." She glanced around the enormous room.

"Board games are my life," the man said.

"Really?" I asked. "In that case, have you ever heard of a game called Monsterville?"

"Monsterville," he mused. "Ya know, I ain't heard of that one. What does it look like?"

I described it to him, and he shook his head. "Don't ring a bell."

"Well, I'm sure you can help us find something wonderful," Mom assured him, running her hand along a stack of old Monopoly games. "I have a four-year-old at home, and she loves animals. Do you have anything with horses, maybe? Or bunnies?"

"Sure!"

He was off, running to the back of the store on surprisingly athletic legs. He returned with something called Rabbits in the Carrot Patch.

"I invented this one," he said shyly. It was cute how into board games this guy was. "Took me about thirty prototypes."

"Prototypes?" I asked.

"Sure. Takes a lot of versions to get a game perfect. You didn't think Monopoly always looked the way it does, did ya? You used to go around in a big circle to pass Go."

"I didn't know that!" Mom said. "How fascinating." She reached into her wallet, pulling out a ten and handing it to Tom. "Keep the change."

"What a sweet man," Mom said as we left the store, fumbling in her purse for her sunglasses. She put them on and scanned the block.

"Yeah," I replied, thinking of Tom's comment about a prototype.

Someone, at some time, cooked up the idea of a board game about the world of creatures living beneath a kid's bed. Maybe that person knew something about Down Below.

There'd been no company logo on the game—no Parker Brothers or Milton Bradley. Some people pay to get their books published. Maybe that was how Monsterville began—as someone's pet project.

And I'd found it in Aunt Lucy's basement. Aunt Lucy, who believed in monsters.

In movies, there are no coincidences.

SCENE EIGHT:

MONSTERVILLE EXPLAINED

I was so tired when we got home that I crawled into bed with my shoes still on and slept through dinner. When I woke up, it was pitch black outside.

My alarm clock glowed, and I squinted to read the time: four in the morning.

"Ugh," I muttered, swinging my legs over the side of the bed and slipping off my shoes. My face was greasy, and my mouth tasted horrible. I stumbled into the bathroom and spent the next ten minutes washing my face and brushing my teeth. Colgate never tasted so good.

The game shop in Alonquin made me think—*prototypes*. If Monsterville had started as an idea, there might be more information in our basement. Old notes, drawings . . .

I didn't want to go down there. It was dark and clammy, and I didn't trust those dark corners.

Then I thought of Blue. If someone had designed Monsterville based on Down Below, that meant they'd been there. They could know something Blue didn't, something useful.

Mustering my courage, I padded down the hall and eased open the basement door. I pulled the chain on the overhead light, blinking in the harsh glare. A red flashlight rested on a wooden shelf. I grabbed it and tiptoed down the narrow stairs.

Five minutes, I told myself. *If I don't find anything in five minutes, I'll go back to bed.*

When I got to the bottom of the stairs, I sneezed. Not once, but about fifteen times. *Man, there's a lot of dust down here.*

Switching on the flashlight, I played the beam over the room. The lumpy shapes under plastic tarps were furniture—Aunt Lucy's old living room set, a broken cuckoo clock, a wooden hutch with a door that didn't quite close. Everything smelled musty.

Aunt Lucy's old washer and dryer were pushed up against one of the walls. Along the far side was a storage closet with a wooden door that slid open on metal tracks. That looked promising.

I switched the flashlight to my left hand and tugged at the door. It didn't budge. When I placed the flashlight on the floor, it rolled a few inches away, scraping against the rough concrete, then stopped. I yanked on the door with both hands. This time it slid open noisily, the shrieking of the metal tracks echoing off the walls.

I stood on tiptoe to pull the chain hanging from the closet's ceiling. *Broken. Figures.* I picked up the flashlight and shined it on the shelves.

At first glance, I didn't see anything interesting. On the top shelf sat a big plastic container with Christmas paper that had faded from red to pink. I pawed through the rest of the shelf's contents, but it was just holiday decorations—an old wreath, a Nativity set, and a box of glass ornaments shaped like icicles.

Something rustled at the back.

"Ah!" I dropped the flashlight, and everything went dark.

With hands slick with sweat, I fumbled for the light, my fingers groping the cold concrete until my hands closed around the handle. The top had loosened when the flashlight slipped from my hands, and I screwed it back on. A thin yellow beam cut through the room.

I held my breath, aiming the light at the top shelf again. Nothing. Whatever had been there, I'd scared it away.

Taking deep breaths to steady myself, I aimed the flashlight at a shelf that looked empty, playing the beam over uneven wooden boards. There was nothing there but dust.

And a mousetrap. *Gross.* At least it was empty.

The third shelf was crammed with boxes of what Mom calls sentimental junk: old report cards and wedding invitations and high school trophies.

I lifted a box off the shelf. The cardboard was soft, and it looked like a mouse had been chewing on one of the flaps. Inside were just old recipes and cookbooks. I slid it back on the shelf and took down another one.

Books about trees and birds and insects. I remembered what Adam had said about Aunt Lucy letting him and Upchuck explore her woods.

The last box held office supplies. Spiral notebooks with cramped writing detailing grocery lists and things to do. Loose paper, and Post-its, and dried-up pens. Nothing interesting.

I was about to put the box back on the shelf when I had a thought. When I first started writing stories and screenplay ideas, I kept them in semi-secret journals. *Semi-secret* because even though I kept the journals in plain sight, the ideas were hidden behind pages of old math problems or English assignments.

On a hunch, I picked up one of the notebooks and flipped to the yellowed pages near the end. Nothing but a list of ingredients for garden vegetable soup.

I picked up another fat spiral notebook and flipped through it. When I reached the middle, my breath caught.

<u>Down Below.</u>

With a shaking hand, I flipped the page. The top right-hand corner said *August 4* in faded ink. It must have been really old. The rest of the page was filled with the same slanted handwriting I'd seen on Aunt Lucy's Christmas cards every year.

I can't shake the guilt, Aunt Lucy had written.

Guilt? What guilt? I settled onto the floor, ignoring how hard and uncomfortable the cold cement felt.

> *Of the twelve of us, I was the only one to escape. Even now, all these years later, I still ask myself—what spared me? I wasn't special. I wasn't particularly smart. I wasn't easily frightened, but surely that was true of most of the other children taken.*

My mouth went dry and my breath hitched. I hadn't actually expected to find any information down here. I'd just hoped I would, the same way people who buy lottery tickets hope they'll be the big winner.

> *I'll never forget the moment I realized I could only save myself. The look in that one little boy's eyes—it hurts to think of it. I left him! How could I do that? From now on, every time I see green eyes, I'll think of him*

and blame myself, even if I've told myself a thousand times over, there was nothing I could have done.

It's strange to me how much one night can shape your life. How one experience, standing alone, can create a lifelong mission.

It's more than a mission. It's an obsession. It's all-consuming. Perhaps I couldn't have saved the other children taken with me. But now that I am older—now that I know of Down Below and the creatures that lurk there—I may be able to protect others.

Isn't it my responsibility to do so?

A film of sweat coated my skin. I swiped a hand across my forehead, thumbing through the remaining pages. I was almost afraid to read them. Down Below had never felt more real.

To my knowledge, I'm the only human to use the portals to cross between Down Below and Up There. I'm not sure how my portal remains open. Do the monsters desire my company every Halloween?

Halloween. So I *was* right. Monster New Year.

After I escaped, I returned Down Below four more times, always on Halloween. Each time I returned home, but barely. And the last time—I shudder to think of it.

I shuddered, too. My entire body felt ice-cold.

It may have been cowardly not to return after that narrow escape, but I believed— believe—that I have all the information I need. I know the terrain of the paths that lead to the Transformation Room, and I can re-create them.

But I can't simply draw a map for children who might be taken. What good would that do? Small children won't memorize a map. They need something colorful and fun to entice them. Something they'll study and learn without even realizing they're doing so. Something like—

"A game."

A WISH FOR BLUE

I stayed up the rest of the night reading Aunt Lucy's journal. She'd gone back Down Below four times, always disguised as a zombie because it was the easiest monster to impersonate.

Monsterville was only one part of Down Below. Also known as the incubator, Monsterville was where new monsters spent their first year before being given permanent assignments. It was also home to the old school creatures that kept the newbies in line.

I wish I could share this with someone, Aunt Lucy had written in one entry.

> *Having this secret is so lonely. But I'm not foolish. If I were to confide in someone, they'd think me insane. How could they not? This is a secret I'll keep forever.*

Poor Aunt Lucy! Suddenly I realized how lucky I was to have Adam. If no one else knew about Blue, I'd go nuts.

But I couldn't get over how brave Aunt Lucy was. She went Down Below by herself. That had to make her the most awesome person ever. I felt a twinge of regret I couldn't have known her better.

According to the entries, when she started designing Monsterville, she knew a guy named Stephen who was trying to get her prototype into the hands of a board game publisher, but he wanted her to improve the game to make it more appealing first. Make it more appealing first

Of course I want it to be appealing! I want every parent to buy it, and every child to play it so that if they are taken, they'll remember the game and have a chance of escaping. But how do I make the game both accurate and irresistible?

Based on the drawings that filled the journal's pages, she'd worked hard to answer that question. Monsterville had gone through about twenty versions before becoming the board game now tucked away on Haylie's shelf.

In one version, Trouble Down Below, the monsters looked really scary. A timer was set for ten minutes, and if the players didn't make it around the board in time, they all died.

In another version, players landing on a monster's turf weren't stuck until the right card was drawn. They were eaten. That one was called No Second Chances.

I could understand why Stephen had nixed those ideas, but I could also see why Aunt Lucy wanted the game to be so scary. She was trying to warn kids.

Near the end of the journal, Aunt Lucy wrote about receiving a prototype of the game from Stephen.

> *Stephen called it an early birthday present. I suspect he's humoring an old lady. He knows this game will never see the light of day. He always was terrible at being honest when he knew it would hurt someone's feelings.*

That explained why I couldn't find Monsterville online, and why Game Shop Tom had never heard of it.

I closed the journal and stood up. It was awful that Aunt Lucy hadn't gotten to share Monsterville with the world.

But at least I could share it with someone.

"Wow. Down Below." Blue's long fingers traced the waterslide snaking from the top of the Monsterville board to the bottom.

I'd finished telling him and Adam about what I'd discovered in the journals. We were sitting in Blue's cabin, the game board spread out in front of us. Not playing, just studying it.

"So it's accurate?" I asked. "At least, the incubator part?"

"Yeah." Blue picked up a card and examined it. "Only it looks more fun since it's in cartoons."

"I think that was the idea," I said. "Kids would want to play it."

"I'd play it if I were a few years younger," Adam admitted.

"Haylie's bonkers about it. She hasn't been so obsessed with a toy since Sammy Squirrel." I turned to Blue. "I have a question. Can humans go Down Below by themselves? Aunt Lucy said she went back, alone."

Blue cocked his head, chewing on the inside of his cheek. "I heard an older monster telling a story about that once."

"What'd he say?"

"When a human goes Down Below with a monster, it leaves a mark. Like a—" he floundered.

"Imprint!" I offered, and Blue nodded.

"After that, they can go back Down Below every Halloween, using their portal. Once they use it, it'll glow for them."

"Like a lighthouse beacon," Adam said.

"Yeah," Blue said. "Especially because it glows a different color for the person it belongs to. Yellow for everyone else, blue for them."

"That's actually helpful," Adam said, picking up the Monsterville cards and shuffling them. "No chance of popping up underneath someone else's bed."

I watched the cards in Adam's hands. "There was something odd Aunt Lucy wrote in the margins of the journal: *Undo it by leaving the exact same way you came.* Do you know what that means?"

Blue pouted. "No," he finally said.

"Well, think about it. Maybe it means something."

Adam frowned. "Let me get this straight. A human can only *return* Down Below on Halloween, and through his own portal. So if his house burns down with the portal inside it, he's out of luck?"

"Yep," Blue confirmed. "But monsters have free rein. Any portal, any day. Right?"

"Right. And they can even take a human with them. Through another portal, I mean. So the human wouldn't have to wait until Halloween."

Blue looked down then, but not fast enough. I caught the panic in his eyes.

"What?" I prodded.

"Oh." He picked up his tail and started fiddling with it. "I was just thinking about what Atticus made us do—coming Up There to scare kids, as different monsters each time. If we did a good job, we got treats."

"What if you did a bad job?"

"Then we got locked in the box," Blue responded promptly. "To think about what we did. I got locked in the box four times. It smelled really bad in there."

"Oh, Blue." Adam looked pained. "This Atticus sounds like a real winner."

"He didn't get in charge by being a nice guy. At least, that's what he said when he made one of the other goblins eat a really big jar of expired pickles."

"That's disgusting," I said.

"Yeah, I'm glad you escaped," Adam added. "You shouldn't have to put up with that kind of stuff. No one should."

"He did worse things, too," Blue said glumly. He didn't elaborate, and for once I didn't have more questions. I didn't want to know.

I glanced at my phone. "Aw. I'm sorry, Blue, but I've gotta go. Mom's taking me shopping for next weekend, and everything closes early on Sunday." I dumped the game pieces into the box and climbed to my feet.

"For the big debut, huh?" Adam said, helping me fold the board.

"Yup. My play, onstage—for everyone to see. And judge." My stomach fluttered. "What if everyone hates it?"

"They won't. Stop worrying."

I stood up, brushing off my jeans. "I can't help it."

"I get it." Adam knocked the dust from his pants. "Oh, I almost forgot. Can you come over at eight, after it's dark? I have something to show you."

"Really? What?"

"It's a surprise."

"Can I come, too?" Blue asked. "I want a surprise."

"Sorry," Adam replied. "This one's for Lissa."

When I got to Adam's house, he was waiting on his porch. He'd changed into a sweatshirt and his hair was wet. "Hey."

"Hey. What's this surprise?"

"Follow me." He led me to the picnic table next to his mom's vegetable garden. He wiped some dirt off the top, then laid on his back, his feet dangling over the side.

"Is that thing going to hold you?" I asked.

Adam raised his head. "Oh, thanks a lot. It's fine, it has a metal frame. Climb up here with me." He patted the table.

"Okay, fine." He shifted to make room. I heard his soft breathing and smelled the clean, sharp scent of his sports soap. "I'm waiting to be surprised."

"Look up."

The sky was black, dotted by hundreds and hundreds of stars. Some were bigger than others, and some were brighter. I'd never noticed that about stars before—the differences.

The sky seemed to stretch into forever. Without anything blocking my sight—the outline of a house or the frame of the window—it felt like I was part of it. Like if I reached forward, my fingers might touch a star.

"Wow," I whispered. I didn't know how much time went by. Maybe thirty seconds, maybe an hour.

"Sometimes I come out here at night," Adam said quietly. "When I've had a bad day. Looking up at the sky makes me feel better. I don't know why."

"I know why."

Looking up at something so limitless made me feel like my problems weren't so bad. It didn't matter that I was hundreds of miles away from my friends, or that Freeburg didn't have a mall or a movie theater.

Suddenly, I was really aware that Adam was only like four inches away. If I dropped my hand to my side, would he reach for it? That was a trick Taylor taught me—give the guy the option of making a move, but not in an obvious way that makes you feel stupid if he doesn't.

My hand itched to touch his, to share the moment. It confused me. This was Adam.

"So," he said after a while. "Have you ever seen a view like this in the city?" And just like that, the moment was gone.

"I'll give you this. We don't have the open sky in the city." Then, I sat up. Too fast. Blood rushed to my head, and I clutched my forehead. "Ugh, bad idea."

Adam smiled. "Yeah, don't do that. It's like eating ice cream really quick."

"This was better than ice cream."

We were grinning at each other. Adam really did have exceptionally white teeth. . . .

"Yuck." I wrinkled my nose at the distinct stench of cow poop. "Do you smell that?"

"Never." Adam stretched his arms over his head and yawned. "I gotta go. I haven't started on the reading for history yet."

"Yeah, me neither. But I think I'm going to sit out here for a while longer. You mind?"

"Nah, that's cool. See you tomorrow, Lissa."

Adam loped away, and I climbed back onto the picnic table, stretching out and looking up again.

My mind drifted to bigger problems. What would happen if we didn't help Blue? He only remembered fragments from when he was a kid. It sounded like waking up from a dream—you only remember scraps of it, and maybe later that same day something happens to jar your memory. But once a few days pass, the dream's evaporated.

What if that happened to Blue? What if his life before Down Below just . . . evaporated?

Maybe it would be better that way. If there was no chance of changing him back, maybe it was better if he didn't know what he was missing.

The boards of the picnic table were hard against my back and I squirmed, trying to get comfortable. The stars blurred. When I drew my sleeve across my eyes, I realized I was crying.

A flash of white shot across the sky—a shooting star! When you see one, you're supposed to make a wish. That's what they always do in the movies.

But I didn't know what to wish. I wanted Blue to return Down Below when he was ready. Based on his stories about Atticus, Down Below didn't seem safe. But Blue couldn't stay up here.

I wish for Blue to find a place to call home.

The star was already long gone.

BLUE'S REAL NAME

It was officially jacket season. When I got dressed for school the next day, the hardwood floor was chilly against my bare feet, and wind was blowing through the cracks in the window frames.

I liked this weather, though. Fall has a crispness to it, and the leaves in Freeburg were gorgeous—all orange and yellow and brown.

Haylie liked the sycamore leaves—the really big ones with jagged edges and veins running from stem to tip. She liked ripping them into confetti and tossing them into the air.

When I got to school, Candice was wearing mouse ears.

"Aren't you a little early?" I asked her. "Halloween's Saturday."

She smiled and adjusted her ears. "I know. But it's my favorite. Want a peanut butter cup?" she asked, reaching into her backpack and pulling out a plastic bag.

"Of course."

Todd walked into class and dropped into his seat. "What are we having?"

Candice tossed him a piece of candy. "Here."

"What's your costume this year?" I asked him. "Because, no offense, but your ninja costume looked a little tight."

He shoved the peanut butter cup into his mouth. "Everyone knows it's lame to dress up after sixth grade." He looked pointedly at Candice's mouse ears.

"Whatever. I'll dress up until people stop giving me candy."

I smiled, arranging my pens on my desk. "I like your attitude."

Adam walked in and sat down. "What're we talking about?"

"We're discussing whether this year Todd's dressing up like a fairy princess or a ballerina."

"Does it matter?" Candice asked. "Either way he gets to wear tights."

"If you got it, flaunt it," Todd said.

"Hey." Candice tapped on my desk. "Want to come over after school tomorrow? I want another opinion on my costume. And you dress cool."

I laughed. "Seriously?"

No one had ever told me I dressed cool before. Not when Taylor—who spends an hour getting ready for school every day—was there for comparison.

"If you're asking me, you *must* need help. But sure. I'd love to come over."

Candice's room wasn't what I expected. Candice is little and cute, so I guess I thought her room would be little and cute, too. But it was big and yellow and airy and filled with horses.

Fake ones, I mean. She had a shelf crammed with horse figurines, and a stuffed horse sitting on her bedspread, and about a million award ribbons stuck to a pegboard.

"So," I fingered a ribbon hanging from the pegboard, "what's your favorite animal?"

Candice laughed and flopped onto her beanbag chair. "Dogs! Can't you tell?" She bounced up and down. "Seriously though, I've been doing horse shows since I was five. You can meet Pete if you want."

"Pete?"

"Yeah, my horse. He's in the backyard."

"You have a horse in your backyard?"

The only horses I'd ever seen in person were the ones pulling carriages in Central Park. I always felt bad for them—getting hot and smelly while carting around tourists dumb enough to pay a hundred bucks per ride.

"Yeah, he's awesome. Here's a picture." Candice hopped up from the beanbag chair and crossed the room to her mirror. There were a ton of pictures wedged into the frame. "Let me see, let me see. Here!" She plucked a picture and handed it to me. "That's from this show we did in Red Bud. We took second."

"Cool." A helmet was shoved over Candice's hair, and her white teeth took over the whole picture. She had her arm around a deep brown horse. It was exactly the way Casey and Taylor and I posed together in pictures. I wondered how many they'd taken without me lately.

"You can put it back when you're done looking," Candice said. "I'll be right back. I'm going to grab us some snacks. You good with microwave pizza?"

"Yeah, sure."

After Candice disappeared, I looked around her dresser some more. Every inch of it was covered—a jewelry tree with a dozen necklaces, a big basket of makeup, more horse figurines.

I moved closer to the mirror to look at the pictures. There were a few of Candice and some other girls in class, and one of Candice and Todd during a school field day. She was laughing as she poured Gatorade over his head. I grinned at that one.

In the top corner of the mirror, I saw a picture of Candice making cookies with a little boy. They were both covered in flour and wearing hideous reindeer sweaters. The picture looked like an ad for cookie dough—two adorable blond kids laughing and making a mess.

Carefully, I removed it from the frame. It reminded me of Haylie and me.

Candice didn't have a brother that I knew of. The kid in the picture must be a cousin or something. I looked at his face, which was completely lit up by a smile stretching to his ears. And his eyes—

It felt like I'd been sucker punched in the stomach.

His eyes were brown and warm and happy. Just like Blue's.

Candice walked back into the room carrying a plate and cradling two sodas against her chest. "Food!"

My mouth was so dry I almost couldn't speak. "Hey." I held the picture up. "This is cute."

Something faded from Candice's eyes. "Oh." She handed me a soda. "That's me and my cousin."

"He's adorable."

"Thanks."

"Does he live around here?"

Candice shook her head. "Not anymore. Maybe you heard the story. Colin disappeared last Halloween."

After I got back from Candice's house, I raced to see Blue. It was dark out, but I didn't care.

Dead leaves crunched under my feet, and I realized how different the woods looked now compared to a few months ago. The wildflowers were gone. The trees were still colorful, but they'd lose their leaves soon. The temperature would dip below freezing, and snow would cover the ground. What would we do with Blue then?

"Blue!" I called out when I got to his little cabin. I cleared my throat. "Colin? Colin!" The name felt strange in my mouth.

I heard a scuffling sound, and then Blue appeared in the doorway. "Lissa?"

I squatted to look him in the eyes. "Colin."

He blinked at me. "Huh?"

"Colin. Your name is Colin. Don't you remember?"

Man, I wished I had that picture! Blue frowned, playing with one of his ears. "No . . ."

"Candice. Do you remember Candice?"

"No . . ."

But he looked like he remembered *something*. Like somewhere in his memory, he recognized those names.

"Do you remember making cookies with Candice? Lots of flour everywhere? Eating the dough? Really ugly reindeer sweaters?"

Blue frowned so hard he looked scary, especially

in the dim light, with the shadows playing over him. "No . . ."

I placed my hands on his shoulders. "Are you sure . . . Colin?"

He pulled away from me. "No! I don't remember! I don't remember anything!" He burst into tears—loud sobs—with his mouth opened so wide.

"Shhhh, shhhh." I felt terrible, and I leaned to pick him up. He let me. Carefully, I carried him to his bed and clicked on the lamp on the battered nightstand. "Here, why don't I read you something? How about *James and the Giant Peach*?"

Blue gulped. "Okay." Huge tears splashed down his cheeks.

I stayed with him until his breathing settled into a deep, even rhythm. He clutched Willy Whale, one of his stuffed animals from Haylie. I pulled his quilt over him, brushing my hand against his bald head.

"Sweet dreams," I whispered.

But how would that ever be possible?

SCENE ELEVEN:

CURTAINS UP!

It was Friday, the day of my play. As Dad whipped the car along the back roads out of Freeburg, I kept my forehead against the window. A headache throbbed at my temples, and the cool glass was soothing.

I couldn't stop worrying about Blue. I knew Adam would keep him safe while I was gone, but I hated leaving him.

At least Adam and I had a great surprise planned for tomorrow. One that both Blue *and* Haylie would love.

Colin, I reminded myself. *His name is Colin.* But to Adam and me, he was still Blue.

"You're awfully quiet." Dad glanced at me in the rearview mirror. "I thought you'd be singing with joy."

"She's nervous," Mom said. "Her big debut."

"Nothing to be nervous about." Dad took the exit to the interstate. "Your play was picked. That means it's good."

"Hmm." I rubbed at the condensation on the window, watching it cloud up again.

I watched the trees and fields pass by the window. It had been months since I'd hung out with Casey and Taylor. Would everything feel the same with them? Would there be any weird gaps in the conversation, or inside jokes I didn't get?

The trip took only three hours, thanks to Dad's lead foot. Soon we were zooming through the Holland Tunnel, then blinking into the sunlight on Beach Street.

I rolled down my window and felt a cold gust of wind. "Hello, New York!" I crowed. A guy driving a taxi in the next lane glared at me. In Freeburg, he would have waved.

"Lissa," Mom hissed. "Don't do that."

I bounced in my seat. "But we're here!" I couldn't sit still. Hello, skyscrapers! Hello, billboards! Hello, yellow taxis!

Hmm, at second glance, the city wasn't as bright and shiny as I remembered it. There sure was a lot of traffic. And I'd forgotten about red lights. This was total gridlock. Would our car ever move?

"Only a mile to go," Dad said.

"A whole mile?" I asked. It can take twenty minutes to drive a mile in New York. We only had two hours until the play started.

Adam's voice from the night of the fair pushed its way into my mind. *How long would it take to drive a mile in the city?* I grinned and took in a deep breath of NYC air.

"Gross! Garbage truck!" I held my nose.

"Means it's Friday." Dad gunned through a yellow light.

Thirty minutes later, we pulled into the valet area of the Waldorf. The rest of my family was staying at the hotel for the night, but I was crashing at Taylor's condo in our old building.

We dumped our luggage in our room and took a taxi to Lombardi's. Grabbing pizza, before the show. We had a reservation at Lombardi's, but the maître d' informed us it would still be a twenty-minute wait. I thought of Mom and me sitting right down for brunch in Algonquin.

After dinner, a taxi dropped us off in front of St. Mary's. There were a lot of people there. Right off the bat, I saw ten people I'd known since preschool. They all smiled and waved really big at me, and I realized how much I'd missed everyone.

Mr. Kincaid stood guard near the ticket booth. "Lissa!" he boomed when he spotted me. "The Black family!"

"Hi, Mr. Kincaid." I eyed his red suspenders. "Are you the bouncer?"

"I am." Mr. Kincaid reached into his shirt's front pocket and pulled out an envelope. "And I am the giver. Ms. Casey told me to 'give her' the tickets. The 'her' being you." He extended the envelope to me.

"Free tickets? Cool."

"Well, of course. You're in show business now. Getting free things comes with the territory. But make sure you sit in your assigned seats. Right through that door. Okay?"

"Okay," I said, opening the envelope. "Thanks, Mr. Kincaid."

"Sure. Now you'll have to excuse me. I'm very busy and important." He winked at me and disappeared up the steps to the balcony.

We followed the crowd through the auditorium doors, grabbing programs printed on pastel pink paper on the way.

"I didn't know the seats in the auditorium were labeled," I said to Mom. My ticket had G 1-4 scrawled on it in black letters. It looked like Casey's handwriting.

"I'm sure we'll figure it out," Mom said and, sure enough, seven rows in, four seats had RESERVED signs across them. My pulse quickened. *This is all for me?*

"How nice." Dad ripped the signs off the seats and settled into the one farthest in. They were the same kind of seats you'd see at the movies—all red and squishy. I lowered myself into the one on the aisle. It squeaked.

The lights started flashing, and I took a deep breath. This was it. *My* play. The crowd stopped talking as the overhead lights dimmed, and then stage lights illuminated a kitchen scene. Taylor and Brian Borlas sat at a table, both wearing blue bathrobes and gray wigs.

"What are we going to do?" Taylor wailed. "I'm old! I'm tired! I want to retire in the Caribbean!"

"I want to scuba dive before my arthritis is too bad."

"I want to learn how to surf."

"I want to find sand dollars."

Brian shook his head so violently his fake mustache came unstuck. He slapped it back on, which got a laugh from the audience. "But we'll never get to the Caribbean if Jasper doesn't find himself a lady."

Taylor picked up her coffee cup. "But how is Jasper going to do that?"

Ian Randall strutted in, wearing an orange sweater and a pair of dorky glasses. "Hi, Mom. Hi, Dad. Great news. I got to Level four hundred in Call of Modern Warfare Warcraft. Isn't that great?"

I put a hand over my mouth to hide my smile. The dialogue sounded even funnier coming out of Ian's mouth than it had when I was writing it down.

Taylor stood up and put her hands on her hips. "No, that's not great, Jasper. That's time you could have spent outside, meeting a nice girl."

"I don't need to meet a girl. I'm only thirty-five."

Brian picked up a magazine on the table. "Do you see this? See the boat on the cover? On the ocean next to the white sand?"

Ian glanced at the magazine. "Yeah?"

"What's missing?"

Ian looked at the magazine again. "The captain should have a life vest."

"No. It's missing us! Your mom and me! We want to retire! And we can't do that with you living in the basement."

"I told you. I don't need to meet a girl. Now, Mom, can you make me a Hot Pocket? I'm supposed to lead the next mission." Ian disappeared off the stage.

"I don't know what that means!" Taylor wailed, wringing her hands.

I sneaked a glance at the people around me. Did they like it? Hate it? No one had gotten up and left yet. And everyone was laughing in the right places. But maybe they were just being polite.

Onstage, Taylor and Brian huddled over a laptop, creating an online dating profile for Jasper.

"Hmm," Taylor mused. "Jasper lives in our basement and doesn't pay rent. How can we spin that?"

Brian held up his index finger. "Independently wealthy!"

"What about those coke bottle glasses of his?"

"Err . . . academic!"

"Remember when Cousin Albert bought that picture of him? Since he liked the frame? We can say he's a former model."

They high-fived and bent back over the laptop. The lights on the stage faded to the sound of applause.

One by one, different girls showed up—ones that were there because they thought Jasper was rich, or really smart, or super good-looking. Ian did a great job of getting madder and madder after each date.

It came to the last scene. Ian stomped through a fake park. A fountain and a bridge were drawn on the backdrop. Megan Martin, a girl who'd been in my Advanced English class, sat on a bench in the middle of the stage. She was wearing thick glasses and orthopedic shoes, and was throwing bread crumbs to stuffed ducks. From my row, I could see the Toys "R" Us tags.

Ian stomped across the stage and flopped down on the bench. He sighed heavily and dropped his head in his hands. Megan shot him a sideways look. "Everything okay?"

Ian looked up. "No! My parents won't mind their own business. They're trying to get me to *settle down*."

He made exaggerated air quotes, and I seriously had to resist climbing onto the stage and kissing him. He was exactly how I'd pictured the character.

Megan tossed some more bread crumbs. "That's funny. That's why I'm out here, too. My brother keeps making me go out with guys he knows from work. They're all terrible."

Ian gave Megan a long, appreciative look. It drew a few laughs from the audience. Then he looked away. "That's too bad."

"I know! All I want to do is stay in my room playing Call of Modern Warfare Warcraft."

"You do?" Ian's mouth dropped open, and the crowd roared.

"Yes. I just got to level four hundred. Do you have any idea how hard that is?"

Ian's eyebrows shot up. "Yes! Yes, I do!" Another big laugh from the crowd.

My heart swelled. People were enjoying something I had written. It was the most amazing feeling in the world.

Megan looked up distrustfully. "You do?"

Ian hopped up onto the bench and put his hands on his hips. His stomach poked out. "Commander Davis, at your service." He saluted her. "Level four hundred and counting."

Megan stood up, too. "Really? Level four hundred?"

"Four hundred and two, now." Ian puffed out his chest. He climbed off the bench and raked his hands through his hair. "I'm Jasper." He held out his hand and Megan shook it.

"Anna."

"Well, Anna. What are you doing tonight?"

"Looks like I'm spending it with you."

Megan took his hand, and they strolled off the stage. The crowd started clapping. And kept clapping. And later, when Taylor and Brian and Ian and Megan returned onstage, people stood up. They stood up! It was a standing ovation!

I glanced around, and my eyes welled with tears. I was both happy and sad. Proud of myself for creating something that made hundreds of people clap. And sad that I wasn't a part of putting the production together.

I looked down at my program. I'd been so nervous that I hadn't even looked at it.

Across the front in loopy black lettering, it said: *Hot Pockets and Modern Lovecraft.*

Below that, in slightly smaller letters, it said: "a Lissa Black production."

That was my name! On the front page of the program! I stared at the words.

Mr. Kincaid walked onstage, holding up his hands to quiet the audience. Slowly, the clapping died down.

"Thank you for coming!" Mr. Kincaid's eyes scanned over the crowd, resting on me for a second. *Was that a wink?* "There will be refreshments in the cafeteria. Please purchase in abundance to help pay for our eighth grade class trip." He cleared his throat. "But the real reason I came onstage—other than my need for constant attention—isn't to peddle for donations. I need to honor someone very, very special who has joined us here tonight."

My stomach dropped into my toes.

"As you all know, a play is put on every year by St. Mary's seventh graders as an exercise in creativity. The students do everything—the writing, the set, the makeup, and costume design. This year, the play we presented was written by one of our most talented students." Mr. Kincaid paused so everyone could clap. "Our young playwright is Miss Lissa Black . . . right there in the seventh row."

A light from the balcony settled over my seat, and I raised a hand to shield my eyes from the glare.

"Everyone, let's get her onstage and embarrass, er, I mean *honor* her." Mr. Kincaid grinned at me and pulled at his suspenders.

Mom nudged me with her knee. There were tears in her eyes. "Get up there, Lissa."

Taking a deep breath, I rose from my seat, wiping my sweaty hands on my best jeans. Suddenly, I was glad that I'd put on lipstick and my favorite green sweater.

With the bright stage lights, red spots danced in front of my eyes. I climbed the four wooden steps to join Mr. Kincaid. He put his hand on my shoulder.

"Allow me to introduce Lissa Black!"

The crowd stood up. Again. I was trying so hard not to cry that I almost didn't see Taylor coming toward me from the right side of the stage. She carried a huge bunch of yellow roses tied with a white ribbon, and she looked grown-up and pretty in a short black dress that showed off her dark skin. She crossed the stage and handed me the bouquet, leaning forward to hug me.

I had to wipe the tears from my eyes, because I was seriously starting to bawl. Taylor led me offstage, where the rest of the cast was hanging out in the back hallway. Everyone cheered when they saw us. Ian raced forward and picked me up, hoisting me over his shoulder. "To the party!" he yelled, and he didn't put me down until we were in the school cafeteria. It smelled the same as ever—like Pine Sol. The lunch line was open so people could buy snacks and juice.

"Ian, I just want to say—" I choked up, thinking about how good he'd been playing Jasper.

"I know what you're going to say." He shook his head and pointed at Taylor and Brian. "The verdict is in. I'm adopted." Taylor is Ethiopian. Brian is Mexican. And Ian is a pale white boy with an Afro.

"No." I shook my head. "You were perfect."

"I had good material. Thanks."

"Wait a second. Where's Roland Reed?"

Ian shrugged. "Who knows? He's never around."

Casey pushed through the crowd and shoved her phone at Ian. "Would you take a picture of us?" She squeezed between Taylor and me and put her arms around us. "Everyone look happy!"

I grinned like an idiot while Ian snapped the picture. Even when he handed the phone back to Casey, I couldn't stop smiling.

It wasn't just that the play had turned out so well. It was how everyone had made me feel. I wasn't at St. Mary's anymore, but I hadn't been forgotten.

SCENE TWELVE:

A CONVINCING DISGUISE

The next day, I fell asleep on the ride home. Usually I can't sleep on car trips. I must have been totally zonked.

But I perked up that evening. It was hard not to. Haylie was so excited about trick-or-treating. She kept running around in circles dressed in her fairy princess costume and yelling "poof!" while waving her wand. I love my little sister, but talk about a generic costume choice.

I was a movie director, complete with a megaphone and clapboard.

Adam had refused to be Sound Guy, choosing to dress as a Sasquatch. He knocked on my door at five o'clock wearing his backpack and his furry mask. *"Rrrrrrrr!"* He was dressed all in brown, and wearing animal paw slippers.

I turned toward the living room. "Haylie, c'mere!"

Haylie pranced to the door, decked out in her purple fairy dress, clutching her wand. "What?"

I pulled her onto the front steps and shut the door behind us. Adam shoved his mask into his already-bulging backpack.

Squatting to look Haylie in her eye, I asked her: "If I took you on an adventure, would you promise to keep it a secret?"

Her blue eyes grew huge. She looked from me to Adam. "Yes! Yes, I promise."

"Are you sure? Because it's really, really important that you keep your promise." I dropped my voice even though I knew Mom and Dad were on the back porch, safely out of earshot. "It's about Blue."

When Haylie nodded vigorously, I went on. "If we take you both trick-or-treating, can you pretend he's in costume? Like, he's dressed as a goblin? Not, he *is* a goblin?"

"Yes! Oh, please, please, please let us go trick-or-treating!" Haylie clapped her hands. "I'll be good, I promise!"

Adam and I exchanged a look. Adam's face scrunched up and he rubbed his chin. "I guess it'll be dark out," he said doubtfully. Even though he'd agreed to the idea, he still didn't seem sold on it.

"Trust me on this. People *expect* to see little kids running around in goblin costumes, so that's what they'll see." I turned back to Haylie. "In an hour, Up—

er, *Charlie* will drive us into town. So you need to play it cool. Like Blue's just one of your friends, hanging out. Okay?"

"Okay."

Adam touched my arm. "Come on, Lissa. We need to get going."

As I rose, Haylie looked at her star-topped wand. "He should have this, though." She extended it, cheap glitter drifting to the ground. "It's magic. So long as he has it, no one will figure out he's not in costume."

"Thanks, Hails. I'm sure Blue will appreciate this." She gave me a huge smile and opened the door.

Adam and I rushed through the woods to Blue's hideout. We found him kneeling on the broken sidewalk, drawing with colored chalk. When he heard us crashing through the trees, he stood up.

"You're here!" Like always, he sounded pleased, as if he hadn't expected us.

Adam lowered his backpack and removed a bologna sandwich from the front pocket. "Here you go," he told Blue. "Remember to remove the wrapping first."

Blue *hrumphed,* but he peeled the plastic back before swallowing the sandwich. Without a word, Adam handed him a red Gatorade to wash it down.

"Blue." I sat down in the dirt with him. "Do you know what day today is?"

I held my breath waiting for his reply. Blue might get really upset if he realized this was the anniversary of his being taken.

Blue wriggled his nose. "Saturday?"

"That's right, but it's something else, too. It's Halloween."

"Oh," he responded in a small voice.

"So we're taking you trick-or-treating!" Adam boomed in the same fake cheerful voice Dad uses sometimes. "You'll get a ton of candy, and you won't even have to worry about disguising yourself." Adam rooted through his backpack. "But, just to be safe, I brought supplies. Check it out—clothes, masks, grease paint, a . . . hat," he said, naming each item as he removed it. "You can wear anything you need to feel safe."

Blue fingered a black skullcap. "I don't know . . ."

"I promise we'll take care of you," I told him. "Nothing bad will happen to you so long as we're around. And Haylie'll be there too."

"Haylie?" His face lit up.

"Yeah, of course. She wants to go trick-or-treating with you. And she gave me this for you." I held up the wand. "It's magic," I said, echoing Haylie. "You'll be safe as long as you have it."

"Really?" He took it and studied it like it was Aladdin's lamp.

"Really. You just point it at someone and they'll leave you alone."

Blue took it and examined it in his gnarled hands. "Wow."

Adam glanced at his watch. "Sorry, but we need to hurry. Do you think we can have him at my place by six?"

"No sweat," I said. "Now, Blue, like I said, no one's going to pay any attention to an extra goblin running around on Halloween. But you can't look *exactly* like yourself. We need to B-movie it up—make it *look* like you're wearing a goblin costume. Because your *mask* is too realistic. And your tail looks like a special effect from *Jurassic World*."

"What do we do?" Adam asked while Blue stood there with his hands behind his back, looking confused.

"Leave it to me."

I rummaged through the pile of random supplies. "Here we go!" I pulled out a faded green John Deere sweatshirt and a pair of jeans. "This is a good start."

Adam eyed the jeans. "Those look a little big."

"Yeah, but we need room for his tail. We can put it down a pants leg."

"Good thinking."

Blue wriggled into the outfit, and we crammed the black skullcap over his ears. "Yikes, that does *not* work," I said, inspecting him. He looked like a real goblin in a skullcap, especially considered that the hat barely covered his ears.

"I have something for that." Adam reached into the depths of the backpack and removed a squashed-looking straw hat. He plunked it onto Blue's head. "Tada!"

"Oh, man." I took a step back to survey him. "You look like a DreamWorks reject." A character like Blue in that getup wouldn't get past the drawing board.

"What's he supposed to be?" Adam asked. "Other than himself, I mean."

"He's the Freeburg goblin, of course. Otherwise why else would he wear a straw hat and a John Deere sweatshirt?"

Adam grinned. "Nice."

"Did you bring a grease pencil like I asked?"

"Yeah, here." He removed it from the side zipper. "What's it for?"

"Like I said, he needs to look like a *fake* goblin trying to be a *real* goblin." I rubbed the grease pencil across my palm to get a smooth line. Then I drew squiggly wrinkles across Blue's forehead. He stayed perfectly still while I worked, gazing at me with his big brown eyes.

"That tickles."

"Shh, it'll be over soon."

After a few more dashes, I was finished. "All set." I blew on his face to remove the stray bits of pencil. "Now, let's get you some candy!"

After reloading Adam's backpack, we weaved through the woods. Dead leaves crunched beneath us, and a strong wind gusted around us, cutting through my jacket.

"Adam's brother is giving us a ride," I told Blue once we were close to Adam's house. "Act like you're playing a part—as Haylie's human friend dressed as a goblin. Act casual."

"Casual?"

"Yeah. Remember—casual keeps you safe."

He frowned, nodding.

Five minutes later, I led Haylie to where Adam and Blue were hiding behind a pickup in the Griggs' driveway. "Blue!" she screamed when she saw him, and I shushed her.

"Don't call him that tonight! Call him—" I considered. "Heck, I don't care. Lots of people have weird nicknames. Look at Upchuck."

Speaking of Upchuck, the screen door creaked on its hinges, then banged shut. We all popped up from behind the pickup like curious gophers and scooted from our cover before Upchuck noticed us hiding.

"Hey. Y'all ready to go?"

"Yeah, we're good." Adam was as cool as a cucumber. "Thanks for driving us."

"Thanks," I echoed, and Upchuck's gaze shifted to Haylie and then to Blue. Haylie seemed fine, but Blue stared at the ground like he'd been caught doing something wrong.

"Who's your friend?" Upchuck asked Haylie.

"This is Blue." Haylie nudged him. "Right, Blue?"

Blue wouldn't tear his eyes from the ground. "I'm casual."

"Huh. Well, I'm Charlie," Upchuck said. "Now come on. The sooner you guys get your candy, the sooner I can go home and get ready for the *real* evening."

"Date, huh?" Adam asked. "I should have known. I can smell you from here."

Upchuck lifted his shirt collar and sniffed. "It's not that bad."

"Yeah, if you were born without a sense of smell."

"Hey, you want a ride or not?"

We all squished into the pickup, which was pretty clean—no food wrappers or anything, although the dog smell still hung in the air. Adam was right—Upchuck definitely had a date.

In just five minutes, Upchuck pulled up to a street corner. Lined with one-story houses, the street had already been invaded by miniature witches and

Batmans and pirates. Haylie was so excited, she almost fell out of the truck.

"I'll be back in an hour and a half," Upchuck said. "Meet me on this corner."

Adam pulled four sacks out of his backpack and gave one to each of us.

"You know the drill."

It was so much fun. Who knew that trick-or-treating could be so awesome? Every single house was decorated—ghosts hanging from trees, carved pumpkins. And when we rang doorbells, half the time Haylie did her "trick" before being asked. It was a curtsy, which was sort of lame, but people forgive adorable kids.

After the tenth house I noticed that Blue's sack was empty. "Blue, is there a hole in your bag?"

He smiled at me, bits of plastic wrapper and chocolate stuck to his teeth. Of course.

Someone was playing music a few blocks over, but I couldn't figure out what it was.

I took Haylie's hand. As I strained to place the tune, it occurred to me that banjo music wasn't an appropriate soundtrack to my life, after all. Freeburg deserved more credit than that. Maybe Taylor Swift, since she can do both pop and country—like how I could rock NYC and Freeburg.

As we crossed the street, a superhero posse approached us from the other way—little kids in Batman and Superman and Iron Man costumes. One kid dressed as Iron Man stopped in his tracks when he saw Blue. "Mom!" he wailed. His mother swooped him into her arms.

"Tired already?" she murmured, smiling, but he wouldn't stop crying. He buried his face in her shoulder, peeking once at Blue. He squealed and hid again.

"Poor little guy," his mother said as she passed.

"Adam," I hissed, grabbing his sleeve. It felt like there was a rock in my stomach. "Did you notice that?"

"Notice what?"

"That little kid was terrified of Blue! He looked right at him and started crying!"

"Really?" Adam's eyes looked worried behind his Sasquatch mask. "Are you sure?"

Blue and Haylie had run ahead, and they turned around to make sure we were following. They grinned so big I decided not to worry about serious stuff, at least not right now. They should have their night.

"I might just be paranoid," I said to Adam, smiling weakly. But what if I wasn't? It got me thinking—Blue still acted like a kid, and I definitely thought of him as more human than monster. But that little kid had noticed the monster right away. Would Blue become a full monster? When?

We hit up a crazy number of houses in the next hour and a half. At first, when a door opened, the half-second that followed freaked me out. Would someone scream "Monster!" and faint? But it was just like I'd told Adam: people expected to see a little kid in a goblin costume, so that's what they saw. We even got compliments on Blue's makeup.

"My feet hurt," Haylie complained after the sixth block.

Blue pointed the wand at them. "Abracadabra!"

"I feel better!"

"I guess we should head back," Adam said.

Taking my phone from my pocket, I glanced at the screen. "Yikes, we're fifteen minutes late."

"It's okay. Charlie won't mind." Adam hummed as we walked down the sidewalk.

That's when I spotted Candice and Todd. What if she recognized Blue? Those eyes . . .

There was no time to warn him. "Cross the street!" I said frantically. "Now!"

But it was too late. "Hey look, it's Lurch and Linda." In three seconds, Todd and Candice were standing right in front of us.

"Hi, Todd," Adam said, his voice muffled behind his mask. "What are you supposed to be?"

Todd tapped at the nametag on his shirt. "I'm Bob."

"And *I'm* a shipwreck victim," Candice announced.

Her costume looked great. She even had added dried starfish and sand dollars to her hair.

"Barrettes and hot glue." She shook her head. "You like it?"

"Yeah, that's super original."

"Do you guys want to trick-or-treat with us?" she asked. "We're just getting started."

"I thought trick-or-treating was for babies," Adam reminded Todd, who shrugged.

"Well, you know, free candy." Then he reached and took Candice's hand. My eyes met hers and she sucked in her lips to hide a smile.

It made perfect sense. How had I not noticed the clues?

"And who are you?" Candice asked, turning her attention to Haylie and Blue. "Let me guess—a fairy princess." Haylie nodded.

Candice focused on Blue, eyeing the ridiculous straw hat and John Deere sweatshirt. "Er, are you a goblin farmer?"

Blue didn't answer. He stared at Candice like he was hypnotized. "Candice," he whispered.

She frowned. "That's right. How'd you know that?"

"Oh, haha," I squeaked. "I must have said your name when we saw you. He has a really good memory."

"You look so familiar," Candice muttered, leaning closer. "What's your name?"

Before Blue could respond, Haylie ripped the wand from his hand and smacked Candice. "I want to go home!" she screamed, whacking her again.

"Ow!" Candice let go of Todd's hand and shielded her arms. "What's wrong with her?"

Adam hoisted Haylie over his shoulders and I grabbed Blue. "Too much sugar," I said, tugging him along the sidewalk. "I'm so, so sorry. Haylie, say you're sorry."

"I'm sorry," she said from upside down, waving the wand. Her face was turning purple.

"That's . . . okay." Candice rubbed her arms.

The four of us were already halfway down the street. "Bye, guys!" I called. "See you on Monday!"

Adam put Haylie on the ground as soon as we were a safe distance away. "Violence is not the answer," he told her, snatching the wand.

"But the magic worked!" she insisted. "It kept Blue safe."

SCENE THIRTEEN:

KEEPING WATCH

Haylie and I walked through the front door to the twang of country music. Mom appeared from the master bedroom, fastening a pair of earrings. "Ta-da! How do I look?" she asked as Haylie escaped to her room with her candy.

Mom was Marilyn Monroe. She wore the famous white halter dress—you know, the one Marilyn wore when she stood on the subway grate—one of the most iconic movie moments of all time.

"Woo-hoo, Mom. You're hot!"

She patted her hair, tilting her head. She'd applied a mole to her left cheek. "Thank you. You know, I'd always wanted an excuse to wear this dress, and now I have one."

She and Dad were going to a party thrown by another doctor from Dad's hospital. I might have worried about them leaving us alone on Halloween, but my plan to keep Haylie safe was foolproof.

Mom lifted her foot. "Look at my shoes!" They were silver, glittery heels that looked like they pinched.

"Nice. Dad, what are you?" I asked him as he appeared from the hallway.

"I'm one of Marilyn Monroe's husbands."

"What do you wear?"

"This." Dad picked up his suit jacket lying across the living room couch and stuck his arms into it. "And an expression like I've just won the lottery. Since I'm with the most beautiful woman in the entire world. Which is true in real life, too." He wrapped an arm around Mom's waist and pulled her in for a kiss.

"Gross." I covered my face with my hands. "I don't need to see that."

"Okay, fine." Mom pulled away from Dad and scanned the room. "There it is." She grabbed her clutch and waved it at me. "Be good!"

"Always."

The door slammed behind them, and I headed to Haylie's room. She was sprawled on her bed, empty sack in front of her. Candy covered the bed, and she was industriously categorizing it by type. Everything with a stick—Tootsie Roll Pops and Blow Pops and suckers—had its own pile. So did plain chocolate, chocolate with nuts, gummy candy . . .

"Whoa." I sat on the edge of Haylie's bed, careful not to disturb the piles. "Pretty organized there, Hails."

She looked up. "I have one hundred and thirty-four pieces."

"You made out like a bandit."

She cocked her head. "I'm not a bandit. I'm a fairy princess."

I rolled my eyes. "I know. It's an expression. It means you got a lot."

The doorbell rang and Haylie's eyes widened. "Who's that?"

"Just Adam. Come on." I grabbed her hand and pulled her off the bed.

That was a cardinal movie rule in protecting someone from monsters: never let them out of your sight.

When I opened the door, I sighed. Adam was back to jeans and a sweatshirt. "Aw. I was expecting a Sasquatch."

"Sorry to disappoint." Adam glanced into the living room. "They're gone, huh?"

"Yup. Want anything to eat?"

"Yeah, a celery stick. I've been eating Reese's Peanut Butter Cups all night."

"How about popcorn? I'll put on a movie."

"That'll work, too. Corn is good for you." He looked down at Haylie. "Do you want some popcorn, too?"

"Are you supposed to be here?" she asked innocently.

Adam and I exchanged a look. "Yes, he is," I replied. "See, tonight, Adam and I have a very important job. We have to keep you safe until after midnight."

"Safe from what?" Haylie asked as I led them both into the kitchen, where I removed a package of microwave popcorn from the pantry.

I turned, ripping open the plastic wrapping. I'd dreaded this conversation. "Here's the deal, Hails—there are monsters other than Blue out there."

"There are?" I could tell she was imagining a monster tea party.

"But not like Blue," Adam said. "*These* monsters are bad. They take kids away."

"Hmm." Haylie wrinkled her nose like she didn't understand.

"And because that's a *bad* thing," I said, crouching to look into her eyes, "Adam and I are going to watch you like a hawk until midnight. That's when their time runs out to take you." I pointed to the microwave. "See? The clock says 8:30. That means the monsters have three and a half hours left to try."

Haylie clapped her hands. "Monster games! Monster games!"

I shook my head. "No, Haylie. It's not a game. It's for real."

I needed her to understand she was in danger. According to the movies, when you're protecting someone, you should always give them a proper warning. How else will they know not to get into a villain's car?

"Here's what you do," I said with a sudden flash of inspiration. I didn't need to *actually* scare her, as long as I taught her how to protect herself. "You see a monster, you scream." I threw my head back and screamed. "Just like that."

She screamed.

"Good! That's perfect!" I shoved the popcorn into the microwave. "Haylie, why don't you pick out a movie? Adam and I will bring out the popcorn." She ran to the living room and opened the cabinet doors below the TV.

"What's the plan?" Adam murmured.

"It's easy. We're going to avoid the *Sleeping Beauty* plot hole."

"What's that?"

"In *Sleeping Beauty*—all five million versions of it—everyone knows that Sleeping Beauty's in danger only one day of her whole life. A witch curses her to prick her finger on a spinning wheel on her sixteenth birthday, which will make her sleep forever. So what do her parents do? They hide her away in the woods with a bunch of fairies, and don't tell her, *hey, don't touch any spinning wheels*, and then lose track of her on the one day it matters."

"And . . . ?"

"It's a huge plot hole! Where's the danger if all they have to do is lock her in a windowless room away from pointy objects for one day? *Their stupidity* creates the danger. They don't protect her on the one day it matters. They don't even warn her."

"Oh."

"With Haylie, we do the opposite. *One*, we warn her. Check. *Two*, we protect her by staying with her until midnight. And *three*, we monster-proof any place we sleep."

"How do we do that?"

I waved my hand. "Make sure there's nowhere we can fall asleep that has any space between it and the floor. Remember what Blue said: Monsters can crawl out from beneath *anything*. It doesn't have to be a bed."

"Pretty impressive."

The microwave beeped and the red digits readjusted to display the time. "See that?"

"What's that?"

"The time. If the monsters wanted to mess with us, they could sneak in and reset the clocks so we think it's safe to go to bed. Like how the gremlins messed with the clock in *Gremlins* to trick Billy into feeding them after midnight."

"Good thing you're smarter than Billy."

I swiped at him. "I'll make you watch that movie one day. It's a classic."

We settled onto the couch and started the movie Haylie had chosen, *Frozen*. After it, we put on *Cars*. We were halfway through it when the doorbell rang.

I put Haylie on the floor before I jogged to get it. "Stay there," I told her. "No matter what, okay?" A monster could crawl out from underneath the sofa if she went to sleep there.

It was Upchuck. "I've been sent by the parental units. They figured out you were gone," he told Adam. "Sorry."

Oh, man. "Why don't you *both* stay?" I asked Upchuck. "He's here because I'm scared of being alone. Right, Adam?"

"Right. She's a complete fraidy cat," Adam agreed.

Upchuck scratched his head. "Um . . ."

"I'll give you twenty dollars," I added.

He laughed. "I don't need your money. Besides, Freeburg's about the safest place on the planet."

"What about last Halloween?" I shot back.

"That was terrible, but it was totally a freak thing. Come on, Adam."

I couldn't really be annoyed. Upchuck didn't know why I was so worried.

"See you guys later." I sighed.

"I'll keep my phone by me," Adam said as the door closed behind them.

Once I was alone with Haylie, I assessed the situation. Maybe Adam was gone, but I could keep Haylie safe for another hour. I just needed to stay awake, and not let her out of my sight. Easy-peasy.

"Lissa?" Haylie sat up, rubbing her eyes. "I want to go to bed."

"No, let's finish the movie! Um . . . I'll let you have more candy."

She made a face. "My tummy hurts."

I picked her up and shut off the TV. "I'll get you some medicine." Carrying her into our bathroom, I doled out one level teaspoon of pink liquid. "Swallow this."

She obeyed, and I glanced through the door to her bed. Would it really matter if I put her into it? It was after eleven. So long as I stayed there watching her, surely she'd be fine. Kids only get kidnapped in monster movies when people aren't watching.

I tucked her in and settled next to her, careful to stay sitting up so I wouldn't accidentally fall asleep.

In about three seconds, Haylie's eyes were closed and she was breathing evenly. She clutched her wand like a stuffed animal, and I smiled. Her latest toy obsession. I only hoped she wouldn't hit someone with it again.

"Good n—"

Something grabbed my feet and yanked me off the bed. I landed hard on my butt, my head cracking against the floor a second later. Black spots danced across my vision, and I barely registered what was happening.

A monster crawled out from underneath the bed. Furry and black, it looked like a large, shaggy dog. It didn't even glance in my direction.

"Hey!" I tried to yell, but nothing came out.

I couldn't move. It was like I was nailed to the floor.

It took less than two seconds. The monster grabbed Haylie and disappeared back under the bed. Its feet were the last thing to go—hairy with soft animal pads.

"H-h-how?" I stuttered to an empty room.

I dove for the floor and lifted up the ruffled bed-spread. Nothing but solid wood.

"Noooo." It came out as a gurgle.

When I climbed to my feet, the room tilted and spun. I wasn't sure if it was from hitting my head or from what had just happened—probably a little of both.

As the room stopped moving—and with a wicked headache—I imagined breaking everything in sight: smashing the mirror and tearing the pictures off the walls and bashing the lamp in. I screamed again and again, until my throat burned.

My hands were shaking so badly it took me four tries to hit the button to dial Adam's number.

"Haylie. It's Haylie—" I could barely suck in air. "She's gone."

"What? Gone? How?"

"They took her right in front of me."

"Holy cow." There was a scuffling sound on the line. "I'm getting Blue and coming right over." The line went dead.

I went to my room and pulled on jeans and sneakers. Putting my hair in a ponytail, I stared at my face in the mirror. I looked pale and wild-eyed.

They took her right in front of me. How?

I believed in monsters already. Maybe that was how one could steal Haylie in my presence. It didn't need to hide from me.

That must have been it! It was a monster movie rule I'd overlooked. I felt sick.

Stumbling to the kitchen, I put together an ice pack and swallowed a few Advil from the cabinet next to the fridge. I needed to be clearheaded for whatever was coming next. I walked back to Haylie's room, sticking the ice pack against my head. It was so cold, it burned.

I sat down on the bed. Something hard poked me in the butt, and I shifted and pulled out a plastic figurine that had been snared in the covers. It was the blob from Monsterville. The game was peeking out from under the nightstand, the cover ajar and cards scattered all over the floor. I shoved the missing piece back inside the box.

Dropping to my knees, I pulled up the bedspread again. All I saw was hardwood floor, a brown-haired Barbie in a shiny purple dress, and dust. I slid underneath and pressed my hands against the boards.

Solid wood.

The doorbell rang, and I dropped the bedspread. "Coming!" I screamed, readjusting my ice pack and racing down the hall. I yanked open the front door and burst into tears as soon as I saw Adam and Blue.

"It's okay," Adam said, wrapping his arms around me. "It's okay. It's okay." He kept repeating the words as I clung to him like I was drowning and he was the last life preserver.

My nose was running, and I wiped it with the edge of my sleeve. "You're going to get in trouble for sneaking out again."

Blue hid in the shadows cast by the porch light, clutching his tail. "What happened?"

I ushered them inside and closed the door, bolting the lock. "A monster came out from underneath the bed. *I saw it happen.* And I couldn't even do anything."

"That's a nasty lump," Adam said, moving the ice pack to examine my head. "You might have a concussion."

I waved him off. "I'm fine. The ice helps with the swelling." Tears welled in my eyes again, and I brushed them away. Crying wouldn't help Haylie. "Come on." I stumbled to her room, and they followed.

As I explained what happened, Adam hovered in the doorway, his backpack slung over one shoulder. Blue walked inside and perched on the edge of the bed. He put his hands in his lap and glanced around the room.

I *hated* the monsters. Hated them! Snatching Sammy Squirrel from Haylie's bookshelf, I hurled it across the room. "They have *Haylie!*" I screamed. "How could I let this happen? What is *wrong* with me?"

Headlights washed over the wall. Mom and Dad were home.

"Oh, no." I rubbed my hand across my face. "They're here. They're here. What do we do?" When they walked in and found Haylie missing, they'd call the cops. I'd end up stranded in a police station, unable to go find her.

A car door slammed outside, and I heard Mom laughing. Car keys jangled. I crossed the room and shut the door, my hand trembling.

Blue picked up Sammy Squirrel, cradling it in his long, bony hands. He swallowed hard, his Adam's apple bobbing, and then nodded. "I can take you Down Below," he said, almost inaudibly.

"You can? Seriously?" Mom and Dad's footsteps came up the front steps, and a key turned in the front lock.

"Yes, but we have to be quick." He hopped off the bed and pulled up the bedspread. Reaching underneath, his arm disappeared into the hardwood floor. "Ready?"

The front door opened and closed.

"Wait!" I barreled through the bathroom to my room, tossing the ice pack in the sink as I went. Snagging Aunt Lucy's journal from underneath my mattress, I rearranged my pillows and drew up the covers. Maybe, if I got lucky, my parents wouldn't realize I was missing. I raced back to Haylie's room and did the same thing with her pillows.

On impulse, I dove to the floor and grabbed a fistful of scattered Monsterville cards. Like the journal, they might come in handy Down Below. "Ready," I panted.

Blue dove headfirst under the bed, vanishing through the floor. His head popped up. It looked so gross—a severed goblin head under Haylie's bed. Then it popped back under the floor. "Come on." Blue's voice was muffled. "I'll pull you under."

I scrambled under the bed, scratching around for a trapdoor or a raised edge—something. I felt only hard wood. I rapped on it. "Little help?"

"Lissa?" Adam asked quietly. "What's happening?"

"Nothing yet!" I whispered, just as Blue's bony hands shot through the floor and wrapped around my wrists. I watched my outstretched hands being sucked into the floor. It was like moving through molasses—I couldn't breathe and my body felt squeezed in on all sides, like I was in one of those vacuum bags used to shrink down clothes.

The feeling passed, and I fell, landing hard on stony ground. "Ow!" I yelped, getting to my feet and squinting around me. It looked like I was in a cave— rocky walls and ground, and hazy light. A cold wind chilled my face, and I pulled my jacket up.

Blue reached overhead, grunting and pulling at something. His hands had disappeared into dark shadow.

"One. Two. *Three!*" he counted, tugging hard, and Adam tumbled down next to me.

"Ouch!" he said, catching himself with his hands. He shook his head, looking dazed. "That was weird."

"I'll say." I helped him up. "So. This is Down Below."

ACT THREE
DOWN BELOW

SCENE ONE:

SIX HOURS LEFT

There wasn't much to see, at least not yet. I paused, letting my eyes adjust to the dimness. We were in a twisting tunnel. When I groped to the right, my hand connected with a cold, rough surface, and light trickled in up ahead. Blue nodded, running a gnarled hand along the wall. "This is it," he said softly, then pointed up. A soft light edged the portal we'd come through, like a door closed on a lit room. "See that? Your portal glows when it's open."

"Huh," I replied. I was more concerned with where we were going, not where we'd come from.

Adam dropped his backpack to the ground and surveyed the area. "Let's get down to business," he said brusquely, pulling something small from the front pocket. "This is for you." He extended something to me that glinted in the dim light.

"What is it?"

"It's a Boy Scout Backpacker Wrist Watch. Unbreakable, waterproof, and it glows in the dark."

I examined it. "Thanks! Wow, this is really nice. But you didn't have to buy me this."

"I didn't. I stole Charlie's from his nightstand before I left." Adam grinned. "Now!" He clapped his hands. "How do we get to Haylie? Which path?"

"I don't know yet." I crept forward, keeping my hand against the wall for balance. My whole body trembled. "The middle right path is the shortest," I said. "When we played, the person on that path always won. But Aunt Lucy's journal went on and on about how the spiders will kill you . . ."

"We can't risk a spider bite we can't treat. Not down here."

I nodded. "That's what I was thinking. So . . . middle left path."

"Is that what your gut says?" Adam asked. "Middle left path?"

I made up my mind. "Yeah. Middle left. Sandmen and mummies and zombies. Let's go!"

I sounded just like Dorothy from *The Wizard of Oz*. Only sandmen and mummies and zombies were way more terrifying than lions, tigers, and bears. I cracked my knuckles and took a deep breath.

Then I noticed Blue. His forehead was beaded in sweat and even in the dusky light, he looked ghostly pale.

"Blue? You okay?"

"Atticus," he whispered.

"Don't worry. We'll protect you from him," Adam said, standing up straighter.

Blue managed a weak smile. "Thanks."

"Ugh." I closed my eyes. Being down here still felt surreal. "We're in Monsterville. The *game*."

"This ain't no game," Adam replied quietly.

"No kidding. How much time do we have to get out of here?" I twisted my arm to glance at my new watch. "A quarter after midnight. How long until sunup?"

"Six hours. It'll come up right around quarter after six."

My pulse quickened. Six hours to find Haylie and escape back up through the portal. Six hours before sunup, and then we were all doomed. Panic bubbled up inside me, and I took a step forward.

Adam grabbed my arm. "Wait, we need to feel out the terrain first."

I bit my lip. He was right, of course. Charging full speed ahead was a recipe for getting killed. I knew better than that.

Adam pulled three flashlights out of his backpack. "The batteries in these are good for twelve hours." He handed one to me and one to Blue.

"Thanks," I said. "Blue, do you know how to get to the four paths? You know, how they're laid out in Monsterville?"

"I think so." He pointed. "They're that way."

"I'll go first." Adam switched on his flashlight and aimed it toward the opening at the end of the tunnel. "Everyone ready?"

"Wait." I thrust Lucy's journal and the Monsterville cards at him. "Do you mind keeping these safe?"

Adam glanced at them, his face brightening. "Good call! We can use these." He unzipped his backpack and stowed them before starting down the rocky passageway. He didn't even hesitate, which made me feel a little bit safer.

Without a word, Blue and I followed, our footsteps echoing against the flinty walkway, our breaths coming in shallow gasps.

We were about to enter the depths of Aunt Lucy's Monsterville.

FIVE HOURS AND FORTY-FIVE MINUTES LEFT

The end of the tunnel opened up on a huge area. "Whoa," I said in a low voice, glancing around. "What is this? A landfill?"

We stood on a ledge overlooking a cavernous pit. It was filled with garbage stacked in teetering piles. Peering from behind a large slab of rock, we watched goblins push wheelbarrows along trails that twisted among the piles. One goblin wearing a green night-gown and fuzzy pink slippers picked something off a mound, sniffed it, and tossed it into her wheelbarrow.

A bright yellow beach umbrella protruded from a heap directly in front of us, open and miraculously unripped. It seemed out of place among all the old junk. Too bright and too new.

"Oh!" Blue exclaimed. "This is all from the reaping."

"What's the reaping?" Adam asked.

"Remember how I said that monsters collect old

233

things that humans won't miss? Well, on Monster New Year, monsters deliver what they don't need here. For sharing."

"That's actually pretty smart," I said grudgingly. Even if monsters stunk at life—or nonlife or whatever their status was—that didn't mean they weren't practical.

I cleared my throat, scanning the cavern for the four different paths. I didn't see them. "How do we get around the other goblins? Adam and I should avoid being seen, right?"

"Goblins probably won't hurt us." Blue said. "And monsters rummaging for Monster New Year stuff are distracted. But they might tell other monsters we're here."

"Well, let's avoid attracting attention," Adam said.

"Agreed," I said. "Come on." In my head, I pictured a big clock with the time ticking down, down . . .

We descended a rocky path to the bottom of the pit. It smelled rotten, and I held my nose and tried to breathe through my mouth.

That's when I saw them. Four different paths, each one leading into a different cave. My stomach flipped. Showtime.

"Middle left," I murmured. "Hurry, before someone sees us."

We crept along the path, heads lowered. My legs

itched to run, but I knew we needed to be as inconspicuous as possible.

When we reached the mouth of the cave, Adam pushed Blue and me behind him. "I'll go first. Scout the area."

I thought of the first time Adam and I had explored the woods together. How I hid behind him like a big chicken. "No, I got you into this. I should go first."

Adam glanced back at me. There was a smudge of dirt on his forehead, and I resisted the urge to wipe it off. "I want to," he said. "I'm the tallest, and I know how to handle the wilderness." He flicked on his flashlight and aimed it on the ground in front of him. "Trust me."

"I do." I reached for Blue's hand. He was shaking. "Don't worry," I told him, squeezing. "We'll be out of here in no time." I sounded more confident than I felt.

The trail through the cave twisted and turned. I played my flashlight along the roof where ragged stalactites hung down like huge icicles—glittering daggers of bright purple, pink, and blue. They were so pretty I almost forget how deadly they were. If one fell on me, I was a goner.

I could hear water dripping, and I strained to identify other sounds. Rustling, grumbling, slow footsteps—the classic indicators of trouble in any horror film. Nothing.

We moved effortlessly through the dark. Adam didn't even have to slouch, and nothing attacked us. It was so easy it made me a little uncomfortable. I had the horrible feeling we were being set up.

Soon, the tunnel widened and the ceiling rose. I realized we weren't in the cave anymore. A rocky path wound around the base of a hill. I shivered and pulled up my hood.

Above us, I could see stars sparkling. It felt like I was mountain climbing, only I was underground.

There was a loud hiss, followed by a popping sound. "Cover your head!" Blue warned. Something pelted us from above, shattering when it hit the ground.

"What was that?" Adam asked, crouching low. He reached for broken fragments, but Blue grabbed his hand.

"Don't touch! It's hot!"

Adam straightened. "But what the heck *was* that?"

"A light," Blue said. "Some monsters are really good at electricity, so they rig fake stars."

I peered up. Sure enough, those weren't stars. Underground, they couldn't have been. Strings of light bulbs crisscrossed the ceiling. "Well, at least we won't always need our flashlights."

"Good point." Adam snapped his light off. "Let's conserve power." He reached into his backpack and pulled out a bottle of water. "Anyone want one?"

I shook my head, but Blue took the bottle and

drank it all. No self-control whatsoever. Then again, he *was* a monster. *And* a little kid.

My heart ached for him. We were journeying through Monsterville to save Haylie from his fate. I hoped he didn't realize that.

We rounded a corner, and everything went black. I waved my hand in front of my nose, but I couldn't see a thing.

"Guys?" My voice sounded thin.

A beam of light shot through the dark, highlighting a boulder next to me.

"Guess we'll need these after all," Adam said. "That was weird. How'd it get dark so fast?"

Something scaly touched my elbow, and I jumped.

But it was just Blue. "Atticus said that Down Below, everything changes fast. Light to dark, cold to hot. Desert to arctic, swamp to jungle."

As he finished explaining, I realized I wasn't cold anymore. In fact, my forehead was damp and sweat was trickling down my spine. I put my hood down and pushed up my sleeves.

"Man!" Adam took another swig from his water bottle. "It's getting hot!"

"Can I have a water now?" I asked. He tossed one to me, and I took a long gulp. It was the best water in the history of the planet.

The smell of burning plastic hit my nostrils, and I

sniffed the air. What was that? I aimed my flashlight to the left.

The hills and rocks were gone. We were standing in a desert. A huge cactus rose from a sandy hill, its smooth, green form dotted with enormous, bloodred flowers. And massive needles. If I had bumped against it, it would have been like hugging a porcupine.

I felt something sticky and looked down. When I picked up my foot, a long string of something gummy stretched from the bottom of my sneaker. The plastic on my soles was melting. More sweat trickled down my forehead, but I didn't think it was from the heat.

I shined my flashlight on the ground. It was hard, cracked earth the color of rust. Only a few steps later, the hard dirt turned to sand.

"Blue?" Adam asked nervously. "Do you have normal wildlife down here? You know, like snakes and birds and . . . scorpions?"

I sucked in my breath. *Is that something crawling up my leg?*

"I don't think so," Blue said. "Down Below isn't like Up There. Lots of things don't live so far below the surface."

Adam looked thoughtful. "No ecosystem," he said. "Or at least, not any natural kind of ecosystem."

I sighed. At least I didn't have to worry about bugs

and snakes. Just, you know, huge hairy monsters with eight rows of teeth. No big deal.

"Do you know how far we have to go, Blue?" I asked, tilting my head to look up at the sky. I couldn't see anything. The space could have gone on forever or ended ten feet above us—it was too dark to tell.

"No, I don't remember. Sorry."

"Terrific," I mumbled. "We'll probably get there right in time for Transformation."

"Don't joke, Lissa," Adam said sharply. "We can't think like that."

"Sorry," I said, biting the inside of my cheek. I wished this was a nightmare. Or a scene in a movie, so a director could yell "cut!" and get us out of here.

My legs began to ache. Walking was getting hard. I had to fight to take each step—kind of like wading through deep snow.

Soon, I felt a change in the terrain surface and frowned. What was going on?

"Huh," Adam said. "Do you notice something?"

"The ground," I said. "It's not hard anymore." With every step, my sneaker sank into the sand, and I had to wrench it out.

"Desert quicksand." Adam stopped. "Okay. According to the Monsterville board, what's the first thing we'll run into?"

"The sandman," I said quietly.

"How do you beat a sandman?"

"Can I get into your backpack? I need to see what the card says."

Adam twisted and I unzipped his backpack, digging until I found the pile of cards. I flipped through them quickly, then sighed.

"We don't have that one. I didn't have time to grab them all. Talk about bad luck!" Annoyed, I shoved the stack of cards back into the pocket.

"Do you need it, though? Haven't you played that game a million times?"

"I shouldn't need it," I admitted. "But I can't remember the rhyme." I was too on edge to think clearly. My hands trembled, and my head buzzed. I needed to get it together.

Adam reached into his backpack. "Guess we need to go to plan B."

"What's that?" I asked him.

He tossed me a length of rope. "Here. Hand Blue the other end. If one of us gets stuck in the quicksand, the other two can pull him out."

"Or *her*." I grabbed the middle of the rope and tossed the end to Blue. "Don't let go," I warned him. It was an obvious thing to say, like "don't get hit by a car" or "don't burn yourself," but I couldn't help myself.

The ground got stickier, and our pace slowed even more. I had to wrench my foot out of the ground with every step. My leg muscles were burning.

"It hurts," Blue whimpered.

"Just for a little longer," I replied, aiming my flashlight to see if solid ground was nearby. Nope.

Suddenly, a hand burst through the ground and wrapped around my left ankle, strong and tight. Fireworks of pain shot through my entire leg.

I shrieked, almost dropping the rope. "Adam! Blue! Help!"

The hand's grip was like iron, drawing me into the ground. Gritty sand crept up over my ankles, and before I knew it, I was waist-deep in the muck. I dropped my water bottle and flashlight and clutched the rope, trying to kick my way free.

It was like trying to fight off a five hundred—pound gorilla. I couldn't loosen the sandman's hold no matter how much I squirmed and kicked.

"Blue, get behind me!" Adam commanded. "Hurry!" They braced themselves against the creature's pull.

With each passing second, I sank deeper. Now I was up to my armpits. I would have screeched in agony, but I could barely breathe. The sand was crushing me.

"One. Two. Three. *Pull!*" Adam screamed, and I moved up an inch. "One. Two. Three. *Pull!*" Adam screamed again, and I moved up another inch.

But for every inch I moved when they pulled, I sank three when the rope slackened.

Adam and Blue were using all their strength against the sandman, and it only had hold of me with *one hand*. Unless we could change the rules in this game of tug of war, the monster would win. We needed another strategy, and fast.

My mind raced. I had to remember what that stupid Monsterville card said.

I tried to focus, but sand was pushing in around me. The hand stayed wrapped firmly around my left leg, each finger digging in. I squealed.

"Hold on, Lissa!" Adam yelled.

"Not planning . . . on letting . . . go," I hissed through clenched teeth.

Adam had dropped his flashlight, and though he and Blue were only a few feet from me, they were just silhouettes—silhouettes growing shorter by the second. They were sinking, too.

The rope was rubbing my hands raw. Blisters formed and burst open. Still, I gripped the rope as hard as I could.

Closing my eyes, I pictured the Monsterville rectangular card with the rhyme about the sandman.

The sandman's grabbed onto your shoe
Down, down you sink, it feels like glue—

What came next? A sob escaped me as I racked my brain. But I wasn't good under pressure. That was why I choked at spelling bees.

"Come on, come on," I muttered to myself. Like I hadn't read that stupid card a zillion times.

But sprinkle moisture on the ground
And life will grant another round.

"Water!" I croaked. "Adam, we need water!"

"Are you crazy? This isn't the time!"

"That's how you get the sandman! Water! Tell me you have some left over!"

"It's in my backpack. What do I do with it?"

"Just dump it on the ground," I wheezed. My lungs were collapsing. Sand crept up past my shoulders and I raised my chin.

"Blue!" Adam shouted. "Can you unzip my backpack? Bottom zipper. But wait until I tell you to."

"Okay!"

"He's gonna have to let go of the rope," Adam warned me. "You ready?"

I squeaked.

"I'll hold on tight," Adam promised. "Go, Blue!"

Instantly I was sucked farther into the ground. I gulped a mouthful of air right before gritty sand filled my nostrils. I squeezed my eyes shut, trying not to breathe.

243

The lack of oxygen was making me light-headed. Black spots danced in front of my eyes, and I clenched my fist, pinching the fleshy part of my palm to stay conscious. My lungs burned and the ankle the sandman gripped felt like it was being ripped off.

Then it was over.

One second the hand was pulling me down and the next second it was . . . gone. I thought I heard a roar from somewhere down below, but that could have been my imagination. The bad guy always bellows when he's defeated in the movies. That way, the audience knows to expect a sequel.

When I cried out in relief, my mouth filled with sand. I tried to spit it out but my tongue was too dry.

"Lissa!" someone shouted from above me. "Lissa!" The voice was garbled and sounded far away, like it was coming through a tunnel.

I clutched the rope as my body was pulled upward. Everything hurt. I felt like Augustus Gloop from *Willy Wonka* (either version) who drinks from Mr. Wonka's chocolate pond and gets punished. The image of that kid pressed up against that plastic tube like an oversized hamster always made me laugh. Not anymore.

My hand clutching the rope broke through the sand, and Adam and Blue cheered. "Got her!" Adam crowed.

I stretched my other hand and felt air. Two strong hands gripped my wrists and pulled, and my head and shoulders burst from the sand. I shook my head. Sand stuck in my eyes and man, it burned.

"Hold on." Adam's teeth were clenched as he wrapped his arms around me. In one long movement, he wrenched my entire body free. I scrambled away on all fours and collapsed, gulping in air.

My head was swimming. For a second, I thought I'd throw up, and then the fatigue hit me. I'd been running on adrenaline for so long that I'd forgotten how late it was. I dropped my head, wanting so badly to curl up in the sand and go to sleep.

FIVE HOURS LEFT

I glanced at Adam and Blue. They lay like beached whales, their chests rising and falling in unison.

"Is everyone okay?" Adam wheezed.

Blue and I grunted. I couldn't talk yet. My right foot dug into the warm sand. I'd lost my sneaker and sock in the ordeal. "I'm o—" I began, moving my leg.

"Owww!" It felt tender, almost like it was still being squeezed. I angrily wiped tears away. Haylie was still waiting for us.

"You okay?" Adam sat up, resting his arms on his knees.

"Yeah. Just give me a second."

"You're a terrible liar." He reached into his back-pack's front pocket and pulled something out, tossing it to me. "Here."

"What is this?" It felt like a bunch of tiny pebbles in a sealed paper envelope.

"An ice pack. Just bang it against the ground."

I followed his instructions and then placed my hand in the center. "It's cold!"

"Right. It's an ice pack." Adam grinned. "Wait a second." His smile dimmed. "Where's your flashlight?"

I winced and pointed to the ground. "Down there." The quicksand had swallowed it. "Sorry."

"It's okay, Lissa," Blue piped up. "You had to save yourself."

"I guess." I wished I'd thought to throw the flashlight. Then maybe we'd still have it.

I pressed the ice pack against the bruises blooming on my left leg, gritting my teeth against the cold. My skin was super sensitive, but gradually the cold started to feel good.

I gave myself thirty seconds with the ice pack and then climbed to my feet, shaking sand from my clothes. The open blisters on my hands were burning and throbbing, and I felt off-balance without my right sneaker. I looked down at my watch. "It's one thirty! Only five hours left! We have to keep going."

"Five minutes won't kill us. If we recharge, we'll move faster." Adam groped for his flashlight, which had rolled a few feet away. Blue was still holding his.

"I guess you're right," I grumbled, gingerly lowering onto the ground. My head throbbed and I lay back, pressing my temples and willing the pain to go away. I needed to stay focused.

"Adam?" Blue asked hopefully. "Did you bring food?"

"Trail mix, apples, and Fruit Roll-Ups. Preference?"

"Fruit Roll-Up, please."

"Stat." I struggled into a sitting position. "Our hero deserves quick service."

"Hero?" Blue tugged on his ear, his face turning pink. "What did I do?"

"You saved me. If you hadn't been so fast with that water, I might be halfway to the core of the earth by now."

"Yeah. And you managed not to chug our weapon," Adam joked.

That was a good point. Given Blue's history, I was lucky he hadn't pulled that water from Adam's backpack and suddenly remembered how thirsty he was.

"I can control myself," Blue said, taking the strawberry Fruit Roll-Up Adam held out to him. He tossed it into his mouth and swallowed it whole. "When it matters."

"Fair enough," Adam said, leaning to hand me a Fruit Roll-Up. It was apricot, which isn't my favorite flavor, but I choked most of it down anyway. I needed plenty of energy for whatever lay ahead. I stood up and tossed the rest of the snack and the wrapper on the ground.

Adam stooped to pick up my trash. He held it out

to me. "Don't litter. Not even here. That's a rule of exploring nature. Take nothing but memories, leave nothing but footprints."

"Yeah, yeah, yeah. Of course we should respect Monsterville. It's been super nice to *us*." I stuffed the balled-up garbage in my pocket and took off my other sneaker. "I'm looking forward to walking around with bare feet. That's really safe," I scoffed.

Adam reached into his backpack again, pulling out a small plastic box and a rolled-up pair of black socks. He tossed the socks to me. "Here, these are super durable. Not quite shoes, but better than nothing."

"What else do you have in there?" I asked, craning my head. "Seriously. This is getting ridiculous."

"Just survival basics." Adam popped open the box and took out a small plastic tube of ointment. "Here, hold out your hands," he said to Blue, but Blue shook his head.

"No, you guys use it. My skin's tougher than yours. See?" He stretched out his hands, and they weren't all blistered and bleeding like Adam's and mine. Just dirty.

Adam bandaged our hands—expertly, of course— and I fumbled to pull on my new socks. They were thick with padding on the bottom. Adam was right. Shoes would have been better, but these weren't bad. Like mittens for feet.

"Okay." I closed my eyes, picturing the Monsterville board. "After the sandman is the . . . mummy."

"Mummy? Like pharaohs, and pyramids, and Egypt?" Adam zipped his backpack of tricks and stood up.

"Exactly. Crypts, and basements, and enclosed spaces."

"What did the cards say about mummies?" Adam asked. "We should figure that out before we go any farther."

I pictured the game card. This one came easily.

A relic of the ancient past
Odd measures make a mummy last
But all those things which keep it so
Will be the key to make it go.

"Huh?" Adam asked, frowning. "Go? Go where? What's that supposed to mean?"

"I dunno. What's used to preserve mummies? Formaldehyde and bandages?"

Adam patted his backpack. "I have Band-Aids. But those don't really strike me as lethal."

"Mummies like the dark," Blue piped up. "Does that help?"

I shrugged, taking Adam's flashlight when he held it out to me. "I have no idea. Let's just keep going, okay? And watch out for mummies."

SCENE FOUR:

FOUR HOURS AND FORTY-FIVE MINUTES LEFT

It was still hot, and my skin itched. I hoped we would stumble upon a nice little oasis with a clear pond, but I wasn't counting on it. Plus, I knew I probably shouldn't consume anything I found here. If I came across a little Drink Me bottle like the one Alice chugged in *Alice in Wonderland*, I'd be lucky if all it did was shrink me.

As we raced along the path, it turned from loose sand to hard, flat stones. I gripped Adam's flashlight, paranoid that I'd drop it. I'd already messed up enough tonight.

The path twisted to the right, and I stopped, my heart thumping.

Blue bumped into my back.

"Sorry," I said. "I just remembered something."

"What?"

"The tagline of the game! 'A monster around

every corner.' We just turned a corner." I shined the flashlight ahead, but the beam cut through black nothing.

Adam glanced around nervously. "So the mummy's gonna show up now?"

"Soon."

We'd only gone about thirty more steps before a huge stone wall blocked our way.

"What is this?" I played the flashlight over the wall, trying to find where it ended. I couldn't.

"Should we try walking around it?" Adam asked doubtfully.

I shook my head. "I think we have to stay on the path."

Stepping forward, I felt around the wall's surface. It was made of large, square blocks about three feet wide and two feet high. Whoever had stacked them had done an incredible job—the blocks were perfectly even.

"This is a pyramid!" I exclaimed, remembering the cute little cartoon pyramids on the Monsterville board. "The mummy's gotta be *in* the pyramid. But how do we get in?"

Adam rubbed his hand over his jaw. "Isn't that a question for our monster expert?"

I was stumped. Mummy movies have never been my thing, and Aunt Lucy's journal hadn't mentioned mummies. "Maybe there's a secret password or something?"

"Too bad we don't have the script."

"Or, maybe this is like *Goonies*. Remember when they were going after the treasure, and they kept setting off all those booby traps?"

"Never seen it." Adam moved farther from the wall. "Shouldn't we be trying *not* to set off booby traps, though?"

"Maybe that's the wrong example. Maybe this is more like in *Batman Begins,* where Bruce Wayne played a few notes on a piano to open a secret passage." I shined my light over the stones again. "There's always a sign. . . . There! This one's a different color." I glanced back at Blue and Adam. "You guys ready?" They both nodded.

I tapped on the stone. Nothing happened.

I tapped harder. Zilch.

Adam stepped forward. "Allow me."

"Sure."

Adam backed up, made a running leap, and rammed his shoulder against the pyramid. It didn't budge. I had a sinking feeling this wasn't the right way to get inside.

"Check the ground," I said. "Maybe there's a lever or a string—something to push or pull to make a door appear."

Blue crouched down, rubbing his hands along the sand. He squealed. "I found something!" He brushed sand away from a long length of wire embedded in the ground. "Look!"

"Go for it, Blue," I said, squinting at my watch. Two thirty.

Blue gripped the wire with both hands, straining to lift it. It rose an inch before Blue let it go, snapping it against the sand. He cocked his head. "Listen!"

A scraping sound came from inside the pyramid.

"Get back!" Adam yelled, pushing us out of the way. A second later, a stone drawbridge dropped down, crashing where we'd stood just seconds before. We coughed in the dust.

"Ladies first." Adam gestured to the opening. Gingerly, I stepped onto the drawbridge and peeked inside the pyramid.

"I can see the path!" Torches mounted on the walls lit the way down a long tunnel, casting strange shadows on the ground. I could hear something dripping far away.

We crowded together in the entrance. I put the hood of my jacket up. The pyramid was cold and damp. Cavelike. I peered down the tunnel. "Okay, guys. I don't know mummies, but I know rules for places like this. No splitting up to explore different tunnels. No one's allowed to go off alone. No touching anything we shouldn't. Got it?"

Blue and Adam nodded.

"Actually"—I handed Adam the flashlight and grabbed Adam's and Blue's hands—"I don't care how stupid this looks. I'm not taking any chances."

Over the sound of my pounding heart, I heard our ragged breathing and the crackling of the torches. No dragging footsteps, no moans.

We were toast if something came after us now. I imagined mummies emerging from a dark doorway, forcing us to retreat . . . only to face more mummies and a dead end. My pulse quickened, and I forced myself to breath evenly. *In, out, in, out.*

"I hope this leads back outside." Adam's voice echoed eerily off the walls. His hand was sweaty against mine.

"It'll lead *somewhere*," I responded quietly.

The tunnel branched into three passageways: one to the left, one to the right, and one straight ahead. I couldn't see farther than three feet down any of them.

"Which one?" Adam asked.

Blue stood up straight, aiming his flashlight. "I'll go look to see which one's the best."

"No, no, no!" I shook my head. "Didn't you hear me? No splitting up."

"Oh." Blue squinted. "Well, how about straight? That one might be the shortest."

"Good thinking! And since Aunt Lucy drew the path in Monsterville as a straight line, it's probably the right path." I squeezed Blue's hand. "Way to go." He flushed with pride.

"We should conserve battery power." Adam handed me his flashlight and grabbed a wall torch, dislodging a cascade of red embers. They danced in the air before turning to gray ash.

The middle tunnel sloped as it approached the center of the pyramid. My stomach twisted. What if this was the wrong path? What if we couldn't find our way out?

"The hall's getting smaller," Adam muttered.

I felt above my head and touched the ceiling. Twenty feet later, we had to duck to keep going. Soon we were crawling. I went first, gripping the flashlight in my left hand. The hard floor hurt my knees.

I raised my hand to block a bright glare. "What is that?" The tunnel opened to a large room. Climbing to my feet, I stretched my legs, then gaped.

Gold and jewels filled the room—tables and tables piled high with riches I never dreamed I'd see in real life.

Bars and bars of gold were stacked on a wooden table in the center of the room. It sagged under the weight. Strings of jewels—jade and diamonds and emeralds—glittered from where they were scattered on another table. Mounds of old coins covered a third table, a rusted balance scale perched atop one of the piles. The left side of the scale rested against the table, weighed down by rubies.

"Did we die?" Adam asked finally, after we'd stared at the room for a full minute.

"I don't think so." I glanced down. A beautiful multicolored rug decorated the floor, edged by gold tassels. I shook my head to clear it. "This has to be a trap. A distraction."

"It sure is a good one," Adam said, approaching the table with the gold bars. He picked one up with both hands. "Wow, this is heavy."

"Don't touch anything! It might set off a booby trap." I stared at the rubies on the scale. They couldn't weigh more than an ounce each. For a split second—despite every instinct screaming it was a trap—I imagined pocketing one. I could finance my first movie.

I forced my eyes from the rubies. "This isn't real! None of this is. Where would monsters get gold and jewels? They have to be an illusion. Fake, like the stars."

Blue reached toward the jewels glittering on a table. "Shiny . . ."

I gently slapped his hand. "No, Blue. We have to keep going."

On the opposite side of the room, a doorway led to another tunnel. "Come on. This way."

"Aww, man," Adam protested, but he followed me.

I took one last look at the riches before heading toward the tunnel, trying to permanently imprint the sight in my mind. I'd never see anything like that again.

This tunnel was shorter. We had only walked about fifty steps before it opened up into another room with a bare, uneven floor coated with dust. Shelves lined the walls, holding jars containing murky substances. I went to get a closer look and then wished I hadn't. The jars held pickled brains and organs, bloated and discolored from the chemicals they floated in.

Blue saw them, too. His fingers met mine and I grasped his hand, leading him back into the tunnel and shielding him with my body.

It reminded me of all the times I'd held Haylie's hand—taking her across the street, guiding her to the counter at Starbucks, walking her into the shallow end of the pool. I always felt needed, protecting my little sister like that. If only I'd protected her tonight, none of us would be in this mess. I forced myself to breathe evenly.

If we got out of this, I'd never miss the chance to hold Haylie's hand again. I'd walk her to school until she was eighteen years old, ignoring her while she complained about how much I was embarrassing her.

If we got out of this.

The tunnel opened to a third room, which was empty except for a sarcophagus resting at its center. The sarcophagus was rectangular and carved out of smooth, white stone, dripping white candles lining its base.

"Maybe if we walk past it really fast, nothing will happen," Adam whispered.

"I want to stay between you guys." Blue's voice shook.

Without a word, Adam took Blue's torch, and we each grabbed one of his gnarled hands. We tiptoed across the room. The doorway loomed thirty feet away. Then twenty. Then ten. . . .

Something scratched from inside the sarcophagus.

Stopping to see a monster close-up was always a fatal error in horror movies. "Just go!" I whispered sharply. We raced through the doorway and into the tunnel. I had to bend in half to fit. I raced along with one hand trailing along the ceiling, the other clutching the flashlight, Blue and Adam huffing close behind me.

I twisted to look over my shoulder, just in case this was another movie trick: a character hears heavy breathing and assumes it's one of her friends.

Meanwhile, said friend has been quietly eaten and replaced by a monster craving dessert.

Two sets of familiar eyes blinked back at me. "What?" Adam panted.

"Nothing." I turned again just in time to see that we'd reached another fork, two paths this time. My stomach dipped.

"Crud!" Adam yelled. "Now what?"

"Let's go left," I said.

"Why?"

"Because there's a fifty-fifty chance it's the right choice." We escaped into the left tunnel, gasping for air, keeping our ears pricked for the sound of a murderous mummy hot on our trail. The silence was unnerving.

We emerged in yet another room and came to a halt.

Adam raised his torch to get a better look. "You've gotta be kidding me!"

This room was filled with sarcophagi. At least two dozen lined the walls, all identical, with painted-on faces, staring eyes framed with blue and orange headdresses.

Blue tugged at my sleeve. "Come on. Fast. Like before."

We sprinted across the room, our feet pounding

against the rough floor. Behind us, one of the sarcophagi lids clattered to the ground. We whirled around.

A decaying mummy had fallen out, groping on its hands and knees. It lifted its head in our direction.

Another lid clattered to the ground. Then another, and another. Mummies fell heavily to the floor, groaning through their bandages.

"Go!" I screamed, hustling to the other side of the room where we reached a wall. Dead end. "Other way!" I shouted, and everyone followed as I threaded a path around the mummies scrabbling for footing. One clutched at my ankle as I darted past, like a dude with bad eyesight groping for his glasses. I stepped over the hand and darted out of the room.

Retreating up the tunnel, I tried to remember how far away the fork was. My chest burned, but I refused to slow down. Then I saw it.

"Stop!" I yelled. Everyone froze.

A mummy was advancing on us. The pharaoh.

"What do we do?" Adam shouted.

I opened my mouth.

A relic of the ancient past
Odd measures make a mummy last
But all those things which preserve it so
Will be the key to make it go.

The pharaoh blocked our escape. The bandages around its head had begun unraveling, and a decaying skull grinned at us. As I stared, a hairy spider crawled out of its eye socket and perched on its head.

I took a deep breath, hoping I wouldn't throw up. "But all those things which preserve it so, shall be the key to make it go. What preserves a mummy?"

"Chemicals? Formaldehyde?" Adam muttered, wielding his torch like a weapon. "The Egyptians embalmed mummies. That's how they stayed preserved for centuries."

"Yeah, but what can we do with chemicals and formaldehyde?"

"Fire!" Adam cried. "That's it! Stand back!"

Adam threw his torch at the mummy, and it burst into orange and blue flames. The mummy bellowed, staggering toward us with its arms outstretched. Fire crackled, and the horrible smell of rubbing alcohol filled my nostrils as smoke burned my eyes.

"Go around it!" Adam yelled. "Now! Now!" He pushed Blue and me forward.

As we skirted around the pharaoh, it groped for us, its fingers closing around Adam's backpack.

"No!" I screamed as Adam pinwheeled his arms.

"Leave the backpack!" I shouted. I could see the indecision in his eyes, and I yanked at his arm. "Not worth dying for! Take it off!" My heart wrenched as I said it. Aunt Lucy's journal was in there.

An orange flame snaked from the mummy's loose bandages and onto Adam's sleeve. I watched in horror as it caught fire. "Adam! *Please!*"

Finally, Adam shrugged out of his backpack and broke away. We raced down the tunnel without looking back. Behind me, Adam beat at his fiery sleeve.

I came to the fork and raced into the right-hand tunnel, training the flashlight on the path before me. Behind me, Blue and Adam gasped for air.

The hard ground turned to sand. I raised my arms above my head and didn't hit anything. We were out in open air. Boy, did it smell sweet.

"Lissa!" Blue yelled. "Your back!"

I whirled around, expecting to stare into a mummy's soulless eyes.

"Wha—?"

That's when I felt the heat. I was on fire! I'd been so concerned with Adam that I hadn't even noticed. The smell of scorched hair filled my nostrils as my scalp started burning. Shrieking, I beat at my head like angry bees were attacking me.

"I've got you!" Adam yelled, slamming me to the ground and knocking the breath from my lungs.

"What are you doing?" I shrieked, spitting out sand.

"Just a second." Adam patted me, hard. "Okay. It's out."

I rolled over and sat up, touching the back of my head. The hair below my ponytail had been singed off. It felt nubby. This would never happen to a leading lady.

"Thanks!" I shook my head, trying to clear it.

"Sorry, I know that was a little rough. You all right?"

"Yeah," I said shakily. Aunt Lucy's journal—gone. We'd not only lost our road map, but everything—Aunt Lucy's detailed observations about Down Below, her confessions of guilt over leaving that little boy, her drawings of the Monsterville prototypes. It was all gone forever.

Adam was watching me carefully. "Don't think about it," he said. "We have to keep our eyes on the goal. I have some supplies in my jacket. Now come on!"

FOUR HOURS AND FIFTEEN MINUTES LEFT

Our feet slapped against the trail. My throat was dry and my lungs burned, but I kept pushing myself forward. *Haylie, Haylie, Haylie,* I thought with each step.

Finally I stopped, bending over and resting my hands on my knees. "We're running out of time."

"We're okay," Adam said. "We just need to go as fast as possible. Focusing on the time won't help." He unzipped his jacket pockets and poked through them.

"What are you doing?" I asked.

"Taking inventory of the remaining supplies."

"Anything good in there?"

"Not really. Some trail mix and dried fruit, my Swiss Army knife, and my pocketknife."

"Oh." I looked up. If I didn't know better, I'd think I was truly seeing a black sky spattered with stars. It was hard to accept that it was all fake—like we were in a planetarium.

Mom and Dad must have realized we were gone by now. I pictured them in a tiny police station, drinking black coffee from Styrofoam cups and describing what Haylie and I had been wearing when they last saw us. I wished I'd left them a note, but what would it have said?

> *Dear Mom and Dad,*
> *Gone to save Haylie from monsters. Back*
> *before dawn. Would appreciate pancakes*
> *for breakfast. Make lots extra for Adam.*
> *Love,*
> *Lissa*

Adam was looking at me. "What's the matter, Lissa?"

"Well, other than the obvious . . ." I swallowed hard. "I was just thinking about how Mom and Dad must be freaking out right now."

Adam reached for my hand. When our fingers connected, I felt a small charge. "It's okay. Your parents will be so happy to see Haylie again that they'll forget how scared they were."

Tears filled my eyes, and I wiped them away. I couldn't get over how nice Adam was being. I'd put him in horrible danger, and *he* was comforting *me*.

"Look." Blue pointed ahead. "The path's different."

The path wasn't stones anymore. It had turned into

a wide asphalt road similar to the ones leading out of Freeburg. Ditches lined either side. Above us, a white ball hung from the ceiling. The moon?

There were night sounds, too. An owl hooted from far away. A cawing crow. A horse neighed, and a frog went *ribbit*.

"What on earth—" I frowned. "I thought Monsterville didn't have normal wildlife."

"Sound effects," Blue suggested. "Humans play music. Monsters like animal sounds."

Though it was ridiculous to think of cars passing us, we stuck to the right-hand side. Habit, I guess. Our feet crunched on fake grass (Astroturf?), the night still except for the sound effects. It must have been on a loop because we kept hearing the same sounds in the same order: owl, crow, horse, frog. Pause. Owl, crow, horse, frog. The monotony was almost soothing.

We'd been walking for what felt like a long time when Adam pointed across the road. "Do you see that?" Before us was a rickety wooden bridge. "What do you think, Lissa?" he asked. "It doesn't look too safe to me."

The bridge was made of slats held together by long ropes. It stretched over a wide chasm. There were gaps where wooden slats had rotted away, like missing teeth—that was the only part of the bridge we could see. The rest disappeared into fog.

"It looks really unsafe," I said. "I doubt this thing can hold one of us, let alone three."

"And that's a rule." Blue kneeled to inspect the bridge. "No splitting up."

"This way's a shortcut." I tried picturing the game. "There's only a troll, and that's at the end of the path. The other way is longer and has zombies."

Adam stepped onto the first wooden slat, testing it. "I vote we go the long way."

"Me, too," Blue said.

"You guys are right." I ran my hand over my forehead. I hated losing time going the long way, but I knew it was too dangerous to take a chance on the bridge.

"I'm hungry. I wish we still had the backpack," Blue said sadly.

Adam unzipped his jacket and tossed Blue a package of dried apples. "Eat slow."

He didn't.

We started back down the road, Blue's flashlight trained on the gravel in front of us, mine off to conserve power. I kicked a piece of rock. Looking up at the fake moon and breathing in the cool air, I could almost believe I was traipsing down Mine Haul Road.

The soles of my feet throbbed. At least the socks I'd borrowed from Adam were thick. "I'm tired," Blue said and, without a word, Adam bent so Blue could crawl up and ride on his back. Blue looped his arms around Adam's neck, and my throat tightened. It was the same way Dad gave Haylie piggyback rides.

I resisted the urge to check my watch. We were walking as fast as we could. Checking the time wasn't going to make us go any faster.

Finally, I couldn't stand it any longer. I raised my wrist to my face, squeezing the side so the face would light up. I groaned.

We'd been walking for thirty minutes. Thirty minutes we couldn't get back.

And we still had zombies ahead.

THREE HOURS AND FORTY-FIVE MINUTES LEFT

As we reached a curve in the road, my feet started vibrating. At first I thought they were throbbing because they hurt, but then the pulsing intensified. It reminded me of what it felt like to sit on Adam's four-wheeler.

A monster around every corner. Bright yellow headlights lit up the road, and an engine growled. "Ditch! Get in the ditch!" I yelped.

We dove off the road just as a loud vehicle rumbled by. Cautiously, we raised our heads. All I saw was black smoke belching from the tailpipe and tires that had to be six feet tall.

"Who would drive something like that down here?" Adam asked as it rolled away.

"Someone who doesn't care about the environment," I muttered, wrinkling my nose. Dark gunk covered me. I could probably pass for a swamp monster.

"But zombies come next," Adam said doubtfully. "Do they drive tricked-out cars?"

We both turned to Blue, who shrugged. "Monsters get all sorts of things from Up There, and when they take parts from junkyards, no one notices."

"Scavengers. I'll make sure I take a good souvenir from *them*," I said.

"It doesn't go both ways. You can't take things from Down Below to Up There."

"Huh," I snorted, fiddling with my zipper. "That hardly seems fair."

We climbed out of the ditch and kept walking. My hands were clammy and I kept rubbing them against my jeans. Up ahead, very close, zombies were waiting. What had the Monsterville card said about them?

Oh no, a zombie comes for you
With it in tow, a hungry crew
 The way to escape the undead?
With all your might, swing for the head!

I narrowed my eyes. "We're going to face a whole bunch of zombies—*a crew*. We need something hard to hit them with."

Blue whispered, "Shhh!" He put a gnarled finger to his lips. "Do you hear that?"

Laughter filtered toward us, along with rough voices singing. "Sounds like a party," Adam said.

"Monster New Year. Monsters celebrate all night," Blue explained. "At least, that's what Atticus says."

It was getting lighter. Blue's flashlight beam had looked bright cutting through the dark. Now, it disappeared ten feet in front of us, swallowed by hazy shadows.

"Turn that off," I said. "We don't want to be spotted. And it's not much help, anyway."

Up ahead, indistinct shapes rose from the gloom. As we crept closer, I realized we were entering a town. To the left was a trailer park, and to the right I saw a white building with a wraparound porch that had orange lights strung across its awning.

A small sign welcomed us to the town: ZOMBIE STATION. It was scrawled in messy writing. POPULATION 35.

As I examined the words, the number 35 disappeared, and a 38 materialized in its place. HAHA appeared underneath.

My skin crawled. "Guys. The zombies know we're here."

Adam went pale, but he straightened his shoulders and lifted his chin. "So what? The mummies knew we were inside the pyramid and we're still standing. Bring it on!"

Even though his voice trembled a little, he still

made me feel better. If anyone could whack a zombie into submission, it was Adam.

I wanted to help, too. What could I remember about zombies? "Zombie rules." I laughed grimly.

"What's funny?" Blue asked, his eyes darting all around us.

"Zombie rules. They're kind of mean. Travel in a group—"

"Check," Adam said.

"—because chances are someone will run slower than you, so they'll get eaten first."

"Oh."

"And travel with dumb people. Ditto on getting eaten first."

"Your rules aren't very helpful. Got any better ones?"

"Yeah, don't draw attention to yourself. Zombies aren't super great when it comes to using their senses. If we creep along instead of screaming and making a big scene, we might have a shot at getting out of here."

I tried not to think about Zombie Station's welcome sign. It didn't mean anything. It was just Down Below trying to psych us out.

We walked along a cracked sidewalk, stepping over a tricycle with a bent frame. Apart from the voices coming from way off in town, the whole place felt deserted. A cold wind blew through the streets, rattling a broken shutter and whistling through a cracked window frame.

Adam nudged me. "This town's pretty dead. Get it? *Dead?*" He wiggled his eyebrows.

"Haha." I shivered as we passed a boarded-up house with a collapsed wooden porch. I hoped Haylie hadn't seen any of this.

We came to a gas station. Tufts of grass pushed through the cracked pavement, and the lettering over the doors was faded and falling. It was now "GA 'N RAB."

Adam stopped. "Hey. Think we could stock up here?"

"What do you mean?"

"Maybe inside we can find gear to use as weapons. Broken broom handles—whatever works."

"I don't know," I said doubtfully. "When people stray off a path, they bite it." I glanced down the street. I didn't see any zombies, but I knew they were around. And in a horror movie, when monsters can close in around you, every second counts.

"Yeah, but we're going against Zombie Town unarmed. I think that's a bad call, too."

He had a point. "Okay, fine. Let's go around the back," I said. "Maybe there's a rusted-out door we can force open. But we have to be crazy-fast. Got it?"

"Hey, you don't need to tell *me*." He grabbed my hand, his fingers strong and warm around mine.

My stomach fluttered, and I wasn't sure if it was just because we were in the thick of Zombie Town.

We rounded the side of the building and found a supply door. I tried the knob. Locked.

"Allow me." Adam released my hand and stretched. "Here goes." He backed away about ten feet and charged, turning and slamming his shoulder against the door. It detached from the frame, hitting the ground and raising a cloud of dust. Adam climbed to his feet and stepped over the door.

"Looks like brute strength worked this time," I commented.

As I followed Adam into the store, something grabbed the bottom of my jacket. "Ah!" I squeaked, then relaxed when I realized it was only Blue.

"I don't like this," he announced, holding tight to me, twisting the fabric in his fingers. "I have a bad feeling. We should have taken the bridge."

A sour taste filled my mouth. I didn't know exactly why, but I had a bad feeling, too. In monster movies, it's important to trust your instincts.

"Blue's right," I whispered. "I'm getting a weird vibe. Something's . . . wrong."

Adam led the way into the store area. "What is it?"

"I can't put my finger on it. . . ."

As we crept inside, I glanced around the room. Dust coated empty shelves, and the glass freezer doors along the back wall were so dirty I couldn't see through them.

"I know it's creepy, but the other path was worse. That bridge wasn't safe," Adam said.

This place was straight out of a horror movie. The beige linoleum floor was cracked and filthy. Part of the ceiling was caving in.

Something rustled behind the counter. I sucked in my breath and aimed my flashlight at the sound. "Did you hear that?"

Adam cocked his head. "No. What?"

"I don't know." I strained my ears, but everything was quiet again. "Maybe I'm hearing things." Clicking off the flashlight, I rubbed my hand across my eyes. "But in the movies, when someone hears a noise, it's better to assume something's there, even if no one else hears anything."

For a moment, we stood rigid. Nothing.

We crept deeper into the store, Blue still clinging to my side. "It's okay. Two minutes and we're gone."

"That's what I'm afraid of," he whispered back.

"Here!" Adam bent to pick up a metal pole. "This'll work."

The rod was part of a broken, rusted display. Adam ripped a metal shelf from three remaining poles, tossing it toward the freezer section. He twisted two metal poles free from the bottom frame, handing one to Blue and one to me. "Here you go."

"Great, we're armed. Now let's get out of here." My skin felt like bugs were crawling under the surface. I'd never wanted to leave a place so badly before. "Maybe we—"

Something heavy—a brick or a rock—smashed through the window. The object landed at my feet and I jumped back.

"The light! They must have seen the flashlight!"

Stupid, stupid, *stupid*! I knew better than to use the light in a store with windows, even if only for a second. But I was tired and on edge, and that's when people make mistakes that cost them their lives.

The window by the cash register shattered, followed by the glass doors at the front of the store. Blue shined his flashlight toward the back door. Lurching, stumbling figures blocked the way. We were closed in on all sides. It couldn't end like this.

"Quick!" Adam cried. "Into the fridge!"

There wasn't time to protest. We raced to the refrigerators lining the back of the store.

Adam flung one open, revealing metal shelves. "Through here!" He tossed our metal poles first. I heard them clatter on the other side, and I winced.

Blue dove onto a shelf, and I shoved him, hard.

"Eeee!" he screeched, sliding across and landing on the other side.

I went next, headfirst. As I grabbed for the shelf's edge with my one free hand, my fingers slipped against the slick surface. Fingers grabbed my wrists and slid me forward across the cold metal.

I fell in a heap on the floor, banging my elbow. "Ow!" I winced and flexed my arm, gripping the flashlight. I tried peering through the shelves behind me, but I couldn't see a thing. "Come on, Adam!"

He grunted as he tried to squeeze himself through the shelves. The metal squeaked underneath him. He didn't sound stuck, but he sure wasn't moving fast. Soon his head came into view. "Lissa," he gasped. "Grab my—" His eyes widened. "Zombie!"

"Blue!" I yelled. "Get his hands!" Dropping my flashlight, I grabbed one of the display poles. I picked it up and thrust it into the space between the shelves, stabbing wildly.

"Let go, you stupid—" Adam panted. His hair was wet with sweat, his eyes wild. "It's too strong!"

I couldn't see the zombie, but I could hear and smell it. It grunted and wheezed. I tried breathing through my mouth to avoid the stench of its rotting flesh.

My fingers tightened around my pole. I pulled it back and jabbed it at the zombie. The metal connected with something soft and the zombie roared.

"Yes!" I hissed, and Adam finally scrambled through, almost landing on top of Blue.

Drawing the pole back, I looked at the tip. Something soft and misshapen was skewered there. I moved it closer for a better look.

"Gross! Zombie eyeball!" I flung the pole across the room, shuddering.

"Where are we?" I asked Adam as I retrieved my flashlight.

Every muscle in my body was tense. I'd seen movies like this—the heroes escape the zombies/monsters/unidentified scary creatures, only to light a match and find even worse terrors lying in wait.

"The fridge room." Adam sounded about ten feet ahead of me, to the right. "Where they store stuff that isn't ready to go on the shelves. I'm trying to find the door."

Man, we were dumb. In the past five minutes, we'd broken two major rules. First, we'd let the zombies know where we were. Second, we'd trapped ourselves in an enclosed space.

"Yes!" Adam hissed. "Found the door! You guys ready to run?"

"Yep!" Blue and I squeaked in unison, and I braced myself. If zombies waited for us on the other side, we were toast.

The door's rusty metal hinges screamed as Adam pushed it open.

I didn't hear anything—no scrapes or footsteps or groans. I relaxed a little.

At least there was one good thing about zombies—they're dumb. You always know they're coming.

I wasn't relaxing *too* much, though. You can't let down your guard when you're in the dark, surrounded by monsters.

"Hold on," I whispered, tugging on Adam's sleeve. "We can't just go out there. If one's waiting . . ."

"Do you have a better idea?"

I looked at Blue. "Yes." I ducked back into the storage room and gestured for the guys to follow. "We should disguise ourselves."

"How do we do that?" Adam asked, and I jerked my head at Blue. "Ahem."

Blue's eyes lit up. "Oh!"

"Right." I nodded. "You turn into a zombie. And if we're following you, hopefully these dummies won't realize we're not undead. Let's go!"

I couldn't see clearly, but I felt Blue turn. He groaned softly as he grew taller, stretching out his limbs. And the smell—*whew*! It was like standing next to a seventeen-year-old spoiled pumpkin.

After tucking his flashlight into his waistband,

Blue shuffled down the hall, arms outstretched. With a deep breath, I followed him, making sure I was right behind him. I didn't want the other zombies to catch a whiff of Human.

In only fifteen steps, we were out the door. We lurched away quickly, following the broken sidewalk, just three undeads out for a moonlight stroll. *"Errrr,"* I moaned for good measure, keeping my eyes on the ground.

"Errrr!" a zombie passing us replied. It was so close I could have touched it. I definitely smelled it. *Whew.*

After the monster was a safe distance away, I twisted my head to look back at the store and stifled a gasp.

Zombies were stumbling toward the store from all directions. There were at least two dozen of them, all greenish, rotting, and lumbering at the same target. They descended on the store like vultures on roadkill.

I turned my attention back to the path, and my heart sank.

An army of zombies was staggering toward us, blocking any chance of continuing on our way uninterrupted. We'd have to leave the way we came.

"Faster," I whispered, and we lurched ahead and out the door. In another block, we started running. My feet slapped against the road, and my right foot smarted. I only had to imagine a zombie's moldy fingers grazing my back, and I found the energy to speed up.

When we reached the town limits, we kept going. I counted in my head to one hundred, then started counting again.

Adam stopped. "Do you hear that?"

When I strained to hear, I realized what he was talking about. The night sounds on loop. Owl, crow, horse, frog. We were close to the bridge again.

TWO HOURS AND FORTY-FIVE MINUTES LEFT

The Monster-made stars shined brightly, illuminating the road. We didn't even need our flashlights.

"There!" Blue pointed. "The bridge."

I crossed the road, lacing my hands behind my head and breathing in and out slow, steady breaths. My mouth was so dry it felt like it had been stuffed with cotton.

"I can't believe we got away." Adam's face was damp with sweat, ghostly pale in the fake moonlight. "If you hadn't thought of pretending to be zombies . . ." He shook his head. "How'd you think of that? From some movie?"

"Actually, no. I mean, I've seen zombie movies where people try that to get away. But I remembered what Aunt Lucy's journal said when she came Down Below—she dressed like a zombie."

Adam bent to pick up a piece of gravel and chucked

it through a hole in the bridge. "Man. You know, and all this time I just thought she was the nice lady who lived next door. She was like . . . a superhero."

I adjusted the nub that was now my ponytail. "She was better than that. Superheroes get to use powers. You think Peter Parker would have been scaling buildings and rescuing people if he wasn't bitten by that spider?" I felt a swell of pride. Aunt Lucy was amazing.

"Probably not."

"How'd you know about the fridge room?" I asked. "If you hadn't bought us time, the zombies would have been on us right away."

Adam wiped his forehead with his sleeve. "Charlie. He used to work at the Gas Mart in town. He gave me a tour once."

"I knew Upchuck would serve a purpose. In good horror movies, even the throwaway characters are there for a reason."

"I'll let him know you said that." Adam stood at the edge of the bridge, his hands resting on a wooden post. "Who goes first?"

"Me!" Blue piped up immediately.

Adam and I looked at him. "I don't think that's a good idea. . . ." I said slowly. The bridge looked even longer and flimsier than I'd remembered. And the fog was a creepy special effect.

How could we let Blue go first when we knew that

he was actually a little kid? I wouldn't let Haylie cross a bridge like this in a million years.

"I'm the lightest," Blue insisted. "The lightest one should go first."

"You're also the youngest," I said. "We should be protecting you."

"I came down here to help Haylie. Let me go first."

"No," I said again, but this time less forcefully. We were running out of time. Regardless of who went first, we needed to get moving.

"Humph." Blue stuck his nose in the air. "No one ever lets me do anything." He walked into the ditch and plopped down facing away from us, drew up his knees and clicked his flashlight. On off, on-off.

"Blue!" I called after him. "We're not deciding who gets the first piece of cake here. This is dangerous."

"I know that! I've been here before."

Adam and I looked at each other. Maybe Blue was right. Adam twisted his wrist to look at the time. He inhaled sharply.

"What?"

"After three thirty."

Less than three hours left, and we weren't even halfway there. We still needed to save Haylie and retrace our steps.

And getting to Haylie wasn't like crossing a finish line. We weren't going to arrive at the Transformation

Room and have the monsters say, "Our bad, of course you can have your little sister back!" as they handed her over.

Blue stood up, straightening his shorts. "I'm going first," he said firmly, handing Adam his flashlight. We didn't argue this time.

Gingerly, Blue stepped onto the bridge. He held his arms out and kept his legs bowed like he was surfing.

I almost couldn't watch. What if he pitched over the side? What if he fell through a rotted board? What if the twine holding the bridge together snapped?

"Come on, come on," I muttered, urging him along under my breath. He took another step. The bridge held.

I shivered. The temperature was dropping, and white fog was crawling across the ground. It wrapped around my ankles until I couldn't see my borrowed black socks anymore.

The fog was thicker on the bridge. With his next step, Blue disappeared completely.

I didn't know what was worse—watching Blue's every step across that rotting bridge, or not being able to see him at all.

Something touched my hand: Adam. He squeezed. We stayed huddled together, waiting.

"Made it!" Blue's voice sounded like it was coming from far away. "I'm on the other side!"

"Oh, thank goodness," I whispered. My heart pounded as I looked into Adam's eyes. They were really blue in the pseudo-moonlight.

I bit my lip. "I guess I'm next, huh?"

Adam nodded. "In case my big butt breaks the ropes."

I wanted to laugh, but I couldn't. What if Adam really did break the bridge? He was at least fifty pounds heavier than me, and way heavier than Blue.

I turned and faced the path, taking a deep, steadying breath. I'd pretend I was on a tightrope. Like there was a net below, and if I fell, it would be uncomfortable and embarrassing, but not, you know, *fatal*.

Tentatively, and wishing I wasn't weighed down by a flashlight, I placed my left foot on the first board. The bridge rocked, and my eyes flew to one of the wooden posts, which I now noticed looked splintered and rotted.

"You can do it," Adam called behind me. "One step at a time."

"One step at a time," I repeated, my voice low. Narrowing my eyes, I concentrated on the wooden slats just ahead. I counted five until they disappeared into fog. There should have been six, but there was a gap between the third and the fourth ones.

Another step, and the bridge rocked again. The slats felt rough under my feet. I thought for a millisecond about splinters, and then realized I had far worse things to worry about.

Keeping my arms outstretched for balance, I took another step, squinting to see up ahead.

It couldn't be too far. I tried to remember how long it had taken Blue to reach the other side, how fast he'd been going.

With a big step, I passed over the missing section of the bridge. The only sounds around me were the creaking of the ropes and my breathing.

"I'm okay!" My voice was shaky. "The bridge is holding."

As a movie expert, I should have known than to say that. When I took my very next step, my foot punched through a rotten board. I screamed, deciding in a split second to let myself fall forward. My flashlight banged against the wood as my hands connected with the bridge. My right leg dangled through a gaping hole, and I tried to wrench it free.

"Lissa! You okay?" Adam yelled.

"Yeah! The bridge isn't holding everywhere! I'm, maybe, fifteen steps in." I craned my head to look behind me, but I only saw fog.

"But you're okay?" I could tell Adam was trying to stay calm, but panic edged his voice.

"Yeah." I grunted, still trying to pull my leg back through the hole. *Careful, careful*, I told myself. I couldn't afford to damage the bridge more. Adam still needed to cross. Even now, he would be in danger with every step he took.

Every step he took.

"Adam!" I yelled.

"What?"

"You need to crawl across the bridge. That'll distribute your weight better."

There was silence. "Lissa, has anyone ever told you you'd make a fantastic Boy Scout?"

"Not once." I waited until my legs stopped shaking before I started forward again. *Baby steps, baby steps*, I told myself. "Blue! Where are you?" I yelled into the void.

"Over here." He sounded close. I could do this.

I realized I was climbing up, making my way from the dip in the middle. That meant I was more than halfway there. Wisps of fog curled around my feet and hands.

Gritting my teeth, I picked my way forward. I wanted, so badly, to make a break for the other side, but I knew rushing would get me killed.

Patience is a virtue, I thought hysterically, panic bubbling up inside me.

I counted my steps. When I hit thirteen, I felt solid ground under my feet.

"You're here! You're here!" Blue shrieked, hugging me.

I couldn't see him. I couldn't see a thing.

"Adam!" I shouted across the chasm. "Your turn!"

"Crawling!" he called back.

I waited, clutching Blue's hand. He squirmed the same way Haylie does when I hold her too tight, and I loosened my grip. He drew away.

"Don't go far," I muttered.

What if Adam doesn't make it? What if this is my last chance to talk to him? To thank him?

Blue was fidgeting behind me. He kept hitting a stick or something against the ground. I wanted to tell him to stop, but I was focused on the bridge and the thick fog that made it impossible to see what was happening.

Adam screamed, and a horrible snapping sound echoed through the air. The bridge twisted to the right before slackening, then dropping, still tethered to our side of the chasm.

I moved as close to the edge as I dared, straining to hear. When I heard something hit the bottom, I crumpled, unable to support my legs. "No!" The word came out as a whisper.

"Adam!" Blue yelled beside me. "Adam!"

"Don't look, Blue." I covered my face. Blood was rushing around in my ears. Adam was gone. He'd never tease me again, or show me the stars, or point out something amazing about nature I'd never have noticed on my own.

I was having trouble breathing. Adam couldn't be gone. He *couldn't* be.

In the movies, when someone freezes because something terrible just happened, I always scoff. *Move your butt! The killer's still right behind you!* Or, *You still need to complete your quest, dummy!* I would never scoff again. Because, right then, I didn't know if I could take another step.

I heard a scraping sound from below and the bridge twisted. "Hey!"

My head snapped up. I tried to shout but nothing came out.

Blue was dancing. "Adam!" he yelled joyfully, waving his stick like an Olympic torch. "You're okay!"

"Yeah!" I could hear the strain in Adam's voice. "I lost my flashlight. I'm climbing up."

When I got to my feet, my knees almost buckled beneath me. I cleared my throat. "Blue! Grab one of the bridge's ropes, and I'll grab the other. Just in case this side breaks, too." I clutched at the line, wincing as the rough twine scraped against my palms.

After one agonizingly long moment, Adam's head poked out of the fog. He was climbing the bridge like a rope ladder. And he was almost to the top.

"Yay!" Blue cried. The words seemed to motivate Adam because he started moving faster, one hand over the other. I saw his knuckles were bloody. Finally, he pushed himself up with his elbows and rolled to safety.

"Yay!" Blue yelled again, throwing his stick in the air. It cracked me on the head as it came down.

"Ouch!" I rubbed my scalp but I couldn't have cared less. Adam was alive. I curled up next to where he lay on the ground and took his hand, lacing my fingers through his.

There was nothing to say. He could have died, and it would have been because of me.

"I made it." Adam sounded like he couldn't believe it. He stretched out his arm to look at his watch. "Holy cow," he panted. "Look at the time." He hoisted me to my feet. "Let's go."

TWO HOURS AND FIFTEEN MINUTES LEFT

Blue stood on tiptoe to see up the path. It was rocky, winding into thick woods. The branches were bare, outstretched like claws. Thick fog crawled out from the trees, twisting around our feet, daring us to enter.

Like a gentleman, Adam let me keep our last flashlight. I tried to turn it on but it wouldn't cooperate. I banged it on the ground. Nothing.

"Great," I muttered. After all that trouble carrying it across the bridge.

"I have something almost as good." Adam unzipped a pocket in his coat and pulled out a pack of matches. "Find me a big stick. One with some dead leaves."

I scanned the ground and saw a knobby branch. When I picked it up, though, I saw it was still green and remembered Adam's lecture when we'd made a campfire. Green would smoke, not catch fire. I grabbed another branch, one with scruffy, dry leaves, and handed it to Adam.

The first match didn't catch, but the second did. The red glow lit up Adam's face. It was dirty and a long scratch ran along his forehead. I raised my hand to my own face. I must look like a total mess. Not camera-friendly at all.

"How much farther, do you think?" Adam asked, and I screwed my eyes shut, trying to picture the Monsterville board.

"We're close. The troll comes right after the bridge when all the paths connect. And I remember being stuck on the troll spot and thinking that if I got lucky and rolled a six, I'd win the game."

"And the troll is the last monster we're up against?"

"Right." As I said it, our path met with another. This was where all four paths converged. We were almost to the troll.

Roots protruded from the pathway, and the trees grew so closely together they seemed to be pressing in on us. I smelled rotting wood and wet earth.

The monsters hadn't bothered with a sound effects tape here. The woods were silent—eerily silent—and the sky was pitch black. The only glow came from our makeshift torch.

"Do you think we should be using a light?" My

voice seemed loud—a sure way to make the monsters come running. "Someone might see us."

"I don't think we could find our way without it."

Adam was right. Even with the torch, I could barely make out the trail. We weaved around trees, ducked under branches, and climbed over a rotting trunk.

There was something weird about this setting. The bark didn't crumble off the trees the way it did in the woods in Freeburg. And there were no dead leaves to crunch through.

This place reminded me of the zoo. The animals' habitats all *looked* real, but were only imitations. I turned to Blue, who was clinging to my sleeve. "This is all fake, right?"

Adam stared into his torch. "I knew this was burning for too long. These leaves must be made out of something synthetic," he snorted. "Check it out. Down Below did us a favor."

The path twisted to the right, and I moved closer to Blue. "Watch out, guys. We just turned the corner."

This pathway was rockier, and I stubbed my toe. "Ouch!" I said as I stumbled.

Up ahead, a cluster of boulders blocked the path. We'd have to crawl over them to go any farther.

"Wait," I whispered. "This is the perfect spot for a troll."

Adam stopped, shifting the torch from one hand to the other. "What do we do? Just wait for him to come out?"

I shook my head. "We don't have time for that." Crouching, I ran my hands along the ground, gathering a handful of pebbles. "Hey!" I chucked one at the boulders. "Hey!"

Adam grabbed my arm. "What are you doing?"

"Waking up the troll."

"Are you sure that's a good idea?"

"I'd rather wake it up from fifteen feet away than accidentally crawl over its back."

"Good point." Adam picked up a pebble and chucked it at the cluster of boulders. It landed squarely on the middle one. The biggest one.

The one that was now moving.

We all froze. The boulder rose, dislodging two of the others. One hit the path and rolled away. The other split open like a melon. The troll unfolded itself and stretched, naked except for a loincloth. It looked like Tarzan. If Tarzan really let himself go.

"Urrrrrgh," it greeted us, scratching its matted hair.

Really, *really* let himself go.

I cleared my throat and stood up straighter. "Hi!" I flashed a smile. Just because this thing was the size of Upchuck's pickup, that didn't mean it was going to murder us.

"Hi!" Adam echoed. "Mind if we get through?"

The troll glared at us, narrowing its beady eyes. It sniffed the air with a nose that looked like a squashed tomato. Slowly, slowly, it shook its head, its wide mouth parting in a smile that revealed green, nubby teeth.

"This one's easy," I told Adam. "Check it out.

The troll won't sway, insists you pay
Three silver coins to make your way
But bargain yes, and you shall find
He's happy with a mere fruit rind."

When I was done, I nudged Adam. "Hear that? 'A mere fruit rind.' Give him something from your jacket. Trail mix, apple. Whatever's left."

Adam looked like he was in pain. "Umm . . ." He unzipped his jacket pockets and rummaged through them. "I don't think . . ."

"Oh, no," I whispered. "I just assumed . . ."

. . . that Adam, the Boy Scout, always had what we needed. The troll stumbled closer, each step making the ground quake. It exhaled a sour breath.

I grabbed Adam's and Blue's arms. "Step . . . back," I said through my teeth, my brain churning furiously for a solution.

"What do we do?" Adam asked. His face was pale in the the torch's glow. "What are trolls like?"

"Strong," I replied automatically. "Slow. Dumb. Hungry, always."

"I'm really sorry." Adam's voice was tight. "I should have rationed."

"Not your fault." I took another step back, wincing when a jagged rock pierced my heel.

The troll lunged at us, swiping at our feet with a giant, leathery hand. Then, in one jerky motion, it pulled Blue up by one foot, dangling him above the path.

"Lissa!" Blue squealed. "Help!"

The troll lifted Blue higher, sniffing him. It was the same way Mom checks out vegetables at the grocery store.

I couldn't bear to look, but I couldn't *not* look, either. The troll's neck muscles were thick cords, taut and bulging, as it examined the struggling Blue. It could open its mouth at any moment . . .

"Help!" Blue screamed again, twisting and thrashing in the troll's grasp. His face was turning the color of an eggplant.

I scanned the path, searching for . . . something. Something that could be a "mere fruit rind." But I saw nothing but dirt, trees, and rocks. Then I remembered. The Fruit Roll-Up! I hadn't finished the one Adam had given me earlier.

Thank you, apricot, for being the worst flavor ever. It was fate that I couldn't choke you down.

I shoved my hand into my pocket, pulling out the plastic wrapper. There wasn't much left. Would it be enough?

I held the scrap out, trying not to tremble. "Hey!" My voice rang loud and clear. "You want this?"

The troll's nostrils quivered. It raised its head and sniffed the air.

"Mmmm, apricot," I said, waving it around. "Don't you want it?"

The troll took a step closer. The ground vibrated, but I kept my cool. "Here." I nodded at Blue. "Trade, okay?"

The troll just looked at me with its dumb cow eyes. "I give you this. You give me that," I explained, pointing to Blue. The troll jerked its head up and down, and I stepped forward, extending the Fruit Roll-Up.

The troll swiped at the remnants of my snack at the same time that it dumped Blue on the ground. Adam dived to catch him.

I raised my palms at the troll to let it know I didn't have anything else. "All gone. See?" I would have talked the same way to Adam's dog.

The troll snorted and stuffed the Fruit Roll-Up in its mouth, swallowing it, wrapping and all. It smiled at me, the apricot sticking to its teeth.

"See you later," I told it, waving and grinning like crazy. If I acted like we were friends, it might be dumb enough to believe it.

The troll waved and smiled back.

Adam, Blue, and I scrambled down the rocky trail, walking backward so we could keep an eye on the troll.

Another monster rule—never turn your back on something that can eat you.

ONE HOUR AND FIFTY-FIVE MINUTES LEFT

When the troll was out of sight, Adam exhaled noisily. "That was amazing!" he told me. "Like David and Goliath."

"Something like that."

"I'm really sorry I didn't help back there. I can't believe I lost my backpack. How stupid could I be?"

"Are you kidding me?" I swiped at a branch blocking our path. "I'm the one who knew we'd have to face off against a troll. I should have remembered it needed to be fed."

"Yeah, but Boy Scouts are always supposed to be prepared!"

"Uh-huh. But did your handbook cover Down Below? Or getting your backpack stolen by a mummy?"

Adam kicked a rock. "I'm supposed to be ready for all scenarios."

Before I could reply, I heard crying. Blue was ahead of us, his shoulders shaking.

I ran to catch up. "Oh, Blue. I'm so sorry. Are you okay? Did the troll hurt you?"

Blue shook his head. "It's not that."

"What is it, then?"

He looked up with big, watery eyes. "I was just thinking about Haylie. How she has a big sister who'll come Down Below to save her." He dropped his chin. "No one came to save me," he said, so softly I almost couldn't hear him.

"Sure, they did," I told him, hugging him close. "They just looked in the wrong places."

Blue looked up. "What do you mean?"

"Well, no one knew to come Down Below. They thought you were somewhere Up There. Trust me, if they knew to come Down Below, they would have."

"When you disappeared," Adam added, "your picture was on the news every night for a month. And in the paper. And there were even helicopters searching for you."

"Helicopters? For me?" Blue snuffled.

"Yeah. And search parties and radio announcements and private investigators. They did everything they could. Everything."

"Okay," Blue said in a small voice, like he wasn't convinced.

Adam sucked in his breath. "Listen. Do you hear that?"

I closed my eyes. And suddenly, I did—tinny carnival music, far away. We'd made it.

"What does the game say we do now, Lissa?" Adam asked.

"Nothing. You just land on the tent and that's it. You win. Aunt Lucy's journal didn't say anything helpful, either. The only time she was in the Transformation Room was when she escaped from it."

"Huh." Adam blew air out from his mouth, unsatisfied with that answer. So was I.

As we crept forward, the music got louder. Not by much—the notes were delicate, light—like what you'd hear if you wound up a jack-in-the-box.

I only hoped that nothing would pop out of the bushes and eat us.

ONE HOUR AND FORTY-FIVE MINUTES LEFT

As soon as I thought about the bushes, I noticed the trail had changed, narrowing. Blue, Adam, and I had been able to walk side by side, but now we went single file. I led the way, holding Adam's torch.

"Ouch!" something sliced through my sock and into my heel.

"You okay?" Adam asked.

"I think so." I winced, lowering the light to squint at the ground. "I just . . . stepped on something." I didn't see a nail or a piece of broken glass glinting at me. We were surrounded by blades of grass. "I don't see anything, though."

I took another step. "Oh!" I gasped as the pain ripped through my foot. I froze, biting my lip and waiting for it to pass.

"What?" Adam asked.

"The grass," I hissed. "It's a barrier. Literally, *blades* of grass. The monster equivalent of a barbwire fence."

"Can we go around it?"

I raised the torch to see the trees, but they grew so close together they were like a fortress wall. Plus, I didn't like the idea of straying from the path.

"No," I finally replied. "The monsters planned it this way. The only way to avoid the grass is to go back."

No one said anything.

"I'll go first," Blue offered after a while. "My skin's tough. It might not bother me."

"Are you sure?" My feet throbbed like crazy, and I felt something warm running down my sole. Blood.

"Yep."

"Okay, fine," I said, angling myself so he could get around me. "But go fast!"

"Here I go!" Blue inhaled sharply and then took off across the grass, staying on the balls of his feet. He looked like he was hopping across hot coals. "Ow! Ow! Ow! Ow!" he chanted the entire time. About fifteen feet away, he stopped. "It's dirt now."

I looked at the grass. Walking across it would be like crossing a floor covered in broken glass. By the time I got to Blue, I wouldn't be able to walk, let alone save Haylie.

Adam seemed to be realizing the same thing. "Lissa, do you want to get on my back?"

I shook my head. "You can't carry that much

weight—the blades are so sharp they'll pierce right through your shoes."

"They're work boots. Good ones," Adam said, but I couldn't let him risk it. Not after everything he'd done for me already.

"Blue!" I called. "Can you find anything to throw across? Like maybe a log?"

"Be right back!" he replied. I winced at his choice of words.

As Adam and I waited for what felt like an eternity, I heard the tinkling carnival music of the Transformation Room calling to me. Taunting me. Haylie was right there, and I couldn't reach her. I gritted my teeth.

Footsteps approached through the darkness. Soon I could make out Blue's pointy ears.

He was carrying something—a tree that was at least six times his size, with leafy branches and a gnarled trunk. He tossed it over the grass, parallel to the path. "Come on! I'll hold my end so it doesn't roll."

I turned to Adam. "You first. You had to go last on the bridge." I crouched and pulled at the branches protruding from the top. Since the leaves were synthetic, I could grab them without ripping them.

Normally, Adam would have tried to argue, but we were burning night-light. He hopped onto the makeshift bridge and stretched his arms out for balance.

"Okay," he said, psyching himself up. A second later, he took off, moving so confidently that I didn't worry about him falling, not even for a moment. He jumped down to the dirt on the other side.

Adam's self-assuredness gave me courage. I crawled onto the tree and stood up, my feet stinging from where the blades had sliced them. I teetered before gaining my balance. Staring straight ahead, I took a deep breath.

With one step, I almost lost it. My legs shook and I sat back down on the trunk.

"Don't worry about looking good!" Adam called. "If you can't balance, walk sideways and take little steps. Or just sit and scoot."

I exhaled, frustrated. Haylie was waiting for me. I couldn't afford to take my sweet time.

I stood again, turning sideways and taking tiny, jerking steps to inch across the log. I ignored the pain that washed over me. *Pick up the pace*, I told myself.

I was almost there. This was pretty easy! I looked up from my feet to glance at Blue, who was crouched on the other side, frowning in concentration as he held the log, making sure it didn't roll and tip me over.

Then, the second before I was going to jump for the ground, I slipped.

"Ah!" I screamed as I fell, stretching my hands to catch myself. Needle-sharp blades of grass sliced right through the bandages on my palms, then my right knee, as I hit the ground. I almost passed out from the pain.

"Oh!" I gasped as Adam leaned over and lifted me up by my armpits. He dumped me on the dirt, breathing heavily.

I curled up in a ball. Everything hurt—my hands where they'd broken my fall, my right knee where I'd kneeled, the soles of my feet. I felt nauseous, and tears were welling up in my eyes. *How on earth can I walk?*

Then Adam was above me, removing his jacket and tearing off the sleeve of his T-shirt. "Give me your hands."

I held them out, trembling. Adam untied my mangled wrappings, then ripped a sleeve in half and tied a strip around each of my palms. "There. That'll hold better than what you had before." He sighed. "It looks like it hurts. Can you walk?"

I crawled to my feet. My right knee felt like it was on fire, but that was nothing compared to my feet. "I can. But I'm going to be slow."

Gently, Adam took my arm and put it across the back of his shoulders, supporting me. "That's going to have to do."

ONE HOUR AND FIFTEEN MINUTES LEFT

The path ended in a huge clearing. Short grass covered the ground, and I wrinkled my nose as I kneeled to touch it gently. It was fake, but not deadly.

We circled the clearing from the safety of the trees. I was limping, my socks shredded to ribbons. "There it is," I whispered. "See?"

Up ahead, sitting off-center, was a bright purple circus tent. It was at least two stories high, extending hundreds of feet in diameter. And it glowed.

"Whoa. That looks . . . alien," I said.

"That's just the light coming from the inside. The tent is transluscent so it shines through."

We moved closer, trying to keep to the shadows at the edge of the woods. The tent was tethered to the ground with wooden stakes. A gravel path lined with tiki lamps led to an open flap. The lamps cast a cheerful glow that reminded me of Haylie's night-light. Voices and laughter carried from the tent.

I set my jaw. This was all a trick—an illusion of safety and comfort to prevent the monsters' captives from wondering what was going on. Until it was too late.

It wasn't just Haylie being tricked, either. I'd been so focused on saving my little sister that I hadn't thought about the other kids. Even if we saved Haylie, we couldn't save all the others. Some of them—most of them—would be left behind.

Now, I really, truly understood Aunt Lucy's guilt, her obsession with Down Below, and why she'd designed Monsterville. She couldn't forgive herself for leaving the other kids behind.

I didn't think I could forgive myself, either.

"I hate to say this," Adam said, glancing at his watch, "but we only have a little over an hour until sunrise." He swallowed. "I think, well—"

All along, even though I'd known we didn't have much time, that we might not get back before dawn, that risk had never felt *real*. But now it did.

"I failed," I said numbly. "Even if we get to Haylie in time, then what? How do we get back before sunup? This is all my fault."

"No, it isn't," Blue replied instantly.

"Yeah, don't be so hard on yourself," Adam added.

I shook my head. "I *should* be hard on myself. I knew Haylie was in danger, and I didn't protect her. What kind of a sister am I?"

"You're a great one. *This wasn't your fault.* Now come on—we need to focus." Adam squinted at the tent. "How do we do this?"

"We need a distraction," I said. "We can't just go in there and take her." I turned to Blue. "Do you remember anything specific about Transformation? What it looks like inside there? What you were doing?"

Blue shifted from one foot to the other, chewing his lower lip. "Not really. There were a lot of lights. And lots of things to do . . ." He puffed out his mouth. "I think there were balloon animals. And face-painting."

"They wanted to keep you guys happy until dawn," Adam said. "That makes sense. Give you all sorts of fun things to do so you wouldn't ask why you were there."

"If there's so much going on in the tent, we might be able to sneak in," I said. But I wasn't really sold on the idea. It didn't seem smart to barge in without knowing the setup. And we couldn't waste time on half-baked ideas.

Adam was staring at one of the long ropes that tethered the tent to the ground. "You know," he said slowly, "I bet we could make this tent come down."

"Saw at the ropes, you mean?"

He nodded. "I still have my two knives—the Swiss and the pocketknife."

My mind raced. "Okay, that'll be our distraction. But how do we get Haylie out?" I glanced at the tent's open flap. There was shadowy movement and an occasional flash of light, but not much else.

Suddenly a firecracker flew from the opening, exploding in a shower of purples and pinks. Cheers and clapping erupted from inside.

"Seems like a great party," I said grimly. And then it hit me. "A party!" I repeated, whacking Adam on the back with my elbow.

"Ow!"

"That's how we get in. We bring something amazing to the party. Something to draw Haylie out."

"Like what?" Adam looked around the dark woods.

"Not what. *Who.*" I stared at Blue.

"Me?" he asked nervously.

"What do you have in mind?" Adam looked worried.

"Well, *I* can't go in there. The second Haylie spots me, she'll react."

"Yeah, I think you're right," Adam said.

"But if *Blue* shows up in disguise," I continued, "she'll follow him out without attracting attention. No screaming about how excited she is to see him." I touched Blue's arm. "Can you do that?" I asked him anxiously. "Change into something besides a monster?"

"I think so," Blue said uncertainly.

I gazed into his eyes and smiled, looking as confident as possible. "You're going to be great. I know you are." Blue needed to know that we completely, absolutely believed in him.

"What should I change into?"

I glanced at the tent. Assuming that the best kids' party in the world was going on in there, what would it be missing?

I smiled. "Blue, I need you to change into . . . a unicorn!"

"A unicorn?"

"A pink one. Glittery. With fairy wings. Haylie loves that stuff. Anything pink, or glittery, or sparkly—she's totally onboard. And if you're a horse . . . do you know what you do with horses?"

"You ride them?"

"Yes!" I whispered happily. "You ride them." *Thank you, Candice.* I never would have thought of the horse idea without her. "You need to come—*prance* into that tent—and leave with Haylie on your back. And any other kids you can get up there. Got it?"

"Prance," Blue repeated.

"You can do it." I placed my bandaged hands on his bony shoulders. "If you can be a zombie, and a

Sasquatch, and a swamp monster, you can totally handle prancing."

Adam hooted, softly. "Yes, you can. And while you're doing that, we'll be taking this baby down." He made a sawing motion.

"Okay." I turned to Blue. "Curtain's up! You ready?"

Blue stuck his fingers into his mouth and stared into space, like he was trying to solve a hard math problem. Then he removed his fingers and his brow cleared. "Ready."

The change was quick. A pinkish hue lit Blue's skin and then deepened. He dropped to all fours, his arms and legs lengthening into four gangly legs with purple-tipped hooves. A luxurious purple mane sprouted from his head, followed by a yellow horn.

Slowly, Blue's skin began to shine, then glitter like he'd been rolled in tiny diamonds. Sparkly yellow wings unfolded from his back.

"So?" He pawed the ground uncertainly. "Is this good enough?"

"Wow." I clapped my hands together before I realized how much it would hurt. "Ow. You are the prettiest thing I've ever seen. No offense," I added quickly when he glowered at me. He even had long lashes! "Haylie will love you."

Blue tossed his mane. "Thank you. Any tips?"

I shook my head. "Nope. Just sashay in there, get

Haylie, and get out of there. Oh, and kick Atticus if you see him."

"Oh, Haylie will need a ride. I should probably lose these." The sparkly wings disappeared from his back. "Maybe this is better." A multi-seat, pink saddle appeared in their place.

"Smart," I said.

"We need a signal," Adam said. "When you get Haylie outside, whinny as loud as you can."

"Then what?" I asked.

"Then we'll cut the last rope and topple the tent. We'll all meet back here. This'll be our marker." Adam reached into his jacket pocket and pulled out a roll of orange tape. He fastened a strip around a tree branch and patted it into place.

"Good luck," I whispered, touching Blue gently on the nose. He neighed and trotted off toward the tent, disappearing through the open flap with a flick of his purple tail.

SCENE TWELVE:

FORTY MINUTES LEFT

"Come on," Adam said. "It's gonna take some elbow grease to make this thing collapse."

We raced along the edge of the trees, eyeing the ropes. There were at least twenty of them, all as thick as my arm, and stretching from grounded wooden stakes to different locations on the tent—some at the top, some in the middle.

Other than the glow from within the tent, it was completely dark. The pathway with tiki lamps wasn't visible from where we hid. Only a handful of fake stars dotted the sky, and they seemed dull. Maybe they were running out of juice.

"Here." Adam shoved something small and metal into my hand. "My pocketknife. It isn't much, but it'll work."

"Thanks," I mumbled. He'd already flipped the blade open for me. I watched him disappear into the dark.

I began sawing at the rope in front of me, gritting my teeth against my throbbing palms. They would've hurt way more if I wasn't hyped up on adrenaline.

Soon my hands were slick with sweat even under the tatters of Adam's shirt, and I'd only sawed halfway through the first anchor.

To my right, I heard Adam's footsteps as he raced to another rope. At least one of us was useful. I tried to move my blade faster, but it felt like using a butter knife on tough steak.

Finally, only one strand remained. "Come on, come on," I chanted, sawing faster.

The last strand broke. I held my breath as the rope went flying, smacking softly against the side of the tent. The wall tilted very slightly, and I scrambled to my feet and ran blindly through the dark, to the next line.

Adam was crouched about thirty feet away, hacking away with his Swiss Army knife. I could hear him sawing in time to the tinny music. Every once in a while, laughter drowned out the carnival notes—the high, happy sound of kids having fun.

I settled in front of another rope and started cutting. This one was easier—the rope was thinner. Or maybe I was just fueled by rage and desperation. I forgot all about my cuts and how dull the knife was. I just hacked away until it frayed and went flying. Then I was up and running again, hobbling on my left leg.

How many ropes were there? If we were a quarter of the way around and had taken care of five, then maybe twenty? Twenty-two?

I crouched next to another line, but I hurt too much. Footsteps padded toward me, and Adam's breath was warm in my ear. "Just do this one and then run to the other side, okay? I have an idea." He placed a hand on my shoulder before disappearing.

I frowned, concentrating on the rope in front of me. This one was tougher and it took me a few seconds to cut into it. I moved the blade clumsily, my fingers throbbing. My ears were pricked the entire time, waiting for Blue's signal.

The rope gave and smacked against the side of the tent. Done! I rose on shaky legs and ran to where Adam waited on the other side.

"All the ropes on that side are cut," he whispered. "If we take one rope on this side, and pull it hard, this whole thing should fall."

"When should we pull? At Blue's signal?"

"You got it. The second we hear it, jump and grab that one." He pointed at a rope directly in front of us—a long, thick one stretching all the way from the ground to the top of the tent.

A long, low whinny sounded from across the clearing.

"Now!" Adam shouted, grabbing the rope and yanking it.

With a running leap, my fingers closed around the taut cord. I gritted my teeth as the cuts on my hands burned, tucking my legs to apply more weight to the rope.

In a few seconds, the agony had shifted from my hands to my feet. The rope sagged, and my knees grazed the ground. "Adam! The tent!"

We stared as it rippled and fluttered. Angry cries came from inside, and the music halted mid-song.

"Go, Lissa! Go, go, go, go, go!"

We took off, giving the tent a wide berth. Out of the corner of my eye, I saw it collapsing. Call me crazy, but it reminded me of an imploding birthday cake— lazily tilting to the right, fluttering and flattening over the ground.

I could see the outline of horns and heads and hands as the monsters tried to punch their way out, their screams muffled by the heavy canvas.

Up ahead, Blue was waiting at the edge of the trail, still in adorable unicorn form. It had been a good call to make him glittery. He was like a beacon.

I sighed in relief when I saw Haylie perched on his back, her fingers clutching his purple mane. She was really there. And she was okay. Three other kids sat behind her, but I was too far away to see them clearly.

"Lissy!" Haylie cried from across the field. All happy, like I was picking her up from an hour at the playground. I raced to her, my breath coming in gasps. It took me a second to realize I wasn't out of breath because I was tired. It was because I was crying.

SCENE THIRTEEN:

THIRTY MINUTES LEFT

I stood on my tiptoes to lift Haylie from Blue's back, not caring how much it hurt my hands. Her blonde hair was tousled and her pajamas were wrinkled, but she seemed fine. Not even scared. She was even still clutching her fairy wand.

I hugged her tightly. "Let's go home," I said into her hair, and I was shocked to realize that I thought of Freeburg as "home."

She pulled away. "Not now! There's a surprise! And cotton candy!"

"Haylie, you need to listen to me, okay? Those monsters in there"—I pointed to the tent, where some of the monsters were stumbling out—"are not your friends. They're bad. *Really* bad. Like I told you tonight." *Last night.* Gosh, that felt like forever ago.

Confusion knitted Haylie's forehead. "They are?"

"Yes. Just trust me. The cotton candy, the games— all of it—it's a trick."

"They wouldn't do that. They're my friends."

"They're not your friends." I swallowed. I didn't want to scare her. "They've hurt Blue. And if we stay, they'll hurt you, too."

"They hurt *Blue*?" It was like a thundercloud had descended. Her eyes narrowed, and she clutched her wand in her fist.

"Yes. So we need to get away. *Now*."

"Okay," Haylie said. "Let's go home."

One of the other kids heard her, a red-haired girl with big green eyes. "Home? I want to go home."

"Me, too," echoed the two girls sitting behind her, and I pulled away from Haylie to look at them. They both had brown hair and sleepy eyes.

"My name's Lissa. I'm Haylie's big sister. What are your names?"

"Amy," the red-haired girl said.

"I'm Emma," said one of the brown-haired girls. The other kept her mouth clamped shut. "That's Sadie," Emma whispered.

"Nice to meet everyone," I said quickly, lifting Haylie from Blue's back and setting her on the ground. "But we really don't have t—"

Before I could finish, something barreled from the tent, a huge ball rolling toward us like a runaway snowball. It stopped close enough for us to smell its putrid stench as it unfurled into a green, gangly monster at least seven feet tall. Even with its hunchback.

It was wearing a party hat that cast a shadow over its face. All I could make out was a pointy chin and drool dripping from yellow fangs.

"Atticus." Blue whinnied, rearing up, and Atticus grabbed his reins.

"Welcome home. Allow me to show you to the party."

"You let go of him!" Adam screamed, raising his fists. But before he could move another muscle, Atticus put a clawed hand on the center of his face and pushed. Adam flew ten feet before colliding with a tree.

"Adam!" I yelled.

"You!" Haylie screamed, glaring up at Atticus. In the dim light, my adorable little sister's face looked almost demented. "You hit Adam!"

She raised her wand and brought it down on Atticus's bare foot. As it pierced his skin, green slime spurted from the wound. It was just like the stuff they use at the Nickelodeon Kids' Choice Awards. Atticus roared, letting go of the reins.

"And this is for Blue!" This time, the wand got his other foot. Man, Haylie was *lethal*! The wand stuck, like a flag claiming territory of a new country.

I was impressed, but not *totally* surprised. In rescue missions in the movies, it's not unusual for the person being saved to pull her own weight in sticky situations.

"Let's go!" I screamed, running to help Adam up. "You okay?"

He shook his head. "Just a little dazed. I'll be fine. Now what?"

I glanced at Atticus, who was climbing to his feet, a murderous look in his eyes.

"We need a shortcut. We don't have enough time."

"Can we ride the waterslide?" Haylie piped up.

"She's right! There's a waterslide. A huge shortcut. Follow me!" I cried, tearing off to the far right trail.

Please, please let this be the right one, I thought to myself. What if I was wrong? We'd be dead as soon as Atticus and the rest of his monster horde caught up with us.

A branch smacked me in the face and I angrily pushed it away. Jagged rocks cut into my feet, but my pace never slowed. Now that we had a plan—and Haylie—I could handle the pain. I flew down the path at record speed.

Then I heard it. Running water! The current made a sucking sound like it was going into a culvert, and I veered off the path toward the noise, fighting my way through branches and brush.

SCENE FOURTEEN:

TWENTY-SIX MINUTES LEFT

I stumbled and fell into a shallow pool of freezing water, accidentally dropping Haylie's hand for a second before finding it again. "Don't leave my side, okay?" I instructed her. She nodded.

A line of gray rocks jutted up from the ground, forming a semicircle around a frothy whirlpool—Down Below's version of a waterslide.

"You three—in the hole!" I screamed as Adam hoisted the final girl off Blue's back. I felt mean doing it, but I shoved the girls we had rescued into the water. "I know this is scary, but I promise you'll be safe." I pushed them down the waterslide, wincing at the sound of their terrified screams.

I grabbed Haylie's hand. "Just like at Wet Willy's, remember?" I plopped down, shifted her onto my lap, and pushed off. I barely registered the freezing water that sloshed above my waist.

"Ahhhhhhhhhhhhhhh!!!!" The scream tore from my mouth as we plummeted down, and my stomach dipped.

The current swirled around us, shooting us around curves so fast my head was spinning. At one point, I swore we were actually moving *up*, but it was pitch black and I couldn't see a thing beyond the dim outline of Haylie.

Then we were spiraling down again in one long loop like the world's biggest crazy straw. I kept my mouth clamped shut just in case the turns and twists were too much for my stomach. I loved roller coasters, but this took "thrill ride" to a whole new level.

"You okay?" I murmured into Haylie's hair, but she must not have heard me over the rushing water. I was probably gripping her too tight, but that was okay.

The slide veered to the right at such a sharp angle that the left side of my butt lifted off the base. "Hold on," I gasped, half to myself, half to Haylie.

I hoped Adam had made it down the slide before the monsters got there. How much time had Haylie's wand attack bought us? There hadn't been much ground for Atticus to make up.

Water swished around us as we shot straight forward. Suddenly, the cold hit me, the icy water like knives against my skin. I clamped my mouth shut to keep my teeth from chattering.

With a lurch, the slide ended and we were airborne. I lost my grip on Haylie, flailing in the dark. What had I done? What if there was nothing beneath us but jagged rocks? Or sharp sticks? Or—

I belly flopped so hard I heard the *smack* when I hit the surface, and I forgot the pain in my hands and feet for a second.

"Haylie? Haylie!" I screamed, groping in the dark. Water was still gushing from the slide, and I caught a mouthful. It tasted like pennies.

"I'm here." There was a soft touch on my right shoulder, and I reached to drag her away from the waterfall, kicking my legs to stay afloat.

TWENTY-ONE MINUTES LEFT

Twisting to take in my surroundings, I realized the pool was no more than twenty feet wide. The other little girls were clinging to the side, too small to pull themselves out. At least they looked unharmed. Physically, at least.

"I'll help you!" I called to them. "Haylie? Can you crawl on my back? Like a piggyback ride, only swimming?"

"Sure," she said, and I positioned myself so she could wrap her arms around me.

"Hold on tight!" I kept my voice cheerful so Haylie would stay calm.

I glanced at the water pouring out of the slide. Adam and Blue had been right behind us, right?

Paddling to the side of the pool, I twisted so Haylie could pull herself out of the water. I followed, straining to use only my forearms and elbows to avoid opening the wounds on my palms again. At least the cold numbed the pain.

I crouched to help the other girls. Their hair was plastered to their faces, and their lips were blue. I hoped they didn't get sick. Not every little kid was as resilient as Haylie. "You were all so brave!" I said brightly. "I bet that's the bravest thing anyone's ever done."

Discreetly, I checked my watch. Twenty minutes until we all became monsters.

"Wh-wh-where are we?" Amy asked. Her teeth were chattering so much she almost couldn't get the words out.

Good question. Where were we? A huge pile of trash framed the area to my right.

Are we back where we started?

"Almost home," I said. *Almost home.*

Emma smiled. "Detroit?"

"Errr, sure." I crouched down and looked into their small, scared faces.

The water kept pouring out of the slide. It was like someone had opened a floodgate. *Where are Blue and Adam?*

I wrapped my arms around myself. My fingers were numb and my wet clothes felt like frost against my skin.

"Lissy?" Haylie's voice was soft. "I'm cold."

"I know, Hails." I put an arm around her, drawing her against me. Her teeth chattered and her skin was turning blue. "We'll be out of here in just a minute." I only hoped that was true.

"Where are Blue and Adam?"

"They'll be here in a second," I said to reassure myself as much as Haylie. "Hey, let's play a game. Let's count to ten, and by ten, I'll bet Adam and Blue come shooting out of the slide."

"That's not a game," Emma scoffed.

"Well, it's something to do while we wait, okay?"

"Okay."

"One," we counted, our breath coming out in puffs. "Two. Three. Four. Fi—"

A terrified wail echoed from the tube, giving me even more goose bumps. I hugged Haylie tighter.

Adam shot out of the bottom of the slide, hitting the water with a spectacular belly flop. More freezing water sprayed me.

He didn't move, and I jumped to my feet. I was about to leap in when he lifted his head and started swimming away from the torrent. He turned his head to spit out a mouthful of water.

Before he made it to the side, a high-pitched scream came from the tube and Blue shot out. He landed only about a foot from Adam's head, slipping under the surface and bobbing up again.

"Come on," Adam spluttered. "Get on my back."

Blue wrapped his arms around Adam's neck. Huge

circles ringed his eyes and there were scratches on his bare arms. He rested his face against Adam's neck while Adam dog-paddled to us.

"What took you so long?" I reached to help Blue climb onto the bank.

"Nice to see you, too." Adam hoisted himself out of the water.

"I didn't mean it like that. I thought the monsters got you!"

Adam grinned. "We stopped to cover the water-slide with a tree branch. It'll take them at least a few minutes to clear it."

"Won't they just rip it off?"

"It's jammed in there nice and tight."

"Buying us some time—thanks."

Speaking of time . . . I glanced at my watch, and my heart sank. After six o'clock.

"Where to now?" Adam asked.

"I don't know. This looks like where we came in. We're close . . ."

"Well, let's motor." He held out his hands. "Who wants to come with me?"

Blue was already leading the way. Silently, Emma took one of his hands, and Amy took the other.

Adam turned and hurried around the huge pile of garbage. I followed, dragging Haylie and Sadie with me.

SCENE SIXTEEN:

SIXTEEN MINUTES LEFT

When we turned the corner, I recognized the open area from the beginning of the night. Only now, the piles of junk had shrunk, picked over by monsters. A few stragglers remained, making the rounds of the leftovers. Talk about the world's weirdest flea market.

Adam stopped suddenly. "Great. This all looks the same."

"Well, let's look for something we recognize." I tried not to grip the girls' hands too hard. *What if we're too late?*

Then I saw it. Sticking out of one of the piles.

"The umbrella!"

"What?" Blue asked.

I pointed. "I remember seeing that. Right across from where we came in! I was thinking how out of place it was." Thank goodness there was no sun or rain Down Below and the monsters had no use for umbrellas.

"You're right," Adam said. "You found a marker!"

"A marker?"

"Remember? Same thing we used so we'd know where to meet with Blue?"

"Oh, yeah." Had I picked up some Boy Scout skills during this crazy adventure?

"I want it," Haylie said, struggling to wrench the umbrella from the pile.

I didn't have time to argue with her. I grabbed it and hit the button to close it. "Here." I pulled her and Sadie into the dark tunnel we'd left from the beginning of our journey. Willing myself to run, faster and faster, I tried to ignore the rocks cutting into my feet.

"You're going too fast!" Sadie complained.

"Not fast enough. Just a minute more," I wheezed, wincing as something sliced into my foot. If we ever got out of here, I was going to need a tetanus shot.

"There it is!" Blue cried. "That's where we came in!"

FOURTEEN MINUTES LEFT

Up ahead, a rectangular glow came from the top of the tunnel. The bottom of Haylie's bed?

"You first," I told Adam. "You're the biggest. We need to boost you up."

Adam hesitated, and I shook my head. "Adam, this isn't the time to be chivalrous. The whole 'ladies first' thing doesn't apply in Monsterville."

"It's not that," he said. "It's the journal: *Undo it by leaving the exact same way you came.* . . . Could it be referring to . . . Transformation? Is that what she's talking about undoing?"

Blue looked from me to Adam, then back to me. He shook his head. "We don't have time to figure it out."

Adam looked at his watch. "We have thirteen minutes."

I closed my eyes. "It makes sense that she meant reversing Transformation. The whole journal was devoted to saving kids from Down Below. *Leaving the exact same way you came.* How had Blue come?"

My eyes flew open. "Blue came Down Below from under *his* bed." I shook Adam's shoulder. "On Halloween! This is our chance to undo his transformation." I whirled on Blue. "Where's your bed? Do you remember?"

"No." He played with his tail. "But it should be down the same trail since it's in the same town as yours. And if we find it, it'll be glowing."

We were cutting it close. I looked at the small, dirty faces clustered around me. Six human, one monster. If we looked for Blue's portal, and we didn't find it in time, Down Below would claim six more monsters.

I was torn. Then Haylie spoke up. "I want us *all* to go home!"

We didn't even make the decision aloud. Adam and I gripped the girls' hands tighter and we raced down the trail, farther into the darkness. Even without a flashlight, we found our footing. I counted my steps. Fifty, then a hundred . . .

"Look at that!" Adam cried. "Up ahead. Is that—?"

"It's light! And it's blue! That's my portal." Blue sounded like he couldn't believe it.

"Up! Up! Up!" I screamed.

Blue laced his hands together to make a step. Adam stuck his foot in and Blue boosted him up. When Adam hit the ceiling of the tunnel, he went through with a sucking sound, his body disappearing on the other side.

"The girls next," Blue said, and one by one he picked them up and pushed them through the rectangular light.

But the light was fading.

"Hurry, Blue," I moaned.

Just as he moved to help me up, a low chuckling sound rumbled behind us. "You don't want to stay with us?"

I whirled around. Standing there was a gangly, hunchbacked monster—Atticus, appearing for the final showdown. He'd removed his party hat.

SCENE EIGHTEEN:

EIGHT MINUTES LEFT

I stepped forward as Blue shrank behind me. "Get away from us!"

Atticus cocked his head like he was amused. "Why would I do that?"

"There are two of us and one of you. Don't make us hurt you!"

"How cute—a threat." Atticus moved closer, frowning at me like he was trying to solve a puzzle. In the light, he was even more hideous than he'd been near the Transformation Room, his greenish skin covered in lumpy warts and moles.

"You think it's just a threat?" I taunted. "How are your feet feeling?"

"A bit of pain. But nothing compared to what you'll feel . . . very soon."

"Ooooh, I'm *so scared*." I wouldn't show him that I was terrified.

With one more step, Atticus was less than a foot

away, his eyes studying me. "Why do you look so familiar? Have you invaded here before?"

"Excuse me—*invaded*? You stole my sister! And, no, I haven't had the pleasure." I glanced at the light narrowing above me.

"You remind me of someone," Atticus mused, his green eyes meeting mine. His jaw sagged. "It can't be!"

"What?"

"Don't you remember me?" He sounded as whiny as Haylie when she's tired and hungry.

At first I thought he was crazy, or playing some kind of game, but then a flash of realization hit me.

I left him! How could I do that? From now on, every time I see green eyes, I'll think of him. . . .

"Oh," I whispered. "You were taken with Aunt Lucy, weren't you?"

"Lucy?" he said sharply.

"I know. I look like her. She—"

He stepped forward and gripped my arm, his fingernails digging into my skin. Blue shrank back even more, and I used the umbrella to block him from Atticus's reach. "Back off!" I yelled, but Atticus wasn't listening.

"She escaped without a thought for me," he hissed.

"That's not true!" I tried to wriggle away. "I found her journal. She thought about you every day."

"Thought? Why did she stop thinking about me?" he snarled.

"Well," I gasped as he tightened his grip, "she died."

Atticus released me. "She died?" He looked more shocked than sad.

"Yeah. I mean . . . she was old. She had a long life."

His shock turned into smug satisfaction. "She escaped from Down Below and lived a normal life. No glory, no fame—nothing. And here, *I'm* in charge of North American Transformation. *I* have glory. *I* have fame. And I live forever!"

Talk about bad dialogue. Obviously, Atticus was more than a little power hungry. "That's great." I looked into his eyes. There was nothing human there. But I still felt a little bad for him. What turned him into this?

I had no time to waste being sorry, though. I glanced up at the fading light. "You know what you *don't* have?"

"What?"

"An umbrella!" I shoved the tip into his bony stomach, and opened it. Atticus stumbled and landed hard on his back.

"Guys! Look above you!"

I glanced up at the sound of Adam's voice and saw a blue sheet decorated with cartoon astronauts. "Blue! Grab on!" I screamed.

Blue grasped a corner of the sheet and rose in the air, his feet dangling. "Yes!" I cheered, jumping to grab his legs. But instead of staying still so Adam could pull us both up, Blue flailed and kicked me in the jaw.

"Oh!" I fell heavily, my forehead cracking against the rocky ground. Blood trickled into my eyes. Blue vanished through the portal and the sheet descended again. My lifeline.

As I struggled to stand, the ground shook. Was this the end? Had dawn come, and I was transforming? Would I look down at myself and see long, gnarled limbs and translucent skin?

Atticus grinned. "Not long now." I almost expected him to gleefully rub his hands together.

Metal bars jutted out of the rocky ground to surround me. They rose quickly, and in no time at all, they were ten feet in the air and had joined together. The ground below me smoothed into a metal floor. I was trapped in a giant cage.

Clutching the bars, I shook them, not even feeling the pain in my hands anymore. "Let me out!" I screamed.

"Obviously, no," Atticus said. He studied me, his head cocked to one side. "At least not for a few minutes. Not until it's too late."

I looked around wildly for a way to escape—a latch or a broken bar or a padlock. My mind whirred. This was the classic death-trap scenario, like in *Live and Let Die,* where James Bond gets away because the villain takes his sweet time lowering him into shark-infested waters.

When a movie has a death-trap scenario, the hero always finds a way out. If that wasn't true, *Austin Powers* wouldn't have spoofed it. There had to be a way out for me, too.

"You could be the better person, you know," I told Atticus, my head swimming from my new cut. I wiped blood off my forehead. "If you let me go."

"I'm not a person anymore," he reminded me.

"Yes, you are. Just not on the outside."

Maybe I could inspire a villain speech. That's when the villain goes on and on about how smart he is, and why he did what he did, and blah, blah, blah . . . giving his victim enough time to loosen his bonds or unlock his handcuffs or or wriggle from his ropes.

"No," Atticus said, his green eyes hard. "I'm a monster now, thanks to your aunt only worrying about herself."

"Come on, could she really have saved you?" I knew arguing with Atticus wasn't a good idea, but I didn't have a better one.

"Maybe!"

"Maybe. Or would you have preferred you *both* stayed monsters? That seems pretty selfish." I eyed the top of my cage. The sheet poked through the bars. I resisted the urge to grab it. I'd never fit through the bars.

"Lissa!" Adam called to me, faintly.

The light above had narrowed even more. It was just a thin sliver. Desperately, I eyed the sheet, thinking about when this all began. When I got Adam to rig a trap to catch a monster.

My mouth went dry. Could the beginning to all of this also be the ending? I remembered Adam's scornful words when I asked him if a Sasquatch would break his snare.

Of course it won't. I used a clove hitch. As long as Adam braced himself against something and pulled hard . . .

I jumped, grabbing the sheet. "Not yet!" I yelled to Adam. Frantically, I tied the sheet around the top of the cage, using the clove hitch Adam had taught me months ago. It *had* to stay. Then I scrambled up the side of the cage, my palms slippery with blood and sweat. Somehow, I managed to hang from the top, like a kid on the monkey bars. I was less than two feet from the portal.

"Now!" I screamed, my chest burning.

The cage didn't budge.

"Again! As hard as you can!"

The cage tipped to one side and lifted a few feet into the air. Not good enough.

"Again!" Tears poured down my face. Whether they were from pain, exhaustion, terror, or a mix of all three, I couldn't be sure.

The entire cage rose in the air, swaying and shifting. I gritted my teeth, straining to keep my hold on the bars.

"No!" Atticus leapt, but he couldn't reach it. He grasped the metal bars, but he was no match for Adam.

As the cage rose into the portal's glow, I felt myself passing through. This time, it didn't feel like I was going through a too-small plastic tube. It felt like being mangled in a juicer. I squeezed my eyes shut and sucked in my breath.

"Got you!" Adam cheered. I opened my eyes and groped around, feeling wood and the grit of dust beneath my fingertips. I'd been right. As soon as the cage hit Up There, it had disappeared.

Strong hands pulled me, sliding me across the floor.

I blinked. I was out from under a bed. A tall bookshelf filled with bright hardback books stood against the far wall. Haylie had helped herself to one and was sitting cross-legged on the shiny hardwood floor, studying the pictures. The other little girls sat next to her, huddled together and blinking.

And Adam! He was kneeling, looking dazed, staring at a small blonde figure standing quietly next to the nightstand. Colin.

"I'm home," Colin whispered, his huge brown eyes scanning the dim room. "There's my train." He pointed to a circle of tracks across the room. "And my Transformer!" He raced across the room and snatched a toy from a wooden shelf.

As I looked around the room, I choked up. It looked like Colin's parents had kept it exactly like when he'd disappeared. They'd never given up hope that he would come home.

Haylie abandoned her book and stepped toward him, putting her hands on her hips so she could examine him. "You're cute," she announced.

Tears spurted to my eyes, and I let out a half laugh, half cry.

"Look, Adam. It's dawn. We made it."

He glanced at the closed door. "Any second now, that door's going to open. And we're going to have a lot of explaining to do."

I crossed the room, stopping where he was now standing by the window. "I can't get over it. Without you, I would have lost Haylie. And Colin would still be a monster." I gestured to the room. "This room would have stayed like this forever." Another lump formed in my throat.

Adam shook his head. "Nah . . ."

"It's true," I insisted. "You risked everything for us. I can't believe you did that. You didn't have to."

"Yeah, I did. I mean"—Adam wasn't looking at me—"I'd do anything for you."

I grabbed both sides of his face, and pulled him to me in a truly movie-worthy kiss. Only I was missing my shoes and my hair looked like a rat's nest and we both totally smelled from our adventure in Down Below.

It wasn't really all that Hollywood. But here's a secret. Sometimes a real kiss is better.

Footsteps sounded outside the door, and a man's tough voice made us jump apart. "Hello? I heard voices! If anyone's in there, you're gonna regret it!"

We all froze. Colin's eyes went the widest I'd ever seen them go. "Daddy," he whispered, his voice cracking.

The door flung open and a man in blue pajama bottoms and a T-shirt stood there clutching a baseball bat in his rough hands. Hands that looked like they worked in an auto shop. When he saw Colin, the color drained from his face and he dropped the bat.

"Honey?" came a voice behind him. "Is everything okay?" A woman with blonde hair peeked over his shoulder. She looked uncertainly at me before her eyes landed on Colin. Her hands flew to her mouth as she let out a strangled cry.

Colin's parents flew across the room. The man scooped Colin up in his arms, tears rolling down his

344

cheeks as he held his son for the first time in a year. The woman stroked her son's hair, sobbing like the world had ended.

It hadn't. Colin was their whole world, and they'd just gotten him back.

CURTAIN CALL

In the movies, when a main character risks her life to save her loved ones, she always comes out looking hot. Maybe she'll have some dirt on her forehead and her hair will be wild and crazy, but her eye makeup will still look perfect.

But this wasn't a movie, and I looked like, well, a monster. Frankenstein's monster, to be precise. In addition to my singed hair, it took twenty-three stitches to close up the cuts on my feet, knees, and forehead. Dad promised they'd heal just fine, but he could have been lying. He knew my experience was traumatizing enough.

When Blue's—Colin's—parents had opened the door to his bedroom and found us all crowded in there, they called our parents. Only thing was, when they asked the little girls we'd saved—Amy, Emma, and Sadie—what their phone numbers were, they realized that something weird was up. It was the Los Angeles, Detroit, and Chicago area codes that tipped them off. So, after the initial screaming and hugging and crying, our entire crew found ourselves loaded up and en route to Chester County Hospital, with the police on the phone.

Mom and Dad met us there, our SUV parked all cockeyed in the half circle in front of the ER. They were almost to us by the time I'd helped Haylie onto the sidewalk.

"Kids!" Mom's scream was strangled as she tried to gather us both in her arms. After a bone-crushing hug, she started examining us for signs of maiming. "Lissa, your forehead," she murmured, wiping away a tear. I glanced at Dad, and his eyes looked misty, too.

"Oh, man," I said, horrified to see my parents crying. I'd *never* seen Dad cry before, and Mom maybe only once or twice. "We're fine, I promise. And I'm so, so, *so* sorry we worried you. I feel horrible."

Haylie was uncharacteristically quiet throughout all this. Her eyelids fluttered, and I remembered she'd been up all night. Mom cradled her against her chest.

I looked up. The sky was gray, the rising sun streaking it with yellow and pink and orange. With a jolt, I realized that some of the kids taken last night would never see another sunrise. They were goblins now, trapped Down Below.

"Haylie?" Dad prodded. "Want me to take you home? Are you ready to go to sleep?"

Haylie's eyes opened all the way. "Can I have a

pony? I'm good at riding." Her eyes closed, and Mom and Dad looked at each other, frowning.

A black-and-white police cruiser pulled up behind our car, followed by the Griggs' pickup. Adam's parents looked more dazed than anything; I suspected they hadn't known Adam was gone until they got the call.

I kept my eyes on the police cruiser. I wasn't worried about getting in trouble; more about explaining the impossible. Should we tell the truth and let everyone think we were crazy?

Would they? There was no way to account for the three little girls.

Two black-uniformed officers climbed out of the cruiser. They walked toward Colin's parents, who were kneeling down, whispering to the little girls. When they noticed the officers, they stood up. I couldn't hear what they were saying, but there were a lot of hand gestures and head shaking.

Dad noticed the officers, but he put his hand on my back. "I'm taking you inside. If the police have questions, they can find you. Medical help first."

Hours later, after my cuts had been cleaned and stitched up, I sat in a hospital bed, smelling the anesthetic and trying to keep my eyes open. There was a needle in my arm, since I was dehydrated and weak.

Dad had ordered that I stay in the hospital for a day for "observation."

The officers came in to question me, but I played the recovering victim bit, giving only vague answers that didn't make any sense. Something about Haylie disappearing in the dark, and going after her underground and finding the other kids. When they started asking harder questions, that was when I pretended the medicine was kicking in.

After the officers gave up, Mom pulled the thin hospital covers over me, kissing my forehead on an uninjured spot. "You can tell us what happened when you're ready," she said, but I doubted I'd ever be ready.

"Mom?" I asked. "Would you mind lying here with me? Just until I fall asleep?"

She smiled, pushing her hair back from her forehead. "Sure." Careful not to upset my IV or to touch my bandaged feet, she arranged herself in bed with me. "Goodness! Not exactly a Sealy mattress, is it?"

"Ha. If this was a movie scene, that would be obvious product placement." Companies pay big bucks to have characters mention their brands.

I closed my eyes.

For the first time in what seemed like forever, I felt safe.

When I woke up, my head was foggy and my throat felt as dry as the sandman's desert. I turned to where Mom had been sleeping beside me, but she was gone.

"She's getting coffee," an unfamiliar female voice said from in front of the closed door.

"How long have I been out?" Ugh. My tongue felt like sandpaper. Sun glared through the blinds, and I averted my eyes. When I raised my left hand to adjust my covers, plastic hospital tape covered an IV.

Rising, the woman poured a cup of water from a plastic pitcher. In the light, I noticed a small scar that ran above her right eyebrow. "All day." She handed me the water, and I gulped it down. It was warm and tasted like plastic, but I held my cup out for a refill.

Shivering beneath my thin white blanket, I wiped my palms against my scratchy hospital gown. "Are you with the police?"

She shook her head and flashed a bronze badge. "Faye Jacobs, United States Central Intelligence Agency." Her tone was clipped and authoritative.

I swallowed hard. "Central Intelligence Agency?"

I knew I hadn't done anything wrong. Still, just those words—Central Intelligence Agency—made me nervous. I'd never met a real CIA agent before. I wondered if she had a gun.

I glanced at the closed door. How long until Mom got back?

It was like she'd read my mind. "I don't think you want your mother to hear this conversation."

"And why is that?" I tried to sound tough, which was hard considering I was basically wearing paper doll clothes. And if I wanted to escape, I'd have to drag an IV machine along with me. It would be the shortest escape scene ever.

"Because your mother wouldn't believe a thing about Down Below, would she?"

I felt the blood drain from my face. When I opened my mouth to answer, nothing came out.

She raised one eyebrow. "After all, the only people who believe in it are the ones who have been there. Right?"

LISSA'S FILM GLOSSARY

In *Monsterville,* Lissa sees her world through the lens of a camera, often thinking in film terms. The following is a list of some of the film-related terms used in *Monsterville.* Access the full list (and their use in the book) at www.lissablackproductions.com.

AD-LIBBING – A line of dialogue improvised by an actor during a performance; can be either unscripted or deliberate.

AERIAL SHOT – A camera shot filmed in an exterior location from far overhead (a bird's-eye view), like from a helicopter.

ANCILLARY RIGHTS – Ownership of profits made by the sale of action figures, posters, CDs, books, T-shirts, etc. related to the film.

ARC SHOT – A shot where the subject is captured by an encircling or moving camera.

BACKDROP – A large photographic backing or painting for the background of a scene (e.g., a view seen outside a window, a landscape scene, mountains), usually painted on flats (composed of plywood or cloth).

CUE – A signal in a film, usually a line of dialogue, to indicate the next action or line of dialogue.

DEATH TRAP – A plot device in which a villain who has captured the hero, or another sympathetic character, attempts to use an elaborate method of murdering him/her.

MONTAGE – A series of short shots or images that are rapidly put together into a clear sequence to create a whole picture.

PAN – Abbreviation for "panorama shot"; refers to the horizontal scan, movement, rotation, or turning of the camera in one direction (around a fixed axis while filming). A movie can also be "panned," which means it receives very negative reviews.

STAGE DIRECTIONS – Also referred to as "blocking." The positioning of actors to facilitate the performance of a play.

TRIPLE-THREAT – Someone in the entertainment industry who can fulfill a number of roles, such as actor, producer, director, screenwriter, etc.

TYPECASTING – When an actor or actress is commonly (but usually, unfairly) identified with or stereotyped by a particular character role.

VILLAIN SPEECH – Often referred to as "monologuing," where the villain, after having captured the hero or another victim, gives a long speech about why and how he plans on killing his victim.

ACKNOWLEDGMENTS

As a writer who has been on the journey to publication for a very long time, it feels incredible to be in a position to acknowledge those who helped me get there. Boy, am I exhausted, and I am so grateful to all of you! Goodness, the things you've had to endure.

First and foremost, I want to thank my husband, Scott. Honey badger, I love you so much—for all that you are and for all you've done to show your support, to prevent me from losing hope, for trying your best to understand this wacky world of publishing. I can't imagine having done this without you.

Also, thank you to my parents, Bill and Joyce Schauerte, for exposing me to the worlds of books and movies, which ultimately led to *Monsterville's* creation. I will always treasure our movie marathons while camping. Thank you for your special method of filtering movies to ensure appropriateness for children, which shall remain our secret.

Alison Weiss, my editor at Sky Pony—you have been an absolute dream. Thank you for taking this project on and for your insightful notes and input to bring *Monsterville* to life. You've been so respectful of my creative vision, kept me in the loop, answered my (insane) questions. I am so grateful to and for you.

Lauren Galit, my amazing agent—thank you for taking a chance on me. You are a fantastic communicator, editor, friend, and champion of my work, and this book is in print because of you. Thank you for putting up with me.

Caitlen Rubino-Bradway, thank you for your amazing attention to detail and your enthusiasm for this project.

To the teachers at Millstadt Consolidated School, particularly Mrs. Martha Story and Mr. Kenneth Kinsella, thank you for planting the seeds of storytelling and writing. And thank you to Professor Thomas Walsh of Saint Louis University, whose love for the craft will always inspire me.

Thank you to Marianne Reida, for always being a cheerleader for my writing. Thank you for reading everything - good or bad - and loving it.

Thank you to the two writing partners who have been in this with me since 2012. 2012! Veronica Canfield, I treasure our Skype sessions, where we complain and moan and ultimately accomplish real editing. Kate Pawson Studer, I admire your attitude, writing, and treasure our email chains where we overanalyze everything about the process. We don't sound crazy in those emails—not at all! To both of you: there isn't a book of mine you two haven't touched, and I thank you for your role in *Monsterville*.

To everyone at the Sky Pony Press family—I am so proud and humbled to be on your list and part of your team! It's been a true pleasure to work with all of you.